Praise for THE COMPANY SHE KEEPS

"Chambers has created a world of three-dimensional reality… the intrigue-filled corridors of Washington, the romance of Paris, the danger of Tehran. And each page literally brimming with suspense. This is a book I did not want to end, whose story and characters I wanted more of."

— Harold Livingston, *Ride a Tiger, Star Trek: The Motion Picture*

"This is a fabulous book and a fast read… an espionage thriller (that) will pique your interest from beginning to back page. Plots and twists are never-ending. You don't read far to solve the current mystery. But… you'll quickly find the heroine embroiled in yet another more intricate and sticky situation."

— Deb Killarney, *CoastViews* magazine

"A fascinating story about making hard choices and living with the results, as Evelyn and Nick both learn that every decision bears a heavy cost…. When the storyline takes E… to the Iran of the Ayatollahs, a somberness and realism step in that (makes it) impossible to put down."

— Randall Masteller, www.spyguysandgals.com

"A fast-paced tale of a young girl's transition into womanhood. It gives us an inside look at… the shadowy side of The Company. I recommend this book to anyone who likes romantic suspense stories.

— Jennifer Glick, www.myshelf.com

"*The Company She Keeps* is a study in foreign relations. In the course of pursuing her new career… Evelyn Walker takes us around the world, to the exotic and sublime places we dream of, and leads us into the mysterious world of intrigue and shadowy assignations."

— Roy Sallows, *Friday the 13th: The Series, Fall Down Dead*

"*The Company She Keeps* will take you on a roller coaster ride through dangerous relationships, deception, romance, mystery, steamy sexual scenarios, and more!

— Robby Schumacher-Gulledge, *Novel Dialogue* host

Also by Diana R. Chambers

Stinger

The Company She Keeps

Diana R. Chambers

Aventine Press

I with to acknowledge my editors Wayne Arnold and Leigh Walker for their thoughtful contributions. My deep thanks to Sofia Valko for sharing her artistic gifts with me. *The Company She Keeps* could not have been written without the constant support of my traveling companion in life, Everett.

ISBN-10: 1593302541
ISBN-13: 978-1593302542

Library of Congress Control Number: 2005921528
Library of Congress Cataloging-in-Publication Data
THE COMPANY SHE KEEPS

To Everett, who was there from the beginning.

"The truth is rarely pure and never simple."

– Oscar Wilde

Part One

The Meeting

Chapter 1

Washington, D.C.
March 1990

They had told him his cowboy days were over. That rogue operators were an endangered species. But the Director owed him–after Afghanistan. So they brought him home, his reward after all those years in the field. At least, that was what they said.

Some people would see it that way. Comfort and a step up. To him, though, it felt transitory. *Home?* What did that mean? Nick wondered, as was often the case when he found himself parked on a bar stool–this one fittingly temporary, part of tonight's décor.

It was the opening of an Indian sculpture show at the Trocadero Asian Art Gallery, a sleek, glassed-in space on Dupont Circle. In contrast with the cool exterior, the mood inside was hot–spicy, fragrant appetizers and throbbing rhythms–as sensual as the voluptuous Hindu and Buddhist goddesses depicted in wood, stone and bronze. An old Asia hand, he already knew that samosas went great with Jack Daniels.

You could get the Asian food anywhere these days. But the rest... that he did miss. The reds and oranges, the colors of monks' robes, mangoes and chilis. Fires rising out of dung. Green shoots out of mud. Rice and tea and sarongs on swaying hips. Laotian coffee and warm rain on tin roofs. The constant life-becoming-death-becoming-life. It was real, in a way that had nothing to do with Company politics or who was the current Enemy.

Tonight was different, though. Tonight the Enemy was among them–looking just like anyone else.

But then, so did Nick. A sandy-haired regular guy, Nicholas Ross Daley was tall, but not too tall, with a touch of humor around his dark eyes and a stubborn set to the jaw. He was as stubborn as he was patient and didn't mind mixing it up to achieve his goals. He had quieter tactics as well.

Sipping his drink, Nick watched the target mingle with the fashionable Washington crowd–Mike Wilson and his girlfriend, Evelyn Walker, also known as E. She was wearing a pale silk dress, very ladylike, very sexy. Red toenails peeped through skin-toned slingbacks and the silver chain of her evening bag hung over a bare shoulder. Wilson had a more formal appearance, his tailoring immaculate, his manner almost professorial as they moved among images of the mother goddess in her many incarnations, mostly erotic, explicit links to the act of creation itself.

Oblivious to the tinkling of glasses and laughter, Nick had been studying the couple all evening. He found the woman unforgettable–her smile a delight and her complexion flawless, almost lit from within. And her back was spectacular. He stared at the boundaries of silk and skin and imagined all the hidden places just out of sight. He envied the man to have such a woman, noticing that he wasn't the only one to do so.

He saw them pause before a multi-armed bronze with a weird, even demented grin–Kali, symbol of the destructive force, believed to drink her victims' blood from a skull cup. As E winced, Wilson gripped her elbow and they turned toward each other. There was an intimacy that disturbed Nick... her hand on his hip, his hand holding it there.

It was a highly charged atmosphere, filled with sexual imagery. Nick felt it; everyone did... the undulating ragas and curvaceous goddesses with their come-hither looks, tiny waists and softly swelling breasts and hips.

After a too-long moment, the pair strolled toward a beguiling bronze with a serene smile–somewhat like hers. Nick decided to make his move.

Joining them, he extended a palm to Mike. "Excuse me, but aren't you Mike Wilson? We met at Folks Inn down at Norfolk a few months back. Nick... Nick Ross's the name."

The man squinted, regarding Nick with distant caution. After a brief shake, he curtly introduced E. "Evelyn Walker–Nick... uhh–"

"Ross." He held out his hand to her.

As E clasped his hand, her evening bag popped open, affording Nick a quick glance inside.

With a smile, she let go and refastened the clasp, then shrugged. "Too much stuff."

Nick returned the smile, having noted what looked like a man's wallet. Marlboros and a Bic. A comb, no perfume. But she sure smelled good.

Wilson's eyes narrowed. He took E's arm and began edging away. "If you'll excuse us."

"Nice meeting you, Mr. Ross," E said, her dimple returning.

"My pleasure, Ms. Walker."

Mike led her briskly toward the exit. Nick watched them go, following her back as it moved through the crowd. He looked briefly at the sensuous bronze torso next to him, then turned for a final glimpse of E before she disappeared out the door.

He knew he had just met her—his lifelong fantasy. The erotic goddess next to him had nothing on her.

The tall glass door slammed shut, a shot of cold air. *Watch out*, he warned himself.

In this job, you had to be wary of that kind of woman. The kind who could get under your skin, get to you. Or even get you, bring you down. It had been nearly four years since he'd left Afghanistan. Since the journalist got under his skin. Since he got her. That was considered a win in their book. It was a win—for the mission. The loss was just personal.

Nick shook himself back to business; he wasn't here for the women—or the samosas. He'd been investigating the leak for months, long enough to identify the bad guy. But so far there was no evidence. No way to indict. A lot of facts, but no "hook" to hang them on.

They were on the clock now, though, with a Moscow source to protect. And so the boss gave him his marching orders. "Get me a hook."

Chapter 2

Nick had been aware of Evelyn Walker and her potential role in the case for some time. But not her physical impact. What could have prepared him for that? There was something about her he couldn't shake. The young blond under surveillance had become a haunting human being, a haunting woman.

Their target thought so, too.

Maybe Wilson knew something about the woman that Nick didn't. Maybe she was more than she appeared. Or less. It didn't matter; she was the hook.

Nick was taking the scenic route today. The sky was a cool, pale blue, still wintry, but at least not gray. As he drove his Explorer across the Chain Bridge to Virginia, he could see the first hint of green softening the stark branches. Then he reached the other side of the Potomac and was in the country, only a few minutes later at Langley. He never ceased being amazed at the contrast. Eight miles northwest of Washington, these two hundred wooded acres sheltered a remote, self-contained world... one that had come to define most of his adult existence, as much as he would have liked to deny the fact.

He was back again. For now. At least, nearby. Office in Georgetown, Security Consultants International: the Director's payoff for surviving the secret Afghan mission. Or keeping his mouth shut? All he had to do was drop by headquarters from time to time. From time to time was about all he could take.

The Powers That Be needed to keep an eye on him. But not too close an eye. Nick was said to bend the rules and sometimes they didn't want to know. Sometimes it took a certain kind of operative. A lone wolf, creative in tracking his prey.

A ten-foot chain-link fence and three fortified entrances protected the facility. Nick drove through the Dolly Madison gate, parked the car in the south lot and got out, feeling the crisp air on his face. He caught a whiff of cigarette smoke and was glad he'd quit. Briefcase in hand, he walked through the campus-like grounds, passing two red-cheeked, mitten-clad joggers analyzing the recent collapse of the Berlin Wall.

The world had changed. A lot. But then again, maybe not as much as they all hoped. As the French put it, *Plus ça change*. Watching the analysts disappear from view, he reminded himself not to get too comfortable, that changes didn't always stick and things often remained just the way they were.

These thoughts brought his mind back to this case—and her. Evelyn Walker. The girl was striking, yet somehow so damn innocent. Her trusting smile, her open gaze, those sea-green eyes. Nick didn't think it was an act, although he'd been fooled before. He hated to use her, but was there a choice? She was there and he needed her.

Preoccupied, he entered the vast white structure, its air of imperious coolness heightened by Georgia marble. *Our* Georgia—not theirs. No one made eye contact in this great bustling foyer, conversations pitched low and cautious, maybe hatching plans for saving the world. Just like him. There was a purposeful hum here, voices bouncing off the high ceiling, feet clattering on hard polished floors.

As ever, Nick experienced a sense of awe at the power contained within these walls. He was an instrument of that power and, despite it all, it made him feel proud. Sure, you had to walk knee-deep through the bullshit, but he'd lived in Texas and knew his way around the corral. The payoff was that the job gave you a shot at making your mark on the world, making things right. Or half-right. Once in a while.

He'd got the Stingers into Afghanistan, hadn't he? Helped bring down the Soviet Empire. As to unintended consequences, that remained to be seen.

Nick showed his security badge to the guards who checked him out on the computer, then passed him along. Almost instinctively, he paused to read the inscription on the south wall:

AND YE SHALL KNOW THE TRUTH
AND THE TRUTH SHALL MAKE YOU FREE.
– John VIII-XXXII

Nicholas Ross Daley believed those words, always had.

While on the other hand, he knew they didn't apply at all. Truth wasn't exactly a valued commodity at Langley. In fact from what he saw, it got shredded at the end of every day. Or tossed in the burn bag.

His Methodist Sunday School teacher grandma had believed those words. Without the "other hand." Nick wasn't the easiest kid and his folks would send him down to her in Austin, Texas when they were having "troubles." That was most every summer of his childhood. His younger siblings got to visit sometimes, but usually they had to stay back home in El Dorado, Kansas. Family was important, even the semblance of it, even as it was all slipping away.

Nick's father lost his broomcorn processing business when plastic brooms came along, always a day late and a dollar short, too honest for his own good. His mother was a math teacher who had headaches, including her husband. Edwin and Lillian fought and made up and fought some more. Yet they shared the dream of their lakeside cottage outside Austin, a place that would make them whole. It was a dream. A dream that couldn't withstand the diminishing bank balance, her black moods and his bottle.

At the same time Nick's grandma, who saw only God's goodness and grace, was thanking her stars that He had caused them to be born in this free and wonderful country. As tough as life was, Nick's parents clung to those same beliefs, even as they were drowning. But they never thought it was God who let them down.

Those were the people who had raised Nick and those were their values. His parents never let him forget George Washington and the cherry tree.

He never did. Whenever he told a lie, he thought of them. And in his line of work, that was SOP. Lying was what you did. It was in the job description. No one said he had to like it, but he'd gotten used to it. *That* was the truth. Nick cast another look at the noble words on the wall, then turned away. A wiry balding guy stared as if trying to place him. Nick didn't give him a chance and moved on toward the elevators.

He had backed the wrong guy in Afghanistan, at least according to the fundamentalists who did not consider him a friend. Neither did his old boss in Peshawar. So he was wearing a new hat these days. Nicholas Ross Daley meet Nick Ross. Nothing too clever, just different enough to keep him "off the books," as the Director put it.

But available to do his duty. Thus Security Consultants International was born. With Agency proprieties now banned, a slate of clients was lined up, thanks to references from the Director of Central Intelligence. Corporate America had need of protection. They all did.

Technology transfer was a hot-button topic, hot territory with plenty of open space for him to operate. Plenty of covert activities. Plenty of bad guys running around, taking advantage of a free and open society.

Nick headed for the five banks of color-coded elevators, one solely to transport the Director between the basement garage and his seventh floor office, the only floor related to rank. He waited for the blue elevator, then got out on third and turned right down "C" corridor. Despite the primary-colored doors, there was no disguising the Government-Issue vibe. Which was why he preferred having his office out in the "real" world. You lost some of the ability to maneuver politically, but that wasn't his thing.

By contrast, his boss was a master tactician. A division chief and member of the Agency's senior clique, Jay Stiles focused on the one move that mattered at Langley. Nick wondered how long until Jay made it to "supergrade" status on the seventh floor—and if he'd still be reporting to him up there.

After a long hike, Nick reached a blue door numbered 5C33 and knocked.

"Yeah?" came an impatient bark.

"Daley here."

"You mean 'Ross,' don't you?"

"Yeah. Nick Ross. At your service." His *nom de guerre*. At least, this war. He entered, facing a solid, unsmiling man across a tidy desk.

Jay Stiles gestured to the wingchair, while continuing his phone conversation. Nick sat, placing his briefcase on the blue Chinese area rug.

"...A bunch of bull. U.S. regulations never affected you before!" Jay listened, lips tightening in irritation. He swiveled around in his leather seat and gazed down at two trucks and a limousine waiting at the southwest loading dock. "You got a point." He ran a hand over his short silver-gray hair. "Okay. Right. *Shalom*."

Hanging up, he turned back to Nick, who was staring at the miniature ivory and ebony chessboard on a side table. "Those guys are goddamn lucky over there. They don't have our Congress and our laws to deal with."

"No, just a very dangerous neighborhood."

"You should know about that."

"I do." Nick had done some time in the Middle East. He had watched the Iraqi build-up, while everyone else was still obsessed with the Ayatollahs. But it was not his territory, and he had to keep his mouth shut.

"*Shalom* and *Salaam*. Good guys on both sides." Jay studied his fat black fountain pen. Hovering somewhere around sixty, he cultivated a patrician, old money image. He wore Brooks Brothers to the office and L.L. Bean while sailing in Chesapeake Bay. His current wife, Muffie, was F.F.V.–First Families of Virginia. "Sometimes I think I could play on either team."

"I suppose you could."

"*You* couldn't?" Jay shrugged, and began drafting his "Eyes Only" memo.

"I just don't like thinking of it as a fucking game."

"But it is. It's real and it's dangerous and it's one we can't afford to lose." As a young law intern, Jay Stiles had been recruited by "Wild Bill" Donovan for his elite new Central Intelligence Agency, offspring of World War II's glamorous OSS. Stiles had been the "right sort" to fit into the CIA.

Nick knew he was the "other sort," a token something. While Stiles finished the memo, he glanced at the silver-framed photos on his desk, one of a youthful Jay doing a Maltese Cross on the rings. It was dated England, 1948.

Setting down his pen, Jay picked up the picture and flicked off a bit of dust with his handkerchief. "The Olympics. I was eighteen. Those days, I thought hardship meant getting up at five to work out. I learned plenty from those goddamn Brits about endurance–and I don't mean athletics." He placed the photograph back next to one of him and Donovan, staring a moment.

"Wild Bill was a streetfighting Irishman. He warned us: 'In an age of bullies, we cannot afford to be a sissy.'"

"And so the Cold War was born."

"We didn't start it," Jay said. "The Reds began pushing. We had to push back. To protect our values. To keep the peace."

"Or what passes for peace."

"That's where you come in—Ross."

"Exactly." Whereas Stiles found intellectual satisfaction in the arcane, chess-like world of counterintelligence—the webs of truth and lies, strategy and deception—Nick was a more pragmatic sort who just liked to nail the bastards. "Mike Wilson."

"Aah, yes. I've heard that name before. So have the Feds. Your pals. Have they learned to tie their shoes yet?" Jay smiled thinly.

"Velcro." Nick shook his head in frustration. A deep-cover Company source in Moscow had led them to the target. It was their case, but they couldn't go it alone. Domestic counterintelligence was FBI territory, territory jealously guarded, and their CI division had jurisdiction over any spies operating at home.

Jay steepled his fingers. "They have anything for Justice yet?"

"Working on it." He shrugged. "In the meantime, Wilson is making mincemeat of the USDS and we're wide open." Intended as the wireless upgrade to SOSUS, the Navy's creaky Sound Surveillance System, the Undersea Sonar Defense System was being penetrated under their very eyes. "I don't know about you, but I do not relish the idea of some goddamn Russian submarine popping up for drinks on my deck."

"I don't serve vodka." Jay regarded Nick closely. "What else's on your mind?"

"I've finally got an angle." He shifted in his seat.

"Dollars to doughnuts, the 'angle' wears a skirt."

"Right. The SOB has a new girlfriend." Nick opened his briefcase and took out Evelyn Walker's file.

Jay smiled. "Ah, a little 'honey pot' operation you're cooking up. Let's see what the ingredients are."

Nick pulled out an 8x10 color print of a teenaged blond wearing jeans, an Atlanta Braves T-shirt and a big smile. He frowned, then handed it to his chief.

By now, Nick knew a great deal about Evelyn, also known as E, daughter of a twenty-year Army man, a one-eyed vet of the old school. He showed Jay pictures of her family, briefing him on their background, including the move to Alert, North Carolina upon Sam Walker's retirement, the small business to supplement his pension—a contract post office with a one-pump gas station. "Other than the wife splitting, it was an apple pie life. Little League, Sunday church. The old man raised that flag every morning, taught his kids to salute." He sighed, remembering the days. "Then along came Mark Randolph."

"Who?"

Nick stared. "They call him 'the Man.' Guy's a big rock star. *Big*."

Jay shrugged. "Sorry, but I'm stuck in the groove between Mozart and the Modern Jazz Quartet."

"So your kids'll know you're cool." He pulled out an 8x10 of the singer in his usual black. "One day, on his way to a Capital Centre concert, Randolph stopped for gas and left with E. Nicknamed her Everlovin' E."

"I like that."

Nick's eyes flickered. "After he dumped her, the old man cut her off, so she stayed in D.C. Got a roommate, job at a fancy boutique, grew out of Everlovin' E and enrolled at Georgetown. Smart girl, good on her feet. A year later, she met our friend." Nick slapped down another photo. "Milos Wasilova, aka Mike Wilson. Born Prague, 1958. Employed by SeaTech, Inc., Boston. You know how it is, a good mole is a valuable resource—too valuable to let the end of communism get in your way."

Jay nodded. "Governments come, governments go. But the game continues." The spy's photo was followed by a two-shot of him and E at Kennedy Center. Jay checked her out thoroughly, then put the picture back down. "She is some goddamn looker!"

Nick gazed at her image as if he'd never given it much thought before. "I was there that night. *The Iceman Cometh*. Wilson fancies himself a bit of a high-brow."

Jay raised an eyebrow. "He must have something else going to connect with a girl like that."

Nick shrugged. "Late last fall Wilson moved in on her—and moved her in. That's it. Bottom line? She's a good old gal, honest, loves her country. Maybe not too discerning as to whom she loves and why, but I'm willing to swear she has no idea what he's up to."

"How can you be so sure?"

"I'm sure."

Jay shook his head in mock sympathy, mock distress. "What would the old one-eyed vet say? His daughter not only loose, but mistress to a spy!"

Nick regarded Stiles with cold distaste. Moral conflicts were nothing new to him, but they were only for midnight, when you couldn't sleep. His day job was about doing his duty. And his duty was to defend his country against its enemies. "You got it. I think she'd be willing to help get the guy if only to make the old man proud."

"Or keep him from knowing." Jay tapped his closed lips with an index finger.

The problem was "the duty" could leave a bad taste in your mouth. And what he was about to do with her tasted real bad. "Not that."

"Did I ever tell you my first assignment?" Without a beat, he continued, "In Taiwan we trained four-man teams to be airdropped into Red China. Some didn't get out. Many. I learned: you do what you have to do. Use what you've got."

"I've been there," Nick said, thinking of those who'd died for his duty. His loyal Afghan agent–and friend–Taj Akbar, husband and father of two.

"Exactly. Correct me if I'm wrong, but she's all you have. So give her a try." Jay picked up his pen. "We don't have much time. Word from Moscow is he's moved from 'top-secret' to 'cosmic' material."

"Holy shit! How'd he get that kind of clearance?"

"Obviously, a man to be trusted. Your little southern belle seems to think so." He picked up the Kennedy Center photo of E in a black evening gown. "Everlovin' E, huh? Wonder if she's as good as she sounds?"

Expressionless, Nick retrieved the picture, closed her file and dropped it in his briefcase.

Jay watched him, amused. "We used to call them 'broads'–before the PC vigilantes made us afraid to open our mouths. Can't live with them, can't live without them. Right, Nick?" He gave him a pleased little smile.

Nick rose to leave. "Vigilantes... or broads?"

"Work it out." Jay picked up a chess piece and made a move.

Chapter 3

Wearing jeans and a yellow sweater, E left the ivy-covered building. Nick watched her slip a textbook in her backpack, then wave at a couple of friends. She set off down the cobblestone path, making way for a bicyclist and a pair of rollerbladers. The lawn was dotted with shirtless guys tossing frisbees. It was a fine day.

A newspaper under his arm, Nick began walking in her direction, the historic charm of the two-hundred-year-old university lost on him. He liked how she moved. "Evelyn?"

She paused and gave him a blank look.

He could see she didn't recognize him. "Nick Ross," he said. "We met at the Trocadero opening. The Indian art?"

"Oh, yes." She nodded cautiously. "I thought you were a professor just now, in your corduroy jacket."

He laughed. "A professor. Not hardly." He noticed the second dimple on her chin as her face relaxed in a smile.

"I guess there could be worse things. Nice seeing you again, Mr. Ross."

He shook her hand. It was just cool enough… just warm enough. "Good seeing you, too, Evelyn. And please call me Nick."

"Okay, Nick." She smiled again. "My friends call me E."

Flattered in spite of himself, Nick fell into step with her, sticking the newspaper in his back pocket. "Thank you, E."

She cocked her head, listening. "You a southern boy, Nick?"

"Texas, sort of."

"Close enough," she teased.

"Lot of folks'd call you on that, ma'am."

"Long as you don't," she said, eyeing his made-to-order in Bangkok boots. "I've always been partial to cowboy boots. Especially beat-up ones."

And cowboys? he wondered, warmed by the music in her voice. "You?"

"North Carolina."

"Nice state–almost nice as Texas." They ducked as a frisbee sailed overhead. Then a yellow lab dashed across their path in hot pursuit, barking all the way.

"Dangerous place," she said, having fun.

"Really. So, how'd you like that exhibit, E?"

"It's what I love about this town–great new things to learn, people to meet. I even tasted those Indian appetizers."

"What'd you think?"

"I'm not much on fancy foods, though Mike's trying to teach me. Guess I'm more a meat-and-potatoes girl." She gave him a sideways look. "As in 'just plain folks.'"

He thought maybe he caught a saucy twinkle in her glance. *Careful.* "Then I know just what you'd like."

E waited as a bicyclist raced by with the ring of a bell and an "on your left."

"Trust me." Nick flashed a big, good-old-boy grin.

"Okay." She shifted her backpack to the other shoulder.

"But let's be straight about one thing, E." He gazed at her–slim yet rounded, golden and glowing like a Christmas ornament. "About what you just said? Folks, yes. *Plain,* never."

She replied with a faint coloring of the cheeks, but also a little nod of acceptance.

Nick liked that too, how easy she was about herself, how she wore that spectacular body like an old sneaker.

They strolled through the gracious campus, the joggers out in force. The sun was a pale lemon yellow, mild and encouraging, set in a milky-blue sky. They talked about the cherry blossoms now in bloom, how they were looking forward to the opening of baseball season. It turned out they both had a soft spot for the Braves. She told him how Mike was too busy for baseball, more of an intellectual, always reading and making reports.

"He's a serious guy, pretty conservative actually. Can you imagine, he warned me about making friends? *Here?*" E glanced around. "Said you can never be too careful."

"Maybe he's right."

She took a deep breath. "I love this time of year. You can almost see the green pushing up through the earth. And the daffodils! I think I'll buy some later. Mike's coming home tonight."

"It's none of my—"

"Boston. His office is up there. SeaTech," she said proudly.

Nick nodded. They were in residential Georgetown now, following mossy brick sidewalks past restored row houses and dogwood trees blooming clouds of pink and white. Soon they reached Wisconsin Avenue, dodging preppies, punks and hare krishnas.

"Now we just follow our noses," he said. And sure enough, seductive smells beckoned them from around the corner—hot dogs, chili, relish and onions.

"Little League Games." She sighed.

"Yeah," he agreed. "I played shortstop."

Her face lit up. "My brother, too!"

Hal's Hot Dogs was an M Street fixture, a portable stand loaded with condiments, chips and soda cans. Hal was short and skinny with a bald head and booming voice. "Well, if it ain't Prince Charming and Snow White!"

"Hey, Hal. How you doing?"

"How'm *I* doin'? Haven't seen you for days! Something wrong?" He stared at E. "Or right?"

"Just too busy. But now I'm back—with a brand new customer who doesn't know what she's been missing."

"She will." Hal grinned. "The usual?"

"And don't skimp on the chili. She's a very fussy lady."

E watched Hal prepare the first chili dog. Adding a final squiggle of bright yellow mustard, he presented it to her gallantly. "Here you go, angel, best kosher dog this town—or any other."

As she dug right in, Hal beamed, his face shiny from the steam.

Nick glared dramatically, holding out his empty hands.

"Oh, yeah, you." Hal's eyes remained on E. He made one for Nick, then added a bunch of napkins and two Cokes.

E waved as they set off down M Street. Another thing Nick liked: the way she devoured her hot dog. The women he knew were always on diets, but this one had a healthy appetite. He felt good around her.

Finishing, she turned to him, smiled and handed him a napkin. "You have a little mustard moustache, just like my brother used to get."

He watched as she licked her lips and mouth area to clean off, completely unselfconscious. She was erotic, yet innocent at the same time, her complexion fresh, almost dewy from the garden. *Sugar and spice... and everything nice.* He looked away.

"Boy, that was good! Haven't had one in ages. Mike is more of a gourmet," she said, tossing some trash in a bin. "Where did you say you know him from?"

"We met down in Norfolk near the naval base... some mutual friends."

"My daddy was stationed there. He was a hero, decorated in Vietnam."

"You must be proud of him."

"Yes." Her eyes darkened. "Sorry. It's just—I haven't seen him in awhile."

"Oh." Nick cleared his throat, studying his Coke can. "It was a different kind of war." That, he knew. "Hard to figure out."

"My Pop always told me we have a duty to serve our country, even sometimes when we don't understand why."

"Yeah. We have a duty to serve. Even sometimes when we don't understand why." He repeated her words slowly, feeling like a real shit the way he was playing out his line, waiting to reel her in. "Those Nam vets never got the credit they deserved—no parades to welcome them home."

"Down south they did. Least in Louisburg, our county seat. Mama was proud that day. He was a hero to her... for a while." As he gazed off, she added, "That's okay, I don't mind. She told me before she left, tried to explain." E frowned. "But now that I'm here—in the big world—I understand how our old one seemed kinda small."

"Ever see her again?" he asked with sympathy.

E made a wistful shrug. "Can't blame her. Pop wouldn't let her call. Maybe someday." She forced a brief smile. "You're a good guy, Nick. Down to earth."

They continued on in silence. After a while, they reached the southern edge of Rock Creek Park, which accompanied the creek as it wound through the city. Soft light filtered through the oaks and maples. Everything a pale shimmering green. A gentle breeze picked up.

E lifted her face into the air. "Like the flutter of a sparrow's wing."

"Yeah." Nick stared straight ahead, feeling slightly ill—and it wasn't the chili dog. "I didn't run into you by accident."

E nodded, not surprised.

Feeling her warm look, Nick turned to her gravely. "It's not what you think, E. Believe me, I wish to God it were." She was so simple, so trusting.

Why did he have to take that away from her? Why hadn't she just picked some other guy? "I'll give it to you straight. I work for the government—and my job is to make sure our flag keeps flying long after I'm gone."

"Well... sure." E watched him, confused.

"That flag *means* something to me—as I know it does to you. You said your father was a hero, how proud you are of him. Now is *your* chance to serve your country."

"Nick," E said weakly. "I don't understand. Any of this."

"How could you understand, a nice patriotic girl like you? The truth is, E—you're living with a spy."

"*What?*"

The least he could do was give it to her straight. "We've learned from a high-level Moscow source that a SeaTech employee is passing top-secret data about the USDS—our new Undersea Sonar Defense System. He doesn't know the spy's name, just that he's a naturalized American. There is only one such employee at SeaTech—Mike Wilson."

She shook her head in disbelief, then abruptly laughed. "Get out of here!"

Nick just stood there, admiring her spirit—her loyalty—then looked off at some kids kicking a soccer ball in an open patch of green.

"Who are you—*really?*"

"Like I said. I work for the government. This is a matter of national security."

"National security? I thought the Cold War's over—Gorbachev and all..." Her voice trailed off in bewilderment.

"So they say. But if any of the old boys are hanging on? Put it this way. You can be sure their fingers are very near that atomic pistol. And it's still pointed at us—over land and sea." His face hardened. "The world changes, all right. Technology, too—and suddenly we were vulnerable. We've been upgrading our underwater security, thought we were on the right track—until Wilson penetrated our systems."

E glared, hands on her hips. "You're wrong!" Then she dropped her arms and the angry light became cloudy. "So what if he is naturalized? Mike's just like anyone else. Doesn't even have an accent." She shook her head. "I have to go now."

But she didn't move.

"Would you like to see my ID?" Nick asked quietly, still watching the kids. And the black and white ball spinning through the air... looking suddenly very goddamn gray.

"No, I believe you are who you say you are–Mr. Ross. I just don't believe what you say." She stared at the children, her shoulders drooping. "I suppose I should thank you for the hot dog."

Nick reached to touch her, then backed off. His conscience was troubled and he felt uneasy. He had no right. But he did. It was his job. Just doing his duty–and it sucked. "Listen, E. Evelyn. I really wish it had been a coincidence and a casual hot dog, but we're desperate for hard evidence. I need your help! Your country needs your help."

E was still looking away, but maybe she heard something in his voice. Her body softened slightly.

Nick pressed his advantage. "You have no reason at all to trust me, but I feel your instincts are good." He paused. "All I ask is that you keep your ears and eyes open, and if anything–any little thing–strikes you as being unusual in *any* way… Please, give me a call." He was a pro and had recruited many agents, so he'd saved his best for last. "Your father would want you to help." He handed her his business card.

E gazed at the card, then up at his face, then back down. Her fingers tightened around it.

He took out another one. "In case you don't have an iron."

A ghost of a smile touched her lips as she opened her fist and seemed to be studying the crumpled card. But her eyes showed how distressed she was at this first real moral dilemma in her life. "I am mad. But throwing away your card is not going to change that. Mr. Nicholas Ross." A pensive look crossed her face. E sighed. "I guess there's no such thing as a free lunch."

Nick shook his head sadly. "No such thing." He extended his hand.

Small and vulnerable, E stared at it, the golden aura gone. She met his eyes with the faintest of nods. But she sure didn't have to shake hands with him.

"Can't say as I blame you." He lowered his hand. "Well… See you. Evelyn."

She searched his face one more time, then turned away.

He walked off, down the path. As he rounded a bend, he glanced back and saw her still standing there, watching the children. Innocent as those kids. Why couldn't she stay that way? He wished the world were a simpler place. But it never was, and never would be.

Chapter 4

Boston, Massachusetts

Collar up against the gritty wind, Mike Wilson mounted the granite steps. The sky was the color of the building and so were the faces of the other people rushing to work that grim, damp morning. Mike was oblivious to the drizzle, his umbrella unopened, clutched in the same hand as his briefcase. He had a busy day ahead.

His take from tonight's "work" would be the most important thus far. He knew his people would be pleased, their reward generous. Although that wasn't the point. At all. His loyalty could not be bought.

He glanced up at the American flag, sodden and wind-lashed. Only then did Mike notice the weather. He brushed himself off and went inside, making his way to the ninth floor headquarters of SeaTech, Inc.

Located in the former red-light district, the century-old building had found new life during Boston's redevelopment program, financed in part by its thriving high-tech companies. Companies like SeaTech whose research and development projects were funded largely by government contracts. To service the client, the firm had appointed Mike Wilson as Washington liaison.

SeaTech was a key participant in a major Navy/NSA project–the Undersea Sonar Defense System. The USDS would be a powerful upgrade to the current system, replacing the hydrophone arrays positioned along the U.S. seabed with freestanding ones. The wireless sonar network was considered vital to America's coastal security. For despite the new regime, the Russian Navy was still on the prowl, their ballistic missile subs–boomers–ever more silent and deadly.

This project was win-win for everyone, including SeaTech and Mike Wilson.

Born in Prague in 1958, Milos Wasilova grew into an exacting young man of high intellect, studying Marxism-Leninism, literature and history. A staunch patriot, he understood that the future of his ancient land, nearly destroyed by Hitler, would depend upon strong alliances. Recruited by Czech Intelligence, he was later handed over to the KGB for training in clandestine tradecraft. Moscow Center worked on his "legend," blending his real and fictional biography. Then with the necessary documentation, they sent him off to begin his new life.

Milos Wasilova "defected" to Austria in the late seventies and soon entered Canada, a haven for many East European immigrants. Michael Wilson, as he became known, did graduate work at Laval University in Quebec, eventually gaining Canadian citizenship. A few years later, he was employed by SeaTech, Inc. and relocated to Boston. The company helped him obtain a U.S. visa. By then, everyone called him Mike.

He had an aggressive energy and outstanding work ethic. In the mid-eighties Mike received his U.S. citizenship–and top-secret security clearance. A thorough investigation had verified his staunch anti-communism, problems with the Czech authorities and lack of future in his homeland. He blended right into his new life and spoke almost flawless English. People either forgot–or never knew–that he was not born in the U.S.A. With an apartment on Beacon Hill and a condo in Georgetown, he was living the American Dream–but only on the surface. Mike Wilson was a "sleeper," a foreign agent who burrowed his way into his host country. A mole, ready to serve when called upon.

Two years ago that call had come. By then, he had set up SeaTech's D.C. office, a trusted, high-level employee. He was the right man in the right place to defuse the USDS.

Mike had been tense all day and kept as clear as possible from his co-workers. It was long past dusk when he closed his office door and walked down the silent corridor, maybe not the most popular guy but definitely the hardest worker. In fact, other than the janitor, Mike Wilson was usually the last to leave. He knew his employers considered him honest and honorable. But he was never one to question himself or his chosen path. He was a man of clarity and culture.

"Oh, do not ask, 'What is it?'
Let us go and make our visit."

Wondering how many Americans could quote T.S. Eliot, he knocked on a door. "Arthur?"

No answer. He knocked again. Silence.

As he turned the knob, the aroma of pipe tobacco spilled out, but the office was dark, empty. He closed the door, flipped the switch and moved to the file cabinet. Project Director Art Oliver was scrupulous about security, but Mike was a trusted colleague who often transported specifications from Washington. Naturally, he had authorized Mike's access to the locked section whenever he needed data.

So Mike knew the combination and had used it many times. In broad daylight and deepest night. He opened the door, stuffed with documents, tech manuals, drawings and blueprints–all marked *CONFIDENTIAL* or *TOP SECRET*. Even *COSMIC*. Carefully, but not worrying about fingerprints, he searched for the document he needed. He stared at the words stamped across the front: *TOP SECRET–Special Access Required.*

The report, which had arrived yesterday, detailed a major design breakthrough in the system's digital signal processing chip. Beneath it was a nine-page photocopy, dated today and initialed by Art's secretary. She was a stickler for rules and it was SeaTech procedure not to circulate originals. Noting that the copy was complete, Mike straightened the papers, leaving everything as he'd found it. He closed the cabinet door, turned out the light and left.

The copy room was at the end of the corridor. Sounds of the Celtics' game blasted out to Mike. He was accustomed to crossing paths with Joe the janitor at night. The old man, a former alcoholic, was too out of it to be a hindrance. In fact, he was something of a gift–providing inadvertent cover as Mike did his work in plain sight.

Mike entered and saw Joe in the back of the room with the shredder–and his portable radio. "Do you mind? Some of us have to work for a living."

Joe turned the volume down. "Sorry, Mr. Wilson. Didn't mean to cause no trouble." He spoke loudly, being a little deaf.

Mike moved to the Xerox machine. He set his briefcase on the worktable, opened it and removed a packet of receipts to copy for his expense report. After several moments of smooth functioning the red light went on, indicating the paper had jammed.

"Damn machine," he muttered, leaning over to open its side door. He looked in, his back blocking Joe's view.

It made no difference. Joe was in his own world, whistling to a beer commercial.

Mike fussed noisily as he cleared the jammed paper, then removed a small gray object opposite the roller. The magnetic device was the same color as the machine and blended right in with the other components. Looking rather like a pocket calculator, it had an adhesive warning, XEROX–DO NOT REMOVE. He pulled off the decal and stuffed it in his pocket, then dropped the device in his briefcase, and replaced it with another identical one. He closed the machine door with a loud click.

Mike made a few more copies, soon completing his work. He slipped the receipts and duplicates in a manila envelope and then into his briefcase, snapping it shut with an audible sigh of fatigue. He switched off the machine and began walking toward the door.

"Hey! Wait up!"

He froze and looked at Joe.

"They're in overtime–helluva game! Hate for you to miss it!" Joe was all pumped up, the purple capillaries on his nose electric.

Mike contained himself, his smile cold. What mattered now was getting to the airport. Then home–to Evelyn, whom he had come to care for more than he'd ever expected. More than was prudent. Sick of fighting his feelings, he had been thinking of bringing her into his world. There had been some very successful husband-and-wife espionage teams. "I'll see it on the news. Don't work too hard."

Only after Mike walked out the door did Joe turn the sound back up and resume shredding. He began to whistle happily.

Mike was happy, too–or at least, satisfied. Happiness was not an emotion he much valued. It appeared by accident and could not be controlled. But he did allow himself satisfaction at a job well done–and his own cleverness. He passed by his office to collect his coat and umbrella, then left.

In the elevator, he lit a cigarette, burned the crumpled Xerox decal and was still smoking as he reached the lobby where the security man stood guard. "Hey, Mr. Wilson, how many times I have to tell you? No smoking in the elevator."

"Sorry about that, George. You know how it is after a long day's work."

"Yeah. Nothing like a good smoke. Okay, let's have a look at that briefcase."

Mike put it on the table and opened the lid. "Glad to see you're on top of it. Lot of important stuff going on here."

George rifled through Mike's papers, his wallet, cigarettes, lighter and calculator, then closed the briefcase with a loud thump. "Well, no top secret documents in here."

Mike wrapped his fingers around the handle and nodded. "Could've fooled me."

George smiled. "But Mr. Wilson—next time I catch you smoking on that elevator, I'm gonna have to cite you."

Mike shrugged on his way to the exit. "Guess I'll have to be more careful."

Chapter 5

Washington, D.C.

It was an awful afternoon. If only this hadn't been her day off from work; if only she'd cut class. If only she'd never met that damn Nick! *Good old boy, my butt.*

How dare he intrude in her life like that, pretend to run into her, talking about baseball and spring–and *national security*? E had left the park so agitated that she'd barely remembered to buy flowers for Mike. She dreaded seeing him tonight, yet yearned for some reassurance that this was all a crazy mistake.

Edgy and anxious, frantic really, she couldn't concentrate. She did her nails then smeared the polish and had to take it all off. The cookies burned. And forget trying to read or study. She called her old roommate, Cynthia, who didn't answer, probably already at the restaurant. Not that E would have dared mention any of this to her.

As evening approached, she changed into a new silk dress she thought he'd like, wanting to please him out of a sense of guilt and disloyalty. The Willie Nelson disc didn't help any–his voice, full of longing, reminded her of home. Especially "Amazing Grace." More melancholy than ever, she rearranged the yellow and peach daffodils again.

The door flung open. With apartments in both cities, Mike traveled light, just his flat attaché-style briefcase. E rushed into his embrace, wishing to blank everything out. He was strong and solid, and there could be no doubt he loved her. But the other doubts… "How was Boston?"

"Cold." He held her at arms' length. "New dress?"

E posed, hand on hip. "Like it?"

"Pretty. But I'd like it better on the floor, by the bed."

Their eyes met, then their lips. The kiss was a long escape to their own special place. In the background, Willie sang about loving someone, "Always."

Then the music ended.

E searched his opaque brown eyes. "I missed you, Mike."

"Me, too, Evelyn. Everything about you." He traced her mouth with his finger.

"Let's just stay home. I could cook that new risotto dish."

"Home cooking sounds good, but we'll come back for dessert." He nipped her earlobe. "Don't go away. I'll be right back."

Slipping into cozy feelings of normalcy, she watched him walk from the room, then noticed the briefcase in his hand. The bathroom door closed. *A briefcase in the bathroom?* Her smile faded as she tried to recall if he'd ever done that before. Maybe he just had a new toothbrush or something inside. Or a present?

She shook her head, angry at her doubts. Angry at Nick Ross. Grabbing the remote, she punched mute and began flipping through the channels, then stopped on *Hart to Hart*, the show about the rich husband and wife detectives with their beautiful house and clothes, their little yellow Mercedes convertible.

That was the car the rock star had been driving the hot summer day he stopped for gas. Mark Randolph–in *Alert?* She could still feel the moist southern air, smell the fresh paint mixed with honeysuckle, see Bobby sprawled on the office floor with his baseball cards… her annoying kid brother who had warned against going off with the guy. But how could she resist a little trip up to Roanoke Rapids with her favorite singer? Then during the drive, Mark wrote a song for her and promised to perform it that night at his D.C. concert, which she saw from backstage. Although he never did sing the song.

Her daddy still hadn't forgiven her.

All of a sudden, E heard Pop's voice in her ear: *Don't think about where you were. Thank about where you are.* He said it had helped him survive Nam. Probably the loss of his wife too. Their mama.

Mike returned to the living room, looking crisp in his clean shirt, so comfortingly familiar. His cheeks were still damp and he smelled of pine forests. She felt a wave of tenderness. He was all she had, really–until her father let her come back home. "Couldn't you get another job, so you wouldn't have to go away all the time?"

Setting his black briefcase on the coffee table, he stared at her. "I find the going away makes the coming home all the better."

"I guess you're right." With a glance at the attaché case, E turned off the TV and got up. Hoping as never before for a surprise gift.

He opened the case and removed a few items—wallet, Marlboros, Bic lighter—and handed them to her, but nothing else. She put them in her little shoulder bag, then looked back at him. There was something in his left jacket pocket. Some kind of bulge… small, but enough to spoil the otherwise smooth line. Why hadn't he given her that, too? Whatever it was. It couldn't be the car keys. They were in the silver bowl by the front door where he always left them.

Mike offered her his arm and picked up the keys.

Numbers was a lively club with a great sound system and a trendy young clientele. It was dark, smoky and steamy.

Mike was sipping Cutty on the rocks and E an Amaretto. On one of their early dates, she'd tried to impress him by ordering a Stoli—Mark Randolph's drink—but Mike said he never touched the stuff. *Vodka.* She frowned, remembering the night she'd cooked borscht, which he didn't like, either.

When the "Midnight Train to Georgia" came on, Mike tapped out his cigarette. "I think it's that time."

As E nodded, he removed his jacket and hung it over the back of his chair. She gave him a curious look, but just grabbed her bag and slung it over her shoulder.

His hand firm, he guided her to the dance floor. She wrapped her arms around his neck as he took her and held on tight, molding her to him. The lights dimmed. She felt his warm breath in her ear, then his lips. They barely moved.

The lights came up as the music faded. Taking their time, Mike and E disentangled themselves and returned to their table. He slipped his jacket on before sitting, then gestured to the waitress for the check. E handed him his wallet. After he paid, she put it back in her bag. As they rose to leave, E couldn't help but glance at his pocket. The bulge was gone! Everything flat and smooth again, as usual.

Mike took her arm. "Time for dessert."

Their lovemaking was sweet and quiet, each clinging to the other as an anchor... the tug of a safe past against an uncertain future.

She never wanted the night to end, never wanted to face the deceptions of the morning.

E stood at a pay phone on the Georgetown campus and pulled Nick's card from her purse. She studied it a long moment before dialing his number. After three rings, a raspy woman's voice answered, "Good afternoon. Security Consultants International."

"Mr. Nicholas Ross, please."

"Who's calling?"

"Evelyn Walker."

After a few seconds, Nick picked up the phone. "E? I mean–Evelyn? I didn't know if I'd hear from you."

"You almost didn't. If it weren't for my daddy always talking patriotic duty and all that... Anyway, I did notice a few things, probably nothing, but–"

"Would you mind dropping by the office? Or I could meet you?"

"I don't mind. See you."

"I'll be wait–"

After she hung up, E stood there, staring at the card and frowning. Alone.

At his end, Nick too was frowning. The case had been disturbing from the start. Their Russian asset had reported classified data being passed from a private research firm under contract to the U.S. government on the USDS program. He knew the spy was a naturalized American working for the company. And he knew the dates the info had been passed in the D.C. area. But that was it.

Nick had been assigned to the investigating team. Using a mix of modern technology and classic triangulation, they determined which companies were involved in that particular research. Second, they asked, what naturalized Americans might have access to the secrets? Third, who was in Washington on those dates?

Only one name emerged: Mike Wilson. *Bingo.*

It was time to bring in the "crosstown rivals."

FBI counterintelligence, Division Five, had grudgingly accepted the CIA offer of assistance. A joint "mole hunting" unit was set up by Nick and Special Agent Don Angell, but ultimately agents of the Bureau's Washington Field Office would make the collar.

First, however, they needed proof of espionage, one of the most difficult crimes to prosecute. The Justice Department demanded hard evidence it could take to court–nothing circumstantial. So the FBI had to see the suspect pass defense secrets to a foreign agent. It had to catch him in the act.

But *how?*

One thing they knew: Wilson was their man. Nick and his buddy Angell had checked and rechecked everything about him. Mike Wilson fit the psychological profile of a foreign agent. He was a perfect mole, committed and cunning–a slick adversary.

The team kept Wilson under constant surveillance. In addition, they obtained approval from the Foreign Intelligence Surveillance Court to wiretap his home and business phones, but they came up cold. The mole had been well trained in tradecraft.

In the course of the investigation, Evelyn Walker appeared on the scene and Nick resolved to recruit and run her. After first verifying, of course, that she was clean.

He had observed the young woman for a few months before their encounter at the art gallery. Nick had never actually met Mike, but called his bluff by pretending they had, wanting to force him to make the introduction.

By then, Nick felt he knew almost everything about her, except who she *really* was. Maybe she'd be just another pretty face. But no, E was special, her beauty far beyond skin deep. She had a vulnerability that reached out to him. It made the "handling" all the more difficult; he had to resist the desire not to bruise her.

He thought about starting a new relationship with a new agent. He remembered all the people he had used in one operation or another. Those he had lost. Taj. The young Afghan refugee had been a peaceful man, yearning for his old village life, saving Nick's more than once. Sure, he took care of Taj's two orphan boys–and his widow–but that didn't lessen the pain.

What they *taught* you was the antiseptic approach: The case officer was to create a sense of trust in the asset. While keeping his own distance.

The idea was to be close, but not too close. Good in theory, until you put human beings in the equation.

Especially someone like her.

His face softening, he watched her approach through the security TV monitor in the Connecticut Avenue office.

E was dressed all in beige, the color of her blond hair. Her face, too, was pale as she read the brass nameplate, double-checking it against his business card.

Nick nodded. He took a kind of sour pleasure in having calculated correctly, putting all the pieces in place to draw her to him. Like a fly to the spider.

E dreaded this encounter and wondered why she was here. Despite her doubts, she felt compelled. And hated the compulsion. After another moment's hesitation, she sighed and rang the bell.

Mrs. Martin buzzed her right in. A woman of dyed black hair and indeterminate age, she was an old-school Agency secretary. Not an unnecessary word escaped her mouth. Seated behind her shiny desk in the reception area, she gestured toward the double mahogany doors on the left.

E knocked.

"Come on in." Nick rose to greet her. "You found us okay?"

She didn't acknowledge his greeting, her eyes busy scanning the blinking wall of electronic equipment, the dark leather sofa, glossy plants and parquet floor. The computer and stacks of books. The framed maps, both antique and modern, and the row of brass clocks. Set to different time zones! She was impressed but uncomfortable. Nick didn't seem quite so down-home now. "Pretty fancy for the government."

"Actually, I'm a private consultant—under direct contract."

She shrugged. "I feel real disloyal to Mike."

"But you're loyal to your country."

"I'm here, aren't I?"

Nick kept his demeanor professional. "Some coffee?"

"This is not exactly a social call, Nick."

He gestured toward the conversation area. "Won't you at least sit a minute?"

E perched on the edge of the sofa while he sat across the coffee table. She studied her toes, sullen and resentful about being there. His ugly suspicions had slipped inside her reality and poisoned it. But there was no way around it now. The doubt had a life of its own–and she had to get it all out.

"Okay. I did notice a few strange things–not really strange, but a little." She sighed, then pushed on. "He gets home from Boston last night and takes his *briefcase* in the bathroom with him."

"Yes. And...?"

E looked at him scornfully. "A briefcase–in the *bathroom*?"

"Has he done that before?"

"That's the thing. I don't know. I never paid attention before. I thought maybe he had some new toiletries. Or a surprise for me?" Her face fell. "But that wasn't it. And then the next thing–well, first I have to explain. Mike is always so fussy about his appearance. I mean, a perfectionist, suits have to be tailored just so. He gives me the bulky stuff to carry, so I'm the only one with the bulges."

"Bulges?"

"Remember that night at the art gallery," she hurried on, "when my purse popped open? It was a small evening bag, room for just a few things."

"I thought I saw a man's wallet."

"Some fancy designer one." E swallowed. "I'm kinda nervous being here. My stomach is doing flipflops." She stared at the clocks showing the time in various parts of the world and had the crazy feeling she wanted to escape to one of those distant places.

Nick prodded her. "So last night–what did he do with these things?"

"Okay. So he gives me his wallet, cigarettes and lighter, which I put in my purse as usual. But then, I notice there's something *else* in his left jacket pocket–and it makes a bulge as big as the wallet would have."

"What was it?"

"I don't know," E snapped. "I can't figure it out," she added, her voice softening. "Then later, before we start dancing, he takes his jacket *off*– leaves it over the chair."

"So? Those clubs get pretty hot."

Her face twisted in irritation. "He never takes his jacket off. No matter how hot–never even loosens his tie."

Nick waited.

"We finish dancing, go back to the table, he puts his jacket on... and..." She stared down at her nails. "I couldn't help but look–his pocket was flat as normal!" E let out a vast sigh, suddenly drained. She felt weary and old, but also unprepared. Over her head. Foolish. She began picking at a hangnail. "Maybe I'll take you up on that coffee."

"How do you like it?"

"Cream and sugar."

Nick left her to collect herself while he went to the wet bar for the coffee.

As soon as he returned, she looked at him. "What do you think?"

He handed her a cup, then sat back down with a shake of his head. "What do you think?"

"Well... I guess someone could have taken whatever it was from his pocket while we were dancing. It seems farfetched, but why did he give me everything but that—what was so special? And where did it go?" Her brow crinkled as she repeated the questions she'd asked herself so many times since last night.

Nick saw she wished she could talk herself out of her doubts, but couldn't. He was stirred by pity. And shame. They drank their coffee in silence—not tasting it—engrossed in their thoughts. "This bulge? What was the shape?"

"Kinda flat—about this long." She opened her thumb and forefinger a few inches apart. "Square-ish."

A *camera*? "Something he's bringing back from Boston in the briefcase," Nick mused. "Never takes his jacket off." He looked at her. "Are you sure?"

"I'm not sure of anything… *now*. But no, not that I can remember."

"He ever wear an overcoat?"

E lifted her shoulders in a shrug. "Yeah, in the winter. Or a raincoat."

"Does he ever check it?"

"No. He likes to keep it at the table."

That's it. "And when did you move in with him?"

She narrowed her eyes. "Last November."

Nick felt it all click into place. A simple, but deft blend of dead-drop and brush-contact. Always in a crowded public place—always a normal guy with a normal girl. Thank you, E! "But now the weather's getting warmer—no more coats. I think you just gave me what we need, Evelyn." He held her gaze. "I don't want you to call here again. I'm going to put a tail on you, tap your phone, too." She didn't need to know that the Tesur—telephone surveillance—had been in effect for some time.

Tap? She nodded ever so slowly, as if finally realizing the changes facing her.

"Like you say, it may be nothing, but I'll be there the next time you go out–and every time. Until we're sure one way or the other, I'll be watching."

E looked into her coffee cup. Absentmindedly, she took a sip, then set it down. She stood. He followed her up and offered his hand. This time she took it.

"At least you shook my hand this time." He stared at her. Her eyes were an indefinable blend of blue and green, as he always thought the sea should be–but usually wasn't. Clear, but he couldn't quite see to the bottom.

"Evelyn? E? I pray to God I'm wrong."

She nodded, her look telling him she knew he meant it, but so what? He had forced her to betray someone she loved and she felt soiled.

Nick knew about betrayal. Once you moved a person to make that kind of decision, he crossed over to your side, but also away from the side of the angels. It was the end of innocence. There was nothing he could say to make it any better–for either of them. E left quickly, her eyes cast down and away.

Chapter 6

For the next week, Mike and E lived a normal life. He had his job and she had hers at the boutique with a day off for school. After dinner, they usually stayed home; she studied French while he did his paperwork, everything the way it had always been. But not really. When E looked at him, she saw two people: One, her boyfriend–the guy she knew and loved– who loved *her*. The other, a threatening question mark. At times she was lulled into a sort of forgetfulness, but then she would remember. The man who held her in his arms every night was suspected of treason. Of course, it was only suspicion–and people were innocent until proven guilty, but....

She wondered if he had ever concealed the contents of his briefcase after a trip? Had she ever noticed a little bulge before? Where did it go? And was she *sure* about him never taking off his jacket?

So distracted by her questions, E was almost relieved when it was time for him to leave for Boston. Mike promised to come home as soon as possible. He embraced her, stroking her hair. "Perhaps we should start thinking of something more permanent."

Permanent? It seemed that nothing was permanent in this world, nothing fixed, nothing sure. E stared at him. She read the love in his face, the naked feelings. She nodded in silence.

A few days later, Mike called to say he was taking a late flight and would meet her at F. Scott's around ten. In the taxi, she wondered if Nick were following. She turned and stared out the back window, but didn't see anyone. It occurred to her that Nick might not be there. Maybe he'd changed his mind. Maybe he'd found some new evidence and Mike wasn't who they thought he was. Maybe. The *maybe* became a prayer.

E glanced around once more after getting out of the cab. It was a beautiful evening–almost warm, with fluffy tropical clouds–and the Georgetown street was full of people and parked cars. But no Nick.

She walked down some steps to the entrance, then descended a stairway lined with art deco posters. The thump of a dance beat filled the air. Squinting, she scanned the dim room until spotting Mike in a rear corner booth.

E hurried past the backs huddled over the bar, too intent to notice that one of them belonged to Nick. As she approached Mike, he stubbed out his cigarette, pulled her down beside him and kissed her hard without a word. Something jabbed her right hip.

Praying it wasn't what she thought it was, E concentrated on the embrace. When they finally stopped, she murmured, "Welcome home."

His mouth was inches from her. "I thought about you every day–and dreamt about you every night."

"I bet you say that to all the girls."

"I mean it. I've never felt this way about a woman before."

Overcome by guilt and remorse, E glanced away... saw the cigarette pack on the table, the wallet... and then, the little bulge in his left jacket pocket! She kept her eyes down, afraid to meet his.

Mike lifted her chin, gazing at her. Then he poured some wine and raised his glass. "To us."

Her hand was trembling as she lifted her glass, forcing a smile. Nick was not here. It was just a mistake. It had to be.

Nick was nursing his Jack Daniels at the bar, aware of them without really watching. He caught the intimacy of their look and twisted the drink between his palms. Lucky bastard. At least he'd have some good memories. Nick stared into the amber liquid... at his own memories.

Jasmine wafting in with a not-so-innocent journalist in Peshawar. The heat–and ashes. A Thai woman floating above the ground. Unwrapping her sarong. Secrets within secrets. Wet bodies. Air so moist you could drink it. Or drown in it.

In the beginning, things were different. And the same. Slow summer days in Texas. Drive-in nights. Southern girls.

And now there was E. Evelyn Walker, walking wonder, proof positive that the "Made in the USA" brand was as potent as ever. At least to this good old boy.

He put his glass down. Hard.

Maybe he'd catch her on the next go-round—or maybe not—maybe he'd need her again. The Czech mole was about to burrow his way right into the joint, but there were others who would be equally susceptible to those southern charms. After all, Evelyn Walker was his agent now. He was her case officer. His job was to use—*manipulate*—his asset for the greater good. The flipping duty. Nick knew he took the case too personally. He didn't like her going to bed with a spy. Unless it was for a good cause.

As the evening passed, his glass saw more than one refill—he had to wash down all those peanuts.

Mike and E enjoyed medium-rare steak, baked potato and French burgundy. Then cappuccino.

Special Agent Don Angell, in the booth beside them, stuck with Scotch and milk.

Chris Isaak began singing about lost love. When Mike asked if she wanted to start working off dinner, E got a queasy feeling. Sure, she nodded, slipping his wallet in her purse. As they got up, she stared at him—almost holding her breath—waiting for him to remove his jacket. But he didn't. E felt a moment's hope. He took her elbow and steered her to the dance area, flashing with mirrored light. She glanced at his pocket. Whatever it was—it was still there.

When the song ended—love irretrievably lost—Mike pulled her to the edge of the half-moon floor, wiping his forehead. "It's warm in here. Be right back." He winked. "Just remember: you're taken."

With a sick feeling, E watched him walk to their table. She scanned the room for Nick but didn't spot him. She looked back at Mike as he took off his dark jacket and placed it on the seat.

E stiffened in alarm, then smiled gaily as Mike rejoined her and led her back among the dancers.

Nick lost sight of them in the crush of bodies. He exchanged a nod with Angell, then shot a glance at each of the other plainclothes men and women scattered around the club.

As Nick focused on the booth area, a big man in a navy blazer weaved past, knocking Mike's jacket to the floor. He replaced it impatiently and hurried to the exit. Nick looked around to see Angell already on his way after Mr. Blazer.

As he watched them go, Nick bent his head toward the small radio transmitter in his lapel. "Detain large man in navy blazer—Angell in pursuit."

Nick stayed put to keep tabs on Wilson. By some instinct, he glanced back just in time to see a zaftig brunette in red swivel away from a clear path and into a collision with the booth, causing the jacket to fall to the floor. She picked it up and placed it on the seat before moving away.

Jesus Christ. The first guy must have been a real drunk. They'd almost missed the whole thing. "Urgent," Nick barked into his body mike. "Grab curvy brunette in red—on her way to you *right now*!"

He leaped up. Slapped some bills on the bar and followed the woman. At the top of the stairs, she paused to put on her matching red raincoat and tie the belt. Then he opened the door and gestured: *After you.* She turned and gave him a coquettish smile.

"I see we have some rain," she said as he emerged behind her onto the shiny street.

Suddenly, several agents seemed to appear from the cracks of the buildings—most in raincoats or slickers—their weapons all pointing at the voluptuous brunette in the tight red vinyl raincoat. Don Angell flipped his badge in her face. "FBI!"

A young couple wearing safety pins and purple hair turned from the entrance and hurried away.

The broad-cheeked woman thrust her shoulders back, staring at them with disdain. "I do not know purpose why you detain me, but perhaps you are looking for someone else. My name is Hana Stassov. I am Russian diplomat, third secretary of Russian Embassy. I demand immediately to be set free."

Oblivious to the drizzle, Nick zeroed in on the beaded bag she was clutching in her left hand. So did Angell. "We'll call the State Department to verify your identity. They're kind of laid-back over there, though. Let's hope someone's on night duty." He smiled coldly. "While we're waiting, Hana—to kill some time—we'd love to have a little chat about what's in your handbag."

She glared at him.

Taking in her nicely curving figure-eight, Angell shook his head. "You don't seem to be dressed too warmly, Ms. Stassov. Wouldn't want you to get a chill." He turned to Assistant Special Agent Ron Adams, a beefy guy in a yellow windbreaker. "What kinda manners you got, Adams? Leaving a lady standing out in the rain."

Adams nudged her toward a parked white sedan, one of several similar vehicles lining the street. They watched her walk away, no longer swiveling but rigid and stiff, her back bristling with scorn. Careful, however, to keep her red patent heels out of any puddles.

Angell glanced at another Ford four-door. Mr. Blazer was sitting inside, sobbing to a female agent, apologizing for everything he had done–or not done–in his entire life.

Nick shrugged. "Probably just some drunk."

"I'll say, the dude reeks!"

"You FBI types do manage to come through from time to time. Agent *Angell.*"

"That's what angels do. They come through when you most need them. At least, that's what my mama always said."

Nick grinned at his partner, a twelve-year "brick agent" who had tenaciously moved up the ranks at WFO. "I can just see you in your choir robe."

"Adorable." Angell puffed out his chest.

"At least, that's what your mama always said."

"Always. When she wasn't putting a boot in my behind. Anyway, glad to be of service, pal." They both looked at the door. "I wonder how your girl is doing down there."

Nick's mood darkened. He hoped E was okay, that she wouldn't blow it. There were others monitoring her, but none as tuned into her as he was. Then he looked at the cloudy sky, the wet street. "Guess we're the only guys didn't check the weather report."

"Maybe you can keep warm with our new friend," Angell suggested.

Nick nodded and headed her way, with a wink at her bored FBI "escort" leaning against the car. The man moved off. He looked in through the window and smiled. "Hi."

Hana narrowed her eyes. "When do you release me? When do you realize my diplomatic immunity?"

"Soon." He knew the State Department would insist on her release so as not to poison U.S.-Russian relations. But not just yet. Nick opened the door. "Scoot over, Hana." She didn't move, so he squeezed in next to her, leaving the door open. "Cozy."

She turned away. "I like your perfume, Hana." Silence. "I like your scintillating conversation even more." More silence. "But most of all–your watch. Swiss, is it?" Nick placed a hand on her wrist, gave it a quick twist and, grabbing her beaded purse from her lap, hopped out of the car.

"This is wrongful seizure and search!" she shrieked.

"Tell me about it. A shocking disrespect for the law."

Nick had already opened her bag and seen its contents–some keys, cash and a small "calculator"–just the size E had indicated. He reached in his pocket and his hand emerged covered with an inside-out baggie which he placed over Mike's spy camera. Turning the baggie right-side-out around it, he returned her purse. "So sue me," he said. His eyes turned icy. "Or avoid embarrassment and forget it. There's some unprofessional bumbling going on here. Your next posting may be a lot less comfortable than D.C."

Hana's nostrils flared in rage. Then unexpectedly she smiled, revealing a gold tooth that glinted under the neon street light. "We have already plenty, even without that." Long orange fingernails gestured disdainfully at the baggie.

Nick rejoined Angell, who was huddled in a doorway with Ron Adams, a hefty guy who must have purchased his navy suit ten pounds ago. About when he got his windbreaker. Both men were smoking. Nick inhaled longingly. "Y'know, second-hand smoke's just not the same as the real thing."

"That have anything to do with the pleasure-pain principle?" Angell flipped his butt into a puddle as they watched it sizzle.

"There you go, getting all intellectual on me." Nick mock-frowned.

"I'll tell you about pleasure-pain." Adams patted his stomach. "See this gut. Guess what happens every time I try to quit? And we Feds got weight restrictions worse than any stewardess. Excuse me, flight attendant." He stared regretfully at his belly.

Angell straightened his shoulders and cracked his cuffs, then turned to Nick. "The hell with this small talk shit. Get anything?"

"Check it out." He held up the baggie. "The latest in microphotography. Even adds two and two."

Angell grabbed it from Nick, putting the evidence in his pocket. "Tsk-tsk. Illegal search and seizure."

Nick shrugged. "I don't know about you, but I got plenty of cause."

An agent guarding the rear called in. The most exciting action she had to report was the trash going out. Then came a terse communication from a man inside that the only movement of the "package" was on the broad.

"He'd better get it while he can," Angell commented. Nick made no response, but his face told a story. Angell gave him a look. *Oh...?*

They were all used to waiting, but it always seemed long. Eventually, they ran out of shoptalk and just watched the drizzle. Finally, Mike and E walked out the front door and up the steps to the street. Noting the change of weather, he moved his briefcase to the other hand, raised an arm to shelter her and looked around for a cab.

All at once, the FBI agents surrounded them, weapons drawn. Mike made a quick move, which Adams blocked, pinning him against a parked car. Angell flashed his badge, seizing the briefcase. "Nice and easy there, pal. FBI. You're under arrest for violation of the espionage statutes of the United States."

Mike stared at them, his face rigid.

"Step aside, E," Nick ordered.

Mike looked at her... then Nick...

Then her again. "E?" He erupted in fury, throwing off Adams' grasp, and backhanded her savagely. "You bitch!"

As E stood, frozen, Nick lunged at Mike and slugged him in the jaw. Mike recoiled. Ron Adams and Angell pulled them apart. Adams grabbed the suspect and cuffed him. Angell stuck close to Nick to prevent him from lashing out again as new Federal agents appeared, weapons pointed at the spy.

Nick wanted more of the guy and was just barely holding himself back. "No goddamn KGB spy is gonna hit this lady!"

Mike was first to regain his composure. "That is no lady—that is a whore," he said scornfully to Nick. Then he turned and met her gaze.

Her hand on her throbbing cheek, she looked into his eyes, black and bitter. For once his face was naked, no mask to hide his feeling. Mike had given her his heart and she had stomped on it. His contempt hurt worse than the blow. At that moment, E felt a shame she had never known. However pure her motives, she had betrayed a trust.

"One question, Milos. Does our new best friend, Gorbie, know what you're up to? And if not, who's running you?"

His smile was small and tight. "They'll be in touch."

Milos Wasilova didn't look back as they led him away, advising him of his rights.

E watched him go, oblivious to Nick's concern. He stared in her watery sea-green eyes, but they were impenetrable and shut him out. "You all right, E?"

She shook her head. Nick put his jacket over her shoulders, took her gently by the elbow and began moving down the street.

After several moments of silence, she turned to him. "Would you please tell me what this is all about?"

"'Mike Wilson' is really Milos Wasilova, a Czech national sent by the KGB to study in Canada–lived quietly there for many years."

She was still struggling to understand, still finding it almost incomprehensible. "*KGB*? But he seems–just like everyone else."

"That's what a mole does, E. His job is to seem exactly like everyone else. He eventually gained Canadian citizenship, was later hired by SeaTech, then relocated to Boston. He was promoted and D.C. added to his turf. The bastard has ripped off everybody. He's been spying on his friends at SeaTech for the last two years. Don't feel bad. They all trusted him, too."

"Don't feel bad?" E shook her head in dismay. "How *should* I feel? How could you possibly know?" An awful fatigue settled over her. They continued walking in silence. Then she nodded for him to go on.

"He stole secret data from SeaTech, where they design wireless listening devices for the Navy's Undersea Sonar Defense System. The USDS I told you about?"

She stared down at the shiny cobblestones. "I remember, but I still don't understand."

"I was in Special Forces, Evelyn. The way I look at it, the better our technology the fewer soldiers die. Not just on land but sea. Mike's people were trying to penetrate our coastal borders." She blinked. "It's too early to know just how much info he passed, but whatever the damage it would have been much worse without you." Nick looked at her. "Your father would be very proud."

E sighed into the glistening Georgetown night. *Pop.* She wished she could wake up and be who she used to be back home in Alert–her daddy's little girl.

Nick could see she was starting to doubt herself. He wanted to hold her in his arms and tell her it would all go away, that she'd be just fine. But she was his agent, and he had to maintain his reserve. "You're a brave woman, E. You deserve only the best in life. And you certainly deserve the truth: I work for Central Intelligence. CIA."

She turned to him numbly, circuits overloaded.

"We're more than grateful." Pretty lame. But what could you say? He wanted to explain but didn't have the words. "E? I am truly sorry." He guided her to a waiting FBI sedan and helped her inside. "They'll take you home."

Wordlessly, she handed him his jacket. As he closed the door, Nick saw her stricken face staring out the window. He saw the sorrow in her eyes—felt it. He watched the car drive away.

It was an interesting camera the Russians had developed. A technological breakthrough, capable of copying thousands of sheets of paper on the same roll of microfilm. So, as Hana said, they had already gotten plenty.

But not everything, thanks to Evelyn Walker.

Xerox had to redesign its internal mechanism to prevent further unauthorized copying, but they did get a valuable new patent out of it.

The State Department declared Hana Stassov persona non grata. She was deported to Russia where she was reassigned to a desk job in a Siberian town with no nightlife and no place to show off her voluptuous figure-eight.

The Justice Department successfully prosecuted the case against Milos Wasilova. He refused to provide any information about his U.S. operation or his controllers. He made a statement saying he was proud to have distinguished himself as a patriot, proud of his accomplishments, proud of his sense of moral obligation—and proud to plead guilty to espionage. He was sentenced to life in prison.

Nick only hoped he'd never hear of the prick being involved in a spy swap, although he had his doubts. Milos had done excellent work for his people and certainly merited their loyalty. In any case, he wouldn't be needing the contents of his safe deposit box—not the Kruggerands, the car, the financial documents.

So, somehow, the deed to Mike Wilson's condo, his savings account and the pink slip to his all-American red Mustang were all transferred into E's name.

At least she had a roof over her head.

When E returned home that night, she was hit by the enormity of Mike's deceptions and her betrayal. After her tears were finally spent, she spent hours walking through the rooms, reliving those past several months. The lies—on both sides—but also the tenderness, the comfort… the love. The growth she'd experienced. The girl from Alert had been thrown into a world she didn't know existed, but now she was part of that world. There was nowhere else to go.

The next morning, she went to work. Her eyes must have still been red, though, because when E asked if she could switch back to full-time, her silver-streaked boss, Edie, gave her a long look, a longer hug and said anytime.

E burst into fresh tears and, amid the racks of new fall arrivals, sank into Edie's pillowy bosom. "It will be okay, honey. It'll be okay."

She made it through that day and the next. When she was ready, E called her old roommate and—swearing her to secrecy—told her what had happened. Cynthia was stunned, but also kind of turned on. The hostess at a trendy restaurant, she only wanted to know why exciting things like that never happened to her.

"Stick with me," E kidded. The two young women began circulating again.

It was, as Pop would say, just spilt milk. Time to move on.

Part Two

The Company

Chapter 7

Nick kept tabs on E, even when he didn't see her for months at a time. He thought about her often–too often–but knew he had to leave it at that. In his world, a good agent was much more valuable than a good woman. And even more rare. In any case, the tall, untamed bachelor was not hurting for female company, especially in Washington where a single man was a prized commodity. The ladies were vying for the privilege of cooking him breakfast in his rundown cottage, tucked beside a cozy Chesapeake inlet. They had visions of restoring the house while reforming the man.

He did not want to be reformed, though. He knew the woman he wanted. Nick was a good soldier, though, and as it turned out so was she. He hated to take advantage of E's good nature and patriotism, but she was there. She was willing, and he had a job to do. But he only called on her when he had to. And only for a casual date with some guy they were checking out, nothing more. She always handled herself well; sometimes she came up with useful information, sometimes not.

His current case involved a shrewd Greek consultant with whom Langley did business from time to time. Alexis Kaissaris didn't care for exclusivity contracts. Gifted in the ways of global dealmaking, he thrived in a free-market economy that enabled him to buy and sell information, trade favors and put clients together.

The Company had nothing against freelance agents, often finding them quite useful. They had been generous with Kaissaris, hoping to encourage his loyalty. But he had not reciprocated, refusing to offer them right of first refusal. As a result, some very valuable goods had been landing in the wrong hands. "Prior commitments," Alexis cited. Among those prior commitments were the Iraqis, who despite their recent setback with Iran, still had him under retainer. In effect, the Americans had been outbid.

It got worse, though. The latest intelligence indicated new links between him and elements in the Russian Mafia, who were in turn connected to Red Army officers with access to a range of technology–including nuclear. When confronted by Langley about his "business plan," the Greek replied with practiced charm, "I don't want to lie to you. And also I don't want to tell you the truth. It is better for our relationship that way."

Alexis Kaissaris had many relationships, and was shielded by many layers of legitimacy. He was sophisticated in the ways of corporate disguise and cross-border transshipment. Whatever the man was up to, Nick doubted he'd discover any illegalities. Nonetheless, Jay Stiles had made their mandate clear: The Greek wheeler-dealer could not be permitted to pass anything even remotely nuclear to *any* of his clients.

Nick was working a few angles, but knew he'd have to clutch the first straw that came his way. The break finally came through DEA undercover buddy Pete Barnes, a quiet but creative sort who alerted him that something interesting was about to go down outside a D.C. office building the next morning.

Parked across the street, Nick watched two figures huddle near the entrance, coat collars up against the wintry March day. Wearing a wire inside his breast pocket, Pete leaned closer as the other man said, "Man, you are gonna love this stuff!"

"Really good, huh?"

"*Good?*" said Norris Karl, a can-do go-getter in navy blue cashmere. "I promise you, when you argue those cases today, you will sing!"

Smiling, the men exchanged envelopes.

Pete looked at the packet in his hand, then shook his head ruefully. "On second thought, Norris, I don't really want this coke–but you know what I *do* want?"

Norris furrowed his forehead in surprise. "No, what?"

Pete flipped out his I.D. "You. DEA. You're under arrest."

"Oh, shit!"

"Move it."

Nick, seated in the back of the parked white sedan, watched the two men approach, then reached over and opened the door. As the driver slipped out for a smoke, Pete gestured. "After you." Expressionless, Karl slid inside the car.

Pete followed him in and slammed the door with a grin. "Okay, old buddy, we're even now."

"Getting there." Nick turned to the man. "Ross is the name. Nick Ross. Security Consultants International." He didn't offer to shake hands. "You must be Norris Karl. That clever fixer I've heard about?"

The man replied with an indifferent shrug.

"I take that as an affirmative. I bet you even know a little something about the law, do you?"

Karl sat staring straight ahead. His stone-face showed a hairline crack.

"Good. Because I have a proposition I'm sure will interest you: A bit of your highly specialized assistance—or thirty years." Nick looked through his prey. "Right, Pete?"

"Well, maybe twenty. Give or take."

"This's fucking entrapment. I'll walk."

"Maybe. Maybe not." Nick gave him a hard look. "Do you really want to chance it?" The man refused to meet his eye, but Nick definitely had his attention. "If I were you, I'd want to even the odds a little."

"I'm listening."

Nick nodded. "It's about your associate Alexis Kaissaris. Smart guy, but suddenly he gets a hard-on against us—that is, my clients—and won't return our calls. At a time when he has a lot to chat about. We thought maybe you could help. Unless you've got some ethical problem here?"

There was no need to lay it all out for Karl. Nick told him only what was necessary—and that related to one of the more intimate services Karl provided Kaissaris. When the Greek entrepreneur came to town, Norris Karl was his go-to guy. For business—or pleasure.

After Nick finished his explanation, Karl looked back and forth between his two adversaries. He shrugged, then flashed his shark-like teeth in what pretended to be a smile. "As they say on TV—'Let's make a deal.'"

E knew Nick was behind her unexpected windfall, the condo and bank account. The Kruggerands. Probably a guilty conscience. But not only. She felt he had always liked her, so his concern wasn't surprising. It did surprise her, though, why he never called for a date, just business, and then only every few months. As to the past, E didn't really hold it against him. It was his duty. And however much it had hurt, she understood that he'd saved her from a horrible fate. Married to a *spy*? Things had worked out for the best.

Except in one area. Despite her regular Sunday phone calls home–to Bobby, at least–Pop still wouldn't talk to her. She had the hope things would be different in person.

One day in early spring she and Cynthia arranged their work schedules and set off for Alert in the red Mustang convertible. When they pulled into the gas station, Bobby was just walking up with his backpack. E jumped from the car, smothered him in a hug and burst into tears.

He wiped his face. "Girls!" he winced, but couldn't fight the grin.

E felt weepier than ever in her life. It had been over two years since she'd left, and time about slapped her in the face. Bobby was tall–at least three inches taller. "You're so *big*, Bobby." She turned with pride. "Cynthia. You want to meet one heckuva handsome guy?"

Cynthia got out, sleek in her tight indigo jeans. "Hey, Bobby. Your sis never stops talking about you." She cocked her head, studying the two siblings. "You look like her."

"That supposed to be a good thing?"

"Someday you're gonna be glad. Very glad. Trust me." She winked, then looked around. "Say, I really have to go."

"The bathroom's the other side of the–" E felt his presence before she heard or saw him. Pop... standing at the office door, arms crossed. Staring.

"I think I'll go find that john." Cynthia walked quietly around to the bathroom.

E didn't smile, but her eyes were bright with hope. "Hi, Daddy."

He didn't respond in any way, stood there stiffly, looking at her. "I raised you to be better than trash."

"But–"

Her father glanced at the red car. "If you'd a come home before–on the bus? But you couldn't do that, could you, girl? Too independent. Just like your damn mother."

As she moved toward him, Sam Walker held up a hand. "And your shiny friend? Looks like some holiday, only not on my calendar." He shook his head. "I failed with you, and I'm ashamed of that failure. Better go back where ya came from, Evelyn."

Terror filled her being. "But I come from here, Daddy. I just want to talk to you. Talk to Bobby. I miss y'all." Her speech was slowing again, feeling the rhythms of home.

He didn't bend. "You left of your own free will, and no way can I force back the hand of that clock. Even if your mama come home and crawled up this here street, no way could I take her back. People gotta learn. You make a decision and abide by it."

E stared dully, hearing his words, but not hearing them. She turned, gazing at this place that had been her world. "Everything looks the same." The truth was, everything looked the same, but more so. More slow. More quiet. And definitely more small.

"Nothin's the same, Evelyn. Done is done. I'm sorry."

E gazed at him across the abyss. She wanted to run and hug him–make him love her again–but his coldness reached out to her and she was frozen to the spot. Even the tears froze behind her eyes. She could still see Bobby, though. What about the promise to her mother, to explain everything to him? Why she'd had to go.

"Go on inside, son. This here's none a your concern."

Bobby frowned, then shook his head to say he was sorry. E shrugged sadly. He frowned again and shuffled off to the garage, kicking a stone in front of him.

It was a body blow and E could barely breathe. She had truly believed Pop would forgive her if she showed up and asked real nice. "I love you, Daddy," she murmured into the dust.

When Cynthia returned from the bathroom, E was waiting in the car. She didn't say much as they cruised up Main Street... past Ida's coffee shop, the five and dime, the white-steepled church and brick grade school. Past the deep front yards with their porches and rocking chairs, their budding trees and tire swings, their white picket fences and early tulips. E knew who lived in each of those houses and had spent time at many of them, playing dolls and piano and hide-and-seek. That was all behind her now. Over.

Then they passed a sign–ALERT, pop. 1,273–stuck along a tobacco field. Soon the cultivated areas were behind them. Dark oaks and white pines lined the road, all touched with new life. E knew she'd better look forward, because behind her there was nothing. She sighed, let out all the air. But the air she took in was fresh and clean.

It was spring, her favorite season. She thought of the park near her condo, everything just leafing out. It would be nice to get back to Washington. Back home.

When she arrived, there was a message on her answering machine. The woman had a southern accent and called her honey. *Mama.* E listened to the message—over and over—and longed to talk to her, but she didn't leave her number and never called again.

The Norris Karl angle wasn't a great one, but it was the only one they had. After a few more weeks of fruitless investigation, Nick set up a meeting with Jay to brief him.

Their appointment was a Monday in early April, which turned out to be the day of the annual White House Easter Egg Hunt. Since Jay had promised to take the wife and kids, he suggested Nick meet him there.

By the time he arrived, the White House lawn was mobbed with thirty or forty thousand people buzzing around, powered by sugar, even those who never indulged. But today the proud parents needed their energy to chase kids, snap pictures, change dirty diapers and find more goodies seeded among the green—all the painted eggs, jelly beans and chocolate marshmallows. Joining the festivities were jugglers, mimes, clowns—and of course the Easter Bunny in a pink gingham pinafore and beribboned bonnet.

Back in Jakarta when he was starting out, Nick had met and married a charming colleague from Shreveport. It had been a shock when, after two years, the dynamic brunette left him for the soon-to-be-transferred-to-Paris Chief of Station. Jill had seen Nick for what he was: a sincere fellow not at all into Company politics—and not at all likely to rise to stellar heights. It was a distasteful mess, but at least there were no children.

As he made his way through the crowd, Nick did not regret that decision. Maybe one at a time kids were okay, if you were a real family, but otherwise.... Then around the side of the White House, he spotted Jay. "Having fun, chief?"

Jay rolled his eyes. "Christ. I'd rather be behind enemy lines. I've never seen so many runny noses in my life."

Nick waved at Muffie Stiles, kneeling on the grass with their two kids. Wearing a pageboy, penny loafers and pearls, she smiled with what Nick always felt was plastic warmth. He didn't exactly figure in her world.

Then little Sally Ann, all pink and lacy, shrieked with glee. She had just found one of the hidden wooden eggs. Pointing to the White House insignia, she held it up with pride. But Jay Jr., a brute camouflaged in short pants and grass-stained white socks, pushed her and she dropped it. Sally Ann burst into tears.

As Muffie opened her arms to Sally Ann and scolded the boy, Jay gave Nick a nudge. They headed up a small rise where they could still view his family.

"You are lucky to have them, you know." Nick was not unaware of a certain emptiness in his life. But it was the only life he knew and you made your choices.

"That's what she says. Truth is, I'd go back into the field in a minute if I could."

The truth was—that wasn't the truth. Jay Stiles was a politician and a bureaucrat. He loved operating there, at the center of power. However being a field operative was seen to be more macho, so a preference for that life was a pleasant fiction he maintained.

Nick nodded. "We all got our problems. You? The brass likes too much—and me? Well, I didn't go to Yale, you know." He shrugged. "Anyway, looks like we finally got a hook into Kaissaris. His hot shit local fixer, Norris Karl, is suddenly very grateful to us."

Jay rubbed his chin. "How fortunate."

"The guy takes care of the big man when he's in town, gets him the best women and all. It seems Karl has one helluva black book."

"Hmmm. Wouldn't mind having a look-see myself."

"I bet. The Greek is picky as hell, but our guy claims to have his type down cold."

Eyes bright with interest, Jay waved at Muffie and the kids. They held up more eggs to show him, peace evidently restored. "And just what is his type?"

"According to Karl, he likes them fresh and unspoiled, likes to put them through finishing school. And he doesn't often go back for seconds. Usually passes them on to his associates. Party favors, if you follow."

"A connoisseur, huh?" Jay rubbed his chin. "How about Pauline?"

"She—uhh—drowned in Bangkok last summer. They found her body in a canal."

"A pity. Those canals are getting so polluted."

"Yeah." Nick frowned. Pauline was a sweet girl, an embassy secretary who had wanted more from life. She'd jumped at the chance to help out a little and agreed to date a Thai businessman involved in some smuggling arrangement with a renegade Burmese warlord. Unfortunately, the Burmese secret police wanted to send a message. They shot up the taxi Pauline and the guy were riding in, then dumped it in the canal. A drowning "accident" that avoided messy politics. It wasn't his operation, but Nick still grieved for the cheery little redhead from Iowa who died such a lonely death.

"Excuse me. I see I'm being paged." Jay focused on Muffie, who gestured that she and the kids were moving around to the front lawn for the Easter Egg Roll.

As they followed, Jay took out a handkerchief and mopped his forehead. "Whatever happened to spring?" He frowned. "Say, how about that little southern belle with the beestung lips?"

Nick gave him a blank look. "Actually, I was thinking of someone a bit more–sophisticated. Like Suzanne Marchetti. I'm not sure how well E would do in such a fast crowd."

Jay raised a frosty silver eyebrow. "We have an SOS from Interpol and even the fucking KGB. And you're worried about an *agent?*"

Nick shrugged. "I just don't like turning her into a whore. I know what Nick and his crowd are like."

Jay waved at the kids. "And exactly how many guys you think she screwed last year? I've kept track of her, and your little Miss Everlovin' E is no Mary Poppins, that's for damn sure." He turned to Nick with a comradely clap on the back. "I happen to know about those down-home gals. That innocent look? Just a look. Underneath, they're hot to trot."

Little Sally Ann ran up, her pink organza dress now covered with grass stains. "Are you watching, Daddy?"

Jay lifted her into his arms. "I'm watching, sweetheart." He gave her a big kiss, then gazed coolly over her flaxen hair at Nick. "God wouldn't have created women if he didn't want us to use them." He smiled, but the smile contained a warning. "Don't get your priorities mixed up, Sir Galahad. We've been tossed a time bomb–and *someone's* got to defuse it."

He put his daughter down and absently patted her head. His eyes followed her as she ran off to rejoin Mommy and Jay Jr. "In our business, chivalry died a long time ago."

Nick watched Sally Ann, too. It was easier than looking at the chief. "I'll take care of it."

Chapter 8

Nick waited for E in a quiet corner of the Georgetown campus near the C&O Canal. Then he saw her and marveled. She seemed to get better and better. No more the naïve country girl, she radiated a knowing eroticism. Yet she still had that innocent charm. It was a combination that disturbed the hell out of him. Sugar and spice, definitely the right type for their Greek friend–but that didn't mean he had to like it.

E lit up when she saw Nick, moving to give him a hug. But he just held out his hand. They shook, a little longer than normal.

It was a beautiful day, breezy and blue, walkway lined with dazzling yellow. "Daffodils," she exclaimed. "Remember? Last year?"

"You love spring and you love daffodils."

She lifted her chin, visibly pleased.

Nick wanted to touch the dimple in that chin. "How's work?"

"I went back to full-time. Still auditing my French class, though."

He winked. "You must be fluent by now."

"Coming along. I've been reading *L'Histoire de Babar*–the Elephant King, you know. It's supposed to be a kid's book, but I keep *mon dictionnaire* handy." She glanced at him. "And you? How's the–consultancy business going?"

"Same old, same old."

"Umm-hmm."

They set off along the canal, which ran parallel to the Potomac River all the way up to Maryland–George Washington's plan to improve trade by linking the interior with the Atlantic. Traffic these days was considerably less, a barge, a few canoes. Some ducks.

Nick and E shared the towpath with a handful of joggers and other kindred spirits. The tumbling water reflected lush greenery that reminded them both of distant country lanes. It was a treat, this tranquility, far from the urban frenzy. So far, yet so near.

When they reached Wisconsin Avenue, they headed up to M Street. There, in the eye of the frenzy, they grabbed a couple of chili dogs from Hal.

Hal put on an angry face. "Where you been, Evelyn?" She shook her head. "I know you don't need Nick no more for directions," he scolded.

She grinned. "If you forgive me, I promise to come back real soon."

"Deal."

She opened her purse, but Nick insisted on paying. As they ate, they walked back down Wisconsin to the canal, the city sounds gradually muffled by trees and water.

After they finished, E smiled. "You sure know how to treat a girl."

"Noticed, huh?"

"Still, I wish you'd have allowed me to go Dutch—"

"Come on. It's the least I can do."

"Because I have a sneaking suspicion this is another one of those lunches that's going to end up costing. A lot."

The quiet of the towpath was suddenly too quiet. Nick slowed, sensing her sideways glance. Nailed. For some odd reason, he felt naked, embarrassed that she had seen through his BS. Even odder, he felt pleased that she had caught him out. He met her gaze for a brief instant and their look acknowledged long-buried feelings and concerns, thoughts that must remain buried.

Nick recovered and slipped the mask back on. He picked up his pace, realizing what had just happened. It was a spring day and he was feeling good. Beautiful girl at your side. And you almost lose it. Seduced by the pleasure of it all, he had dropped his guard. So much so that he nearly forgot the purpose of the meeting, forgot that he was in the middle of a major operation. Wanted to forget. It was unprofessional. Dumb. He was the one supposed to control the agenda—not the agent.

A mule approached, towing a barge up the canal the traditional way. Just ahead was the landing where tourists boarded. Nick and E barely noticed.

"I'm right then, aren't I?" She crossed her arms in triumph. "Come on, Nick. You don't mind that I beat you to the punch, do you? What's up?"

So much for trying to finesse her. E had pulled the rug out from under him and Nick needed to regain the upper hand. His expression turned sober. "I do have a favor to ask, E. A very important one. It has to do with a Greek businessman—Alexis Kaissaris. A wheeler-dealer who's joint-venturing with the Russian Mafia in the nuclear black market."

"Nuclear?" Her arms dropped, her jaw. "*Russia?*"

Nick nodded. "These days, everyone over there wants to make a deal—even the military."

"But why? Why would a soldier—?"

"Either that or sell pencils on the street. We're talking sixty percent inflation—a month. A lot of cutbacks. A lot of bitterness. A lot of shattered beliefs. So now they're supposed to believe in capitalism, something they were raised to view as evil. It's confusing. Free market—black market—they don't know the difference. Russia's like Dodge City these days, before the marshal arrived."

"But... *nuclear?*"

His mouth tightened. "Exactly. When military and Mafia join forces—well, that's an octopus could strangle us all. And the Russian Mafia makes the Sicilians look like a bunch of priests. Moscow is scared shitless and has asked for our help."

E listened in shock.

"Now, with Alex as middleman, we've got to expect a change in strategy. What he's peddling—and to *whom*—we don't know. He's got a list of customers as long as your arm. Mine, even." He paused a moment, looking at her. "We need to get next to him before the transaction takes place."

She held his gaze. "And you think *I* can get next to him better than anyone else?"

Nick didn't know whether to laugh or apologize. He cleared his throat, then reached in his pocket and pulled out an envelope. "We'd like you to accept this $5000 consultancy fee, maybe use it for some new dresses or something." He didn't quite meet her eye.

E shook her head. "You know, Nick, I don't really need the money. I have a job. And Mike was more than generous." Her gaze was playful, but intimate. "Not to mention you."

Nick gave her a sharp look.

She kept it light. "And I have a great condo. I should have you over to dinner one night. Nice of Mike to give it to me. Don't you think?"

"Oh, yeah. Helluva nice guy." He felt off-guard again and didn't know where she was going. Was she messing with his head? Or just teasing? "E, it's important or I wouldn't ask."

E stared back. She put a gentle hand on his arm. "Have you forgotten what my Daddy taught me about patriotism, Nick?" She swallowed. "And by the way, thanks for putting in the good word. Or do they send those letters to everyone… on official U.S. Government stationery?"

Nick glanced away.

"At least that's what Bobby told me. Commendation for service rendered." Her sea-green eyes were very clear. "It would be an honor to serve my country... but not for the money."

Mission accomplished. Agent launched. Nick was still disturbed, though, by where he was about to send her. "The Greek lives in the fast lane, but likes old-fashioned women. So, uhh, don't be too–clever around him." He lifted a corner of his mouth. "Guess that applies to most men."

She gave him that knowing look. "Including you, Nick?"

He wasn't sure how she did it, or how hard she tried. She kept getting to him, though–slipping sideways under his skin. He wondered what was going through her mind. But this was dangerous turf. "Well, maybe not me."

E pinned him with her eyes and he couldn't escape. "You married, Nick?"

"Was."

"Ahhh." She smiled. "How much money you make?"

He shook his head. "Not enough, E, not nearly enough."

E's smile faded. How did he know what was enough or not enough? He didn't seem the type to care about being rich. And she knew *she* didn't care. Once again she wondered why he never tried to get closer. Then she shrugged. Maybe it was better to have a friend.

Nick leaned down and snapped off a scalloped yellow and peach daffodil. As he presented it to her, their hands met. Neither of them moved for a moment.

"Pretty flower," she said. "You got a girlfriend, Nick?"

"One or two."

Still being the smart ass. "Ahhh," she repeated.

They stood staring at each other awkwardly. Then Nick handed her the envelope. "I'd appreciate it if you'd take this."

A little hurt, although not exactly sure why, E shrugged again and dropped it in her purse. She looked away. "Just let me know, Nick. But right now, I've got a hot date—with my hairdresser." She looked back and met his eyes. "See you, Nick."

"You, too, E."

As she turned to go, a cloud seemed to pass over the sun and the canal turned dark.

It was the first Sunday in May and the warm breeze promised a perfect afternoon. E had selected a filmy, sea-green dress, at once feminine and seductive. Trailing behind some other new arrivals, she moved up the sloping front lawn toward the Federal-style brick mansion. The Dumbarton Oaks estate had been graced by spring—plenty of daffodils along with lilacs, peonies and roses, all in their first, most exuberant flush. Almost as nice as the North Carolina countryside, she thought, feeling a little displaced.

Sounds of music and subdued laughter drifted from the conservatory's open French doors. E ran a hand over her hair and straightened her shoulders. She took a deep breath, then entered. Home to potted plants in winter, the Orangerie was today the scene of a charity event with elegant guests and a string quartet playing Mozart. Pale sun filtered through the high glassed-in roof. Everyone seemed to know someone.

Now what? E made another tentative step, stopped, then commanded herself into action. She moved to the bar and ordered a Chardonnay. Turning, she glanced coolly about, recognized the two men standing beside a ficus-covered wall and picked up her drink, nodding her thanks to the bartender.

E wandered out to a hillside terrace dominated by a great black oak, then opened a wrought iron gate and continued down a brick path to another terrace. She paused to admire a sturdy beech tree and remembered a time, not too long ago, when she would have climbed it. Then she looked down at a quiet, leafy space where a fountain trickled over an expanse of pebble mosaic. She followed the steps to the Pebble Garden and paused, a breeze playing with the hem of her skirt. She felt the sun on her skin and it soothed her. Still, she was anxious.

You can do it, she told herself. You *must* do it. It's your duty. Taking slow, calming breaths, she stared at the shimmering flow of water over cupids and seahorses.

Footsteps approached. "Evelyn?"

As she turned, Norris Karl grinned. "I thought it was you, Evelyn–and looking more beautiful than ever."

"Hello, Norris," she replied coolly, all too aware of the powerful presence beside him, an imposing figure with a thick, silver-streaked mane and broad shoulders. A lion of a man.

Norris took Alexis's arm. "We have a visitor among us, just in from Athens. My dear friend, Alexis Kaissaris. Alex–Miss Evelyn Walker."

"It is a very great pleasure, Miss Walker." His dark blue eyes holding hers, the Greek visitor extended his hand.

"Mr. Kaissaris."

"Alexis, please."

E felt the gentle pressure of his touch, the heat. He didn't let go. A slow smile spread over her face. As Alexis returned it, she noticed his sensual mouth, his olive skin and white teeth. He wore a sleek Italian suit that played counterpoint with his intense animal magnetism. She released his hand.

"Well, I'm off for a refill," Norris said. "Alex? Evelyn?"

Alexis had not taken his eyes off her. "No, we're very fine, thank you." He inclined his head. "Aren't we... May I call you Evelyn?"

E dimpled sweetly and nodded. It was a shock to admit she was attracted by the man, his aura of strength and power. Then she reminded herself that he was dangerous, a threat to her country... that she was playing a role with him, that it was not real.

"Such an unexpected pleasure, Evelyn. You will join me for a stroll in the garden?"

"And perhaps you will tell me something of your country."

"I would like that very much." Alexis plucked her glass away, setting it down beside his own.

E looked in his piercing blue eyes. "My friends call me E."

Alexis offered his arm. She took it, breathing in his smell–some kind of woodsy cologne, very faint, very fine, very male.

Except for a few previous engagements that neither could avoid, Alexis and E saw each other every evening for the next two weeks. She was always demure, asked his advice and laughed at his jokes. She really did enjoy his company, and it showed. He really was smitten–and that too showed.

Then he had to fly to Singapore for the Asian Aerospace show. He told her it was the type of event he usually relished. "But this time I am reluctant to go."

"So you must hurry back soon."

It had been over a year since the earlier message. E was just walking in the door one night when the phone rang. The southern accented-voice was warm and flowing... and the woman called her "honey." It was her mother.

They agreed to meet for Sunday tea at the Four Seasons in Georgetown. E was really nervous, not knowing what to wear, how to behave, or what to say. She finally settled on a beige raw silk suit—*linen wrinkles*—with pearls. Very Miss Proper, she thought as she studied herself in the mirror. Everything but the white gloves. She longed to look in her mother's eyes and see... approval. Acknowledgment that she'd turned out okay.

E arrived early and was seated in a corner armchair of the lounge. Overlooking the C&O Canal, the Garden Terrace was light and spacious, yet cozy. Flowers filled the room. As E stared out the tall windows, the waiter placed a menu on the low, glass-topped table in front of her. She picked it up but was unable to concentrate, words dancing on the page. A distinguished, silver-haired pianist sat down at the Steinway and began a Chopin *Prelude*. E closed her eyes, trying to picture her mother.

When she opened them again, she saw an attractive, self-assured woman appear in a red suit with gold buttons and chains. With an air of bustle and importance, she moved directly toward E. The waiter pulled out a chair and the woman eased it closer.

E sat up straight in her seat.

The woman studied her for a very long moment, then stretched out her strong hands and took those of her daughter. "Evelyn, honey. Aren't you just the most beautiful little thing!"

Every ounce of self-confidence fled. E wasn't even sure what to call her. It was Mommy when she was little, then Mama. Mom. Her lips started to quiver. "I don't know what to say—even what to call you."

"Evelyn, honey. Why don't y'all just start with my name. I think Flo Rita sounds better than Mother, don't you." A statement, not a question.

E nodded slowly. She tried it out. "Flo Rita." *Mama.* Her hair was redder now.

Flo Rita smiled, then placed E's hands back in her lap and patted her knee. "Well, then, what would y'all like to drink?" E shook her head. "How about if I just order then, honey?" Without even looking at the menu, Flo Rita held up a finger for the waiter, then told him they'd have Earl Gray tea, scones and sherry. "And Sweet'N Low, please. Sugar, too," she added with a glance at her daughter. "Looks like you don't need to watch things."

E lifted a shoulder, speechless, feeling as if she were six years old again—in awe of her perfect mother.

"You're healthy, I can see that," Flo Rita said. "Besides being beautiful."

"You're beautiful, too..." E's words trickled off. Calling her Flo Rita just didn't feel right.

"I exercise, watch what I eat, but most of all I'm blessed to be married to a wonderful man."

E took hold of her mother's confident hand, staring into her hazel eyes. "I'm so happy. You know, I think about you all the time, trying to be how I thought you'd be. I've missed you so." Her eyes filled with tears.

Flo Rita reached over and touched E's cheek. "There. There. Well, now we've found each other. You see that I made it, and I see that you did. I think you inherited my survivor's instinct, so I don't have to worry about you, Evelyn."

E remembered back to the phone message. "Was that really you who called last year?"

"Yes, honey, it was me. But it's been a busy year—travel, family. This is the first chance I got to spend some time with you."

"Where do you live now?"

"Mostly Atlanta."

E smiled. "I remember you called it your Mecca. That last night before you left?"

Flo Rita looked startled a moment, searching her memory. "In a way. I found my salvation there, that's for sure. After being so bad, life finally turned good." She paused. "You do know—I had no choice, what I did."

The waiter arrived, his trolley laden with pots of tea and hot water, milk, various sweeteners, scones, strawberry jam and cream. And two small glasses of sherry. They hardly noticed.

E nodded. "I know." Then she thought of her brother. "Bobby will be so excited! Maybe he could come and visit us. We'll all be together again, just like before."

Flo Rita stared, then moved her head slightly and spoke slowly, carefully. "Evelyn, honey. Things change in life. And one thing I've learned, they're never just like before. Can't be. And it hurts too damn much to try."

E remembered seeing her father last year. "Yeah, but...."

"I had an awful hard struggle when I left your old Pop. Had to work as a waitress, live in a rooming house with a bunch of drunks. I went to night school, then got a job as a secretary and found a nice clean apartment. I was lonely, but had no choice–no place to go back to if I failed." She searched her daughter's eyes. "I did charity work, went to church, made a position for myself. I raised myself from poor white trash to somebody. Finally, I was hired as secretary to a lawyer and then he and I fell in love. We got married, and that Georgia lawyer was elected to be a Representative to the United States Congress."

Flo Rita took a deep breath, then reached for her glass of sherry. After a sip or two, she began to tell her story.

There was a time–long ago–when she had seen her future in E's father. Flo Rita Bayless was someone who'd known less and wanted more. Sam Walker captivated her; he was older and had been around. Soon after sweeping her off her feet, he took her to Atlanta on their honeymoon. She was two months pregnant then, but never mind. It was all so exciting, and she forgot about going back to college. Sam doted on her and their little girl. And Bobby. Then he shipped off to Vietnam–and things were different. But when he came home on furlough, he was a tiger–romantic and passionate–with wonderful tales. Flo Rita marked off the days on the calendar, waiting for him to finish his tour and come home for good, then they'd live happily ever after. But it didn't turn out that way.

After his discharge, they moved to Alert–and she began to wonder why she had waited. Suddenly that ten years Sam had on her didn't sit so well. And his stories became old. She really tried, but she couldn't breathe in that small town. She felt white cotton threads winding around her, smothering her. Every day the cocoon got thicker, stickier. She became frantic. She loved her two children–but just had to leave. If she didn't, she might start hating her life so much she'd start hating *them*.

Flo Rita put down her glass and began fussing with the pots, pouring the tea through a strainer, adding milk and sugar to one cup, sweetener to another. She handed the first cup to her daughter.

E took a sip but tasted only bitterness. Really uncomfortable now, she stared at this woman–her mother–the strong, competent stranger who had crossed the lobby with such an unwavering stride. E sensed the stranger was trying to tell her something that she didn't want to hear.

"Evelyn, darlin'. This man thinks I was a childless widow when we met. I just couldn't tell him I walked away from a husband and two little children. I just couldn't."

E blinked, finally starting to see the truth, but fighting that reality. "If he loves you, he'll understand."

Flo Rita met her eyes, face naked. "I'm afraid to take that chance, honey. I can't."

Only then did E realize the extent of her wishes for today. Now she felt bereft, deprived of hope. *Alone.* "Mama." The word escaped her throat and ended in a strangled cry. She grabbed her mother's arm. "But I need you… I lost you. I want you back."

Flo Rita swallowed hard. "I shouldn't have called–I knew I shouldn't– but I needed to see my little girl again, to know how you turned out." Her features softened. "And you turned out fine–beautiful. You'll be fine without me. Better without me."

"Please." E's fingers dug into her mother's arm. Flo Rita raised her arm to smooth her daughter's hair. E's hand stood poised in mid-air, then slowly fluttered down, a fallen leaf.

Flo Rita took a moment to compose herself. "And, Evelyn? If by chance in this small town our paths should ever cross? It'd be best for all concerned if we both just walk away." With that, she removed some money from her purse and tossed it on the table. "Like I'm doin' now. Have a good life, Evelyn, honey."

Wait! E didn't even know her last name.

The words rang in her head–a plea, a prayer–but nothing came out of her mouth. Dazed, E stared after her mother as she walked from the room, self-contained and sure. The pianist began Chopin's "Raindrop" *Prelude.*

Chapter 9

For the first time in her life, E felt truly alone. The dream of her mother being somewhere out there had always sustained her. Now she was an orphan, rejected by both parents. With the loss of her family, she felt untethered and disconnected. There seemed no reason, for anything. Except maybe her job for Nick.

E had no energy, dragging herself out of bed in the morning and off to work at the boutique, where she managed to sell cheery summer dresses as if she really cared. In the evening, she fell back into bed, relieved to escape the world.

It was just as well that Alexis was out of town.

Singapore

He was in Singapore, at the biennial Asian air show, an event drawing buyers from around the world. The government of Singapore had hired Kaissaris as a consultant, hoping to woo investors to its fledgling aerospace industry. As usual, though, Alexis worked for many clients, including Li Chin-Wah, cousin of a highly placed official. Despite his excellent contacts, Li needed capital to fulfill a soon-to-be-announced Japanese contract. Alexis made some suggestions regarding the means to obtain this capital. Li said he would consider any and all options.

Later that evening, relaxing in his Mandarin suite, Alexis heard a tap on the door. He was not surprised to see Li's assistant Julia Chen. Small and slim, she seemed taller because of her proud carriage. She had regal manners and all-seeing, catlike eyes.

Julia regarded him with a red-lipped smile. "Please excuse me for the lateness of the hour."

"Between us, my darling, there is no time, only eternity. And your dazzling beauty."

Her laughter was like wind chimes on a sultry evening. "Alexis, I pray you never lose your silver tongue."

They stood a moment, remembering the pleasures they had taken in each other. Pleasure, however, was expensive in this world, and one had to have the means to pay.

"Again, I apologize for the delay." Julia opened her orange Hermès handbag and removed an envelope. "Li Chin-Wah is a most demanding man. His wife carries with her the morals of the convent. Rather than forcing her to confession, he calls me."

"But you too are convent bred."

She smiled wickedly into his eyes. "Yes, but I enjoy confession."

Nodding in recognition of her sinful gifts, Alexis took the envelope. "I only hope Mr. Li retains the energy to attend to business."

"His Confucian ethics dictate that he work hard in every aspect of life."

"And his Confucian connections bring him work." Alexis understood the traditional Chinese ethic of devotion to family, its honor and success.

"This is true. We are a small island-state and must use everything we have." Then she glanced toward the ice bucket inside the living room. "Will you not offer me a glass?"

"Please," he gestured, moving to open the bottle of Cristal. The champagne bubbled forth like liquid gold. He filled two glasses, handing one to her. "To old friends."

Lifting her glass in response, Julia took a sip and then stepped out of her shiny snakeskin heels. "It has been a long day, darling. Do you know what I would like?" He looked at her. "A hot foamy bath."

"I will draw it for you."

Alexis left Julia to her bath. She was a desirable woman with exquisite talents, but the talent that satisfied him most was her knowledge of business—and businessmen. In this, he was already satisfied. Inside the envelope were shares of privately held stock in Li Chin-Wah's small manufacturing company—and the date it would go public. Kaissaris had some creative notions on the use of this packet, and Julia would be well rewarded, to keep her coming back for more. But as to a late night liaison, he was not interested. His mind was elsewhere.

Washington, D.C.

When the phone rang, E was sitting in bed surrounded by a Babar picture book, an English-French dictionary and French Vogue. She turned another page of *L'Etranger* by Camus, a novel of clear, direct language within her range. But now all she saw were blurs of black and white, its first line still smoldering in her heart: *"Aujourd'hui, maman est morte."* Maman died today. Today, mama died.

Shaky, she stared at the telephone before answering, then finally heard his voice purring across the seas. "I am thinking of you, my beauty. I miss you."

"Yes," was all she could force out of her mouth.

Unaware of her distress, he thought she was playing coy. As much as her indifference continued to excite him, it was beginning to make him angry. He had focused all his skills of seduction on her and yet she seemed unimpressed. He wanted to pierce that indifference. And naturally, he would. He smiled into the phone. "I am returning in two days and hope you will be free to accompany me to dinner."

"Of course," she said quietly.

"I am looking forward to it."

"Me, too."

But her voice didn't sound it, and he felt uneasy. As he rang off, he realized how much he wanted her and began calculating how he would rekindle her passion.

Alexis took her to the Two Continents in the Sky Restaurant and its view of the national monuments did not fail to thrill E, despite herself. The piano music was lovely, too, and the candlelight. She was glad he was back; his return gave her something to focus on. E knew the importance of her work for Nick and the government... for all of them. Literally life and death! It was sobering to realize that the fate of her country might rest on her shoulders. This responsibility was all she had. She had failed with her parents, not making them love her, at least not enough to fight for her. She must not fail here.

She raised her eyes from the menu. "Alex, honey, I need your advice."

"But of course, my beauty. Anything."

"I'm torn between the *blanquette de veau* and *pigeon aux raisins*. What do you think?"

Alexis reached over and touched her lips. "I think *pigeon*, if only to watch you say it."

E tilted her head. "Are you mocking my French?"

"Not at all. It is your southern accent that makes it so delightful."

"I'm not sure my professor would agree with you."

Alexis glowered. "I hope he is not giving you trouble."

"I'm kidding. Actually, I'm an A student," she said with pride.

"I'll bet you are." He gave her that piercing look.

A part of her wanted to sink into his deep blue eyes. "But thank you for offering to defend my honor, Alex."

"It would be *my* honor. You have emerged like Artemis from our ancient myths, an untouchable maiden, never conquered by love. The chaste goddess of *la chasse.*"

"The hunt."

"Exactly, my dear. Makes you wonder if anyone ever caught her."

After dinner an empty wine bottle remained on the table along with coffee and remnants of dark chocolate cake. All at once he leaned forward, touched his mouth to hers and tasted. E felt the light pressure of his teeth and it made her tingle. Then, after maybe seconds or maybe minutes, he pulled away.

Alexis let out a laugh. "It is a long time since I have been so captivated by a woman. And it pleases me. In gratitude, I offer you a small gift." He handed her an oblong box, tied with gold ribbon.

"Why, Alex." E unwrapped it slowly. On a bed of purple velvet lay a long strand of baroque pearls. Holding it up to the candlelight, she marveled at the glow, each pearl slightly different in shape, yet blending together with more richness than a matched set. She began to open the diamond-studded clasp.

"It is a bit tricky, this clasp. You will allow me?"

She smiled. He was charming, unpredictable–and there was something about his eyes, almost hypnotic. "Of course."

Placing the pearls around her throat, Alexis leaned closer, fastening the clasp. He ran a gentle finger along the nape of her neck. Then mouth, tongue and teeth moved in to explore. He reached her ear and whispered, "The earrings to match are in Athens–waiting. Will you accompany me?"

E turned, their faces very close. "What is it they say about Greeks bearing gifts?"

It was dead of night over the Atlantic and Olympic Airway's first class cabin was quiet. Alexis's head was back, dozing. E closed her eyes. Her boss had been happy to give her time off, asking only for every thrilling detail upon her return. E agreed, of course, except the part about being a secret agent.

As to Alexis, whatever was dangerous about him—and she took Nick's word on that—he also happened to be a very special man. Very sophisticated, very sexy. She had to admit, the danger somehow added to his appeal, but more than that, he had given her a new awareness of herself, a new sense of power.

She was playing with fire, but confident she could handle it.

Athens, Greece

Alexis Kaissaris had entered that tiny jewelry shop off downtown Syntagma Square with many women, but never had Kostas responded with such appreciation. The pearl drop earrings suited her, and the jeweler was lavish with his praise.

Then as the two Greeks put their heads together, E studied her image in the mirror, marveling at her journey from Alert to Athens… *Greece*. She was woozy, hadn't slept for hours. Days, it seemed. On their arrival he'd had their bags sent to his flat, immediately setting off to show her *his* city. First, a meal of assorted *mezedhes* in the cool, dark recesses of Gerofinikas, and now here. As promised, a man of his word.

E felt their eyes on her and turned as Alexis handed her a delicate bracelet, woven of white, rose and yellow gold. Then, on the other wrist, he fastened an oval-faced Cartier watch. "So you will never be late."

The men winked at each other, knowing that punctuality was not part of the feminine nature. They then returned to the business at hand. Alexis always did Kostas the favor of paying in dollars, which he would deposit in a nice, safe Swiss bank account, far from the greedy taxman.

The couple left the air-conditioned building, arm in arm. "I have known Kostas for many years. Never has he so envied me." Alexis paused, looking at her. "On our first meeting you wished to know about my country. And so, I give you also this gift." He swept open his hand. "My proud, ancient land: Greece."

"The land of Artemis," she said, their eyes meeting in a secret smile.

The city pulsed around them, everyone gesturing, shouldering, jostling. The sun cast a harsh brightness over Ermou Street, intensifying the din and disorder. E didn't care. With all this light, there was no room for dark. "We studied the Greek gods in school."

"You, my darling, are a goddess."

A memory of the Indian goddess exhibit came to mind, but E shrugged it away as they continued their promenade. Like Alexis, she felt the energy of this place... the electricity and action, stylish people bustling everywhere. It was a kind of fuel that seemed to feed Alexis, recharge him. She had the same sense of life flowing through her. Bringing her back to herself, after all her losses. Her brain was spinning, and she couldn't think straight. Didn't want to.

Alexis squeezed her elbow. "Life is good here. I feel *bien dans ma peau.*"

E nodded. "I know. I feel good in my skin here, too."

"And your skin feels good to me." He stroked the inside of her upper arm. "While we are here, we must enjoy–for tomorrow is Geneva. Business."

E was reminded she had a job to do. "You sure move around a lot, Alex, honey. You never told me *what* exactly you do?"

"A little of this and a little of that," he replied. "Just trying to keep up with inflation. You know, the drachma is worse than the dollar!"

She smiled at his joke, then continued, "Another convention? Like Singapore?"

"One hotel is similar to another," he replied shortly. "But it is not always so amusing to talk about these things." His cool tone warmed up again. "For this afternoon, I had in mind something more pleasant. To know Greece, one must know the sea. And so I've planned a little visit to my beach house."

Hailing a cab, he climbed in and gave the driver an address and a wad of money.

The man gripped the wheel and squealed off, lighting a cigarette en route. The congestion, like the air, was heavy, but he seemed to take pleasure in outwitting the competition. They sped along wide boulevards bordered with new stucco and narrow side streets crowded with old stone buildings.

E enjoyed the ride, too, but wished he would slow down a little. What kind of sightseeing was this?

Awhile later, they reached Athen's southern coast. By now, the air had cleared and traffic thinned. They turned onto a narrow road that hugged Vouliagmeni Bay. It wound upward along low cliffs lined with purple bougainvillea and white villas shuttered in blue. Then the driver hit the brakes. They had arrived.

Alexis escorted her up the steps to his house. He kicked the door closed behind them. The room was all white and glass and oh-so-blue sea. Clean. Pristine.

E turned to him. "Alexis, it's..."

Without a word he threw her on the thick sheepskin rug. The only sound was the crash of waves on rocks. He covered her mouth with his hand and smiled, eyes bright. "Now–*my* turn. You will not speak or move until *I* say."

For a moment, she was too stunned to resist. Maybe he thought this was seductive. She shook her head no and tried to push him off, but his powerful body was like granite.

The pressure of his left hand increased, just enough to hold her firmly in place. He grabbed the front of her dress with his right. The silk ripped. Her teeth dug into the palm pressing on her mouth, but his passion only increased. She kicked his ankle. He clamped down harder.

"Never. *Never* have I waited so long for a woman."

His smile was gone, eyes darkening. Feeling their hypnotic power and the threat of his violence, E froze. She lay there–not moving–body tense with fear and... anticipation.

He placed his free hand on her breast, caressing it as he studied her. His fingers trailed to the other side, teasing, coaxing her response. His mouth replaced the hand on her mouth. His lips and tongue and teeth laid claim to her. She moaned deep in her throat.

"No." He pulled back and slapped her, a slap that became a caress. "You will keep that fire controlled for a very long time, just as I have–until now."

E was stunned by his ferocity, the hint of cruelty. She stared back at him, shocked by the complex blend of emotions running through her.

"Now... once again."

Their eyes locked on. He kissed her deeply. Then his tongue explored the dimple on her chin, her eyes, her ears. His mouth moved along the sides of her neck, her throat, down her chest, eventually reaching her flushed breasts. And lingering there... as her body began to respond, despite herself. His look warned her. "Remember, my darling–you must keep the fire controlled."

He returned to her breasts. She bit her lip, the flesh of her mouth–afraid to cry out. He played with her and teased her, stopping and starting almost willfully. Waves of pleasure rushed over her, but she was angry at this pleasure, angry at him. Her eyes widened, then closed, then opened. She fought him, not wanting to give in.

All senses heightened, she felt the roughness of the rug beneath her back... the sharpness of his fine white teeth... the stubble of his beard moving across her body... and the sensual breeze caressing it. She smelled the subtle mix of his cologne and hers, their bodies, the salt air. She tasted his fingers, the wetness of his mouth, the frightened dryness of her own... and the blood from where she bit her lip. She heard the gentle lap of the waves, then their explosive crash against the rocky shore. She heard his breath. His rising excitement. Her breath. Her heart. The ringing in her ears. Even the rush of her blood. Even her silent gasps. She felt her insides expanding beyond their limits....

And through all this, he made her remain still and silent. Although E resented the way he was toying with her, she wanted him desperately. She hovered on the edge of the cliff–fearing to go over–longing to go....

After what seemed like hours, he raised himself above her, finally ready. His eyes bore into her. "You will never–ever–deny me anything again."

She felt her mind slipping over the abyss. All became dark.

Chapter 10

Geneva, Switzerland

The Geneva Cointrin Airport was tucked snugly in the southwestern corner of Switzerland, just across the border from France. Porters trailing, Alexis and E exited the terminal on the Swiss side. Arm around her shoulders, he guided her to the waiting black Mercedes. As the chauffeur drove east under hazy blue skies, E was quiet and subdued. Confused at her mixed feelings toward the man. Despite her mission, and despite the events in Athens, she was falling deeper under his spell.

It was the force of his personality. He was so vital and alive, so powerful. Passionate. Larger than life. But also protective. He'd cradled her in his arms all night and was being especially gentle today. So many sides to his personality. Flamboyant and sensitive, generous and selfish, tender and cruel. Although she didn't understand him—maybe never would—his charisma enveloped her.

She stared out the window, pretending to sightsee. The green band of suburbs was soon transformed into a crowded city at once provincial yet cosmopolitan—both medieval and postmodern. Window boxes of geraniums coexisted with sleek, no-nonsense buildings. It was mid-morning and the world hummed like a well-made clock.

After a short drive, they reached the shores of Lake Geneva. At the Mont-Blanc Bridge, the lake narrowed into a funnel and the Rhone River poured forth, resuming its course down to the Mediterranean. The Mercedes turned onto the Quai du Mont-Blanc, lined with trees and cheery flowerbeds. The Right Bank of Lac Léman, as the Swiss called it. E stared out at the colorful, boat-filled harbor with its soaring white jet of water.

She was a tourist. An accidental tourist. E thought maybe that was the name of a book, maybe with a character just like her. Maybe someone who had also dreamed about learning and growing and having new experiences. She told herself not to fear the unknown, but to be brave and go for it.

They stopped in front of an elegant, old-fashioned hotel. As they entered the sky-lit, five-story lobby, the couple was welcomed by the owners and staff, always delighted to see the generous Greek businessman.

Once inside their luxurious, shell-pink suite, Alexis threw open the windows, enchanting E with the picture postcard view. He gestured across the lake. "The Old City... Mont-Blanc... the French Alps." Even now in early summer, there were glistening white peaks rising into clear blue. The air was clean, the water sparkled. He pointed to the marble tomb of a man who had so loved this view that he left his great fortune to the city of Geneva if only they would bury him there.

The whiteness of the marble and the snow, the shimmering air… it was all beginning to dance before her eyes.

Alexis peered in her face. "E, *ma belle*, I think you must take some time for quiet."

She let out her breath and felt herself winding down. "I am kind of tired."

"Never mind. You have the day to relax, while I begin my business. Then tomorrow, you will fly down to Milan for some shopping."

"Milan, *Italy?*"

Alexis nodded. "You will take nothing but my Platinum Card. And you must indulge yourself completely. Except one thing, please no furs."

E shook her head, speechless.

"Come, *ma belle.*" As she followed, Alexis walked into the bedroom, pulled back the fluffy down quilt and tucked her into the crisp linen sheets. She was asleep before he left the room.

When E awoke, he was gone. She was awed, as ever, by his energy, his drive. Why wasn't he tired? She got up, showered and dressed in a jet-lagged daze, then reminded herself she needed to contact Nick. Afraid to call from the room, she went down to the lobby and found a quiet phone, a wood-paneled booth with a soft leather seat. She closed the door and sank down so that she wasn't visible through the small window. Spy stuff. She figured out the time change—it would be early morning back in the States.

In his small bedroom overlooking Chesapeake Bay, Nick was dreaming of flying like a bird, over Vietnam's velvety, black-green canopy, so thick you could walk on it... sink into it... bounce back up and take flight again.

The ringing jarred him awake, but it was really the softness of her voice that brought him to life. "*E*? Is that you? Is everything all right?"

E heard the anxiety. "Everything is fine, Nick. Great, in fact. I'm in Geneva now, then tomorrow to Milan for a couple days of shopping, then back here."

"Shopping? Alone?"

"Yes, alone."

They arranged to meet in Milan in two days.

After she hung up, E telephoned the room. Alexis had not yet returned. She looked at her new watch and was not sure what time it really was. In any case, she was starving. On the terrace, the Quai 13 Restaurant was still serving lunch. She ordered *une omelette* with Swiss cheese.

A far cry from the gracious atmosphere of the Beau Rivage, the Inter-Continental was all business. The eighteen-story concrete and glass hotel, located near the United Nations Palace, was host to many international events. Including the annual Euro-Tech Fair. Alexis Kaissaris would not miss it. A consultant to the Matsu division that manufactured surgical and industrial laser equipment, he was attending officially on their behalf—and unofficially on his own—wired and alert for any confidential deals and data that might come his way.

The smoky convention space was filled with tables and displays, bureaucrats, scientists and entrepreneurs. Alexis flowed through the hall like melted butter—kissing, stroking, touching, hugging. No one was immune to his charm.

"Ahh, Dr. Hermann, how good to see you again!" He focused on the pale, hairless CEO of a West German medical concern, grabbing his arm while shaking his hand.

"It is my pleasure, Herr Kaissaris." Dr. Hermann backed away.

Alexis reached into his breast pocket and handed him an envelope. "Price quotes, Doctor, to make you weep. Matsu will underbid any European manufacturer." He smiled with confidence. "So. You give me your order, then relax. Enjoy the pleasures of Geneva, forget business."

"But I have many other suppliers to see."

Alexis moved in on the man again, placing a hand on his shoulder with an intimate look. "Matsu is more than generous to its loyal clients."

"I shall certainly keep that in mind," Dr. Hermann said, noncommittal, although his small, close-set eyes told another story.

"Please don't think I'm being presumptuous, but there's a young medical student anxious to meet you—a rather shy Thai boy. I said you might join us later for a drink?"

Dr. Hermann blinked once or twice. "Perhaps that could be arranged. I do like to give young people a chance." The two men shook hands again and parted.

Moving on, Alexis greeted Samuel Gilbert, the buccaneering venture capitalist. "Samuel. I can't say it's a surprise, but it is certainly a delight."

"Yes, many new and undervalued companies."

"Speaking of which, I have some interesting information."

The small, well-tailored Englishman pulled the cigar from his mouth and smiled. "Information from you, old friend, is always interesting. Despite the eventual cost."

Alexis acknowledged these words as high praise. He looked around, then continued in a lowered voice. "I am just returned from Singapore."

"A fascinating part of the world. Pity we had to let it go. Well, the world changes, does it not? Our job is to keep up with history." Samuel gestured with his cigar. "I have heard of this air show. Impressive how the Chinese have increased their market share."

"Very aggressive, these Asians. Nothing like we imagined." Alexis shook his head. "I have a colleague there—very clever fellow—very connected. His company is up for a big Japanese contract, but needs capital. In exchange for the necessary investment, some privately held stock is available."

"How much?"

Mysteriously. "A great deal."

"Shares are of no value if they remain in the vault."

Alexis wore a sage expression. "I have also the date on which he goes public. With the right promotion, the stock could soar. You know—mutual fund managers, getting in on the Asian future. Let me know. I'll set up a meeting."

Clamping the cigar back in his mouth, Samuel reflected a moment. "Indeed. Funnily enough, I had been thinking of a holiday."

"Keep away from the durian fruit." Alexis winked, then the man walked away.

He stared after the British financier, aware of his recent financial reverses. With the profit he'd clear on this deal, Samuel Gilbert would be back in the black–and very much in his debt. Kaissaris had an inspired plan for repayment.

A fair man with soft undercooked features interrupted his thoughts. "Alexis? I simply knew you would be here stealing my business." Pieter Torssell shook his finger beneath his rival's nose.

Alexis gave the Danish consultant a friendly tap on the chest. "Plenty for all, Pieter, my friend." He reached in his black alligator briefcase, pulling out a bottle of thick amber honey. "And for you, the Greek honey I promised–golden as money, sweet as a good woman."

"Thank you kindly," Pieter said with a bob of his head. "Next time I will bring some excellent Danish cheese. Not so sweet, but more nourishing. For now, you will excuse me. I must meet my clients before you seduce them all away."

"I wish you luck." Alexis grinned as the man hurried off.

His eyes roving the packed room, he spotted another colleague, an Asian woman wearing a tailored brown suit, her black hair in a severe twist. He approached and shook her cool hand. "Dr. Min. May. What a surprise! And quite a lovely one."

She released his clasp, staring through cold dark eyes. "Why should that pertain?"

"But you are lovely," he insisted. "Fortunately or not, we can never escape our senses."

She adjusted her steel-rimmed glasses. "As I can never escape duty. Which you should attend to," she added tartly.

He watched her stride away, a half-smile on his face. It broadened as he found himself enclosed in the exuberant hug of Grigor Dmitryev, a bear of a man bursting from his shiny black leather jacket. "Grigor! How good to see you again."

"Alexis. No, if you will permit, I call you Alexei." Grigor put a hand over his heart. "Good Russian name. For you are one of ours. *Nashe*."

"I am honored."

"And for you, my friend, I bring best pepper vodka in Moscow. As promised. We sample tonight."

"Sorry, but I'm tied-up—business." He winked. "Tomorrow?"

"11 a.m. We get kick-start on lunch."

He nodded at the man's back.

"Alex. Darling."

Turning, he saw his old crony Aldo Pintolli. The men embraced, kissing cheeks. Aldo was stocky, brimming with vitality. An industrial designer, he could escape the tailored uniform, wearing white linen, wrinkled and very fashionable.

"Aldo! To think it takes these tedious events to bring us together! And Gina—how is your gorgeous wife, Gina?"

"Quite well, thank you, busy at home with the *bambinos*. Pregnant, in fact, with another."

Alexis beamed. "Congratulations! Ahh, to be a family man—what I am missing! We are not meant to be alone in life." He shook his head. "This reminds me. I have a friend—a lovely Swedish girl—here by herself. A pity, but I have other commitments and wonder if you would do me the favor of keeping her company."

Aldo regarded him gravely. "A favor for you... is a pleasure for me."

It was a busy afternoon for Alexis. The next day would be more so.

Milan, Italy

The city was smoggy, gray and humid, but E spent little time outdoors. She discovered the Galleria Vittorio Emanuele II, one of the original malls, a lofty arcade tucked between the Duomo cathedral and La Scala. Shopping here was serious business but she was fueled by espresso, a quick sandwich and a few bites of panettone.

E finally made it back to the Hotel Diana Majestic. Late. Formulating her apologies, she lugged her shopping bags through the lobby... a vision in dusty rose, an Armani blend of silk and linen that she had tried on and never taken off. She drew many appreciative glances, and was aware of every one.

The elegant little café/bar was located in the rear, cozy but discreet. Nick was seated at a quiet corner table, his back to the garden. They saw each other at the same moment, faces brightening. He leaped to his feet. There was an awkward pause as they stared, each almost wanting to hug the other, but then he extended his hand.

Arms overloaded, E just shook her head helplessly.

Nick grinned. "Well, then, how about a match?"

She laughed, spreading her bags on the floor and adjacent chairs. "I'm sorry, Nick. I honestly don't know where the time went."

He glanced at her packages. "I think I have a pretty good idea. But what could be better than waiting for a beautiful woman?"

E liked that and smiled happily as she sat down. She liked him too, this down-home guy who could really be her type... another time, another place.

Nick poured her a glass of chilled Gavi and topped off his own. "You don't look like you're doing too badly, lady. Maybe you should pay me a finder's fee?"

"Things are good," E said with a quiet smile. After Athens, there had been no more threats of violence, only tenderness and romance. Alexis was a very attractive man and she hoped to get whatever it was Nick needed–secretly–without damaging him. Maybe her lover didn't realize what he was mixed up in; maybe he'd get out, of whatever he was in. Retire. Maybe she would, too. Although she would miss Nick. A lot.

Nick watched his agent, unable to take his eyes off her. "Thanks for coming." It struck him: Evelyn Walker had become a woman. The pretty girl from Alert had grown up. His emotions were somewhere in the spectrum between parental pride and male jealousy. "No trouble slipping away?"

"Alexis understands about women–and shopping," she said with a twinkle. "Besides, he's busy these days."

"I'm sure. He treating you well?" Nick's pleasure at seeing E was dampened by the knowledge of what he was about to tell her. What he hadn't told her before.

She smiled again. Then raised her glass. "To Milan."

He joined the toast, forcing himself to regard her as a useful Agency asset, nothing more. "Let me update you. Yesterday morning after you left, Alex withdrew three hundred thousand from his Geneva bank. Then at 11 a.m. he met his Russian connection–entering the hotel room with one briefcase–leaving with another."

She put down her glass. "Now that I know him, I just can't believe–"

"*Believe* it, E–believe it!" His eyes blazed across the table. "We faxed the man's photo to Moscow. It seems he's a former Soviet colonel with friends in high places–and low. As in *organizatsiya*. A marriage of convenience that keeps everyone in work–scientists and gangsters. Some kind of atomic

Mafia." He saw her wince and pushed on. "We're still in the dark as to the exact commodity inside the briefcase. More important, who's the customer?" He cleared his throat, uncomfortable. "Kaissaris's MO is that exchanges usually take place while–socializing."

E stared into her wine in silence, then looked up. "That's a lot to take in, Nick. Maybe you could have made a mistake about the briefcase?"

"I wish." He got up and bought a pack of Marlboros from the pony-tailed cashier at the bar. She was very young. He only hoped she never ran into anyone like him. Telling the girl to keep the change, he returned to the table.

E frowned. "So you think he's going to swap it–again? With the 'customer'?"

Nick didn't respond, busy opening the pack, tapping the cigarette and striking the match. "Ever notice how blue the flame is near the source of combustion?"

She watched him light it. Her frown deepened. "What do you mean 'socializing'?"

It was Nick's first drag in years and he made it a good one. Funny how bad it tasted, though. "The guy has a reputation for being a little kinky," he finally answered, studying the growing ash. "Seems to feel that anything goes and–well, I wouldn't want to put you in an uncomfortable situation, at least one you weren't prepared for." He stomped out the cigarette and immediately lit another.

"I know you'd never do that." E was aware of the bond between them, real and important to them both. She wanted to make him proud–to prove that she could do it, to earn his respect. "I appreciate your concern, Nick, but you don't have to worry. I'm sure there's nothing I can't handle. Look at it as a challenge, an adventure. I'm not saying I'm Mata Hari, but…" E shrugged modestly, for to her the spy's name evoked a kind of glamour and mystery.

Nick felt ill. He stared at her–his *friend*–realizing she was unaware the woman had been executed by a French firing squad. He didn't have the heart–no, the courage–to tell her. "You must understand one thing, E. This is much more than an adventure."

"I understand."

But he could see she didn't understand–not at all. For despite her Armani and worldly air, E didn't have a clue. She was not a trained operative, and he had no business using her. Except, that it was his business. They were running out of time and didn't have a Plan B.

"Anyway." She looked at him sideways. "Alex is crazy about me."

"Right." Nick nodded, his conscience torn. Was he a pimp or patriot? He pushed his glass to the side and took another drag. "Okay, then. The tail in Geneva continues—on you both. You and I have no further contact. But when it comes down? I'll be there."

"I trust you, Nick. I know you know your job and I know you always look out for me." E stared at him. "But what *exactly* do I do?"

"One. Watch for anything unusual."

"You mean like a bulge in someone's pocket?"

Nick didn't smile back. He was walking a fine line. He didn't want to scare E off—couldn't afford to—but needed to prepare her, as much as possible. "This is more complex, E. You'll be acting as a decoy to keep him busy."

E looked down at her lap, then back at his eyes, but couldn't see *into* them. The first inkling, the dawn of doubt. "Will it be—dangerous?"

Nick met her wary gaze. "I wouldn't knowingly put you in any danger, E." Yeah, right. The girl could swim, but what about the sharks?

"And Alexis?"

"I don't want to hurt anyone, E. With your help, it should be a piece of cake."

She nodded—slowly.

Nick took out a cigarette and broke it in half. One half was Alexis who would arrive at their meeting place with the briefcase containing the Russian commodity. The other half, the customer, would arrive with the money, presumably in another briefcase. Before they could make the switch, Nick—with E's help—would obtain the Russian briefcase. Because none of the specifics were known, the situation was fluid and she might have to improvise. But no matter what, when or where, she could count on him to look out for her.

Then, feeling like a real lowlife, he began to lay out the various scenarios, how it might go down.

The cold white wine turned warm.

Chapter 11

Geneva, Switzerland

Late the following morning, E walked through the door of the Beau Rivage suite carrying her new red Bottega suitcase. Alexis nodded and hung up the phone. His lips brushed her cheeks in greeting, then moved to her mouth. And stayed there. Finally he pulled away, still holding her in his embrace. "It is very good to see you, *ma belle*."

"And you." She felt that old sizzle between them. And yet according to Nick, this was a man connected with the "atomic Mafia." How could she reconcile both of her lives? As he stared at her, E feared he was reading her mind. She smiled brightly.

"New dress. I approve. I look forward to seeing all your purchases— perhaps a private fashion show—but first I have another little gift. You must close your eyes."

She cocked her head with a questioning look.

"Now," he said firmly.

Closing them, she felt a shiver of fear and then… something heavy on her shoulders. Her eyes popped open. She was wearing a full-length fur, pale and impossibly soft.

"Lynx. A small token of my affection. To keep you warm when I'm not around." As she opened her lips, Alexis held up a hand to silence her. "You may thank me later, darling. First we must pack an overnight bag. I have a little adventure in store."

Much more than an adventure, according to Nick. She felt a moment's alarm. "An adventure? Where?"

"But that is part of the surprise." He smiled. "It has been a most successful week. To celebrate, I have made special plans for the weekend."

Annecy, France

They left in mid-afternoon. With Alexis behind the wheel, the black Mercedes crossed the border into France–her fourth new country in less than a week. Evelyn Walker, accidental tourist. Things were moving a little too swiftly, but what was the choice? The sooner she completed her job for Nick, the better they would all be–and *if* he was right, the world would be safer. Alexis was a question mark, but she decided to go with it for now. There'd be time–later–to sort out her feelings.

It seemed warmer after they left the city. A gentle summer warmth, still and golden. Alexis avoided the motorway, heading south along country roads lined with small farms and villages. He didn't speak much, and she didn't want to. She looked out the window, wondering which car was the "tail." Or was there more than one? After all, this was an important case, a fact underlined by the presence of the black calfskin briefcase in the backseat–the one that used to be alligator.

Then they reached Annecy, a scenic old town sitting at the head of the lake and cut through with little canals. The couple stopped at an outdoor café, watching swans glide through reflections of tiled roofs and ancient stone walls. Despite everything she knew–or suspected–it was terribly romantic, even the fluffy white clouds that drew together, blanketing the sky with silver light.

The clouds accompanied them as they continued around the shores of Lake Annecy and then turned down an unmarked lane. At its end lay L'Auberge du Père Bise, a rustic, two-story inn set amid lush grass growing down to the water, gleaming matte-silver under tentative rays of light.

For an instant, E wanted to kick off her shoes, then remembered the black briefcase Alex carried beside her–the one that had belonged to the Russian. *Heavy*, it appeared, although he refused the valet's offer of assistance. Feeling a similar heaviness settle over her spirits, she shrank back, startled, when he raised a warning finger.

"Do not be fooled by appearances," he said. "The cuisine is *formidable.*"

Just as E began to relax, he added, "I have invited a lovely friend to join us for dinner. I hope you don't mind."

The customer? E's brain kicked into overdrive. "Well, only a little," she said, willing a curve to her lips. "Besides, any friend of yours is a friend of mine."

He squeezed her elbow and moved toward the entrance. "I'm glad you feel that way."

The evening passed slowly for Nick. Seated under the grapevines on the Père Bise terrace, he mulled over the new intelligence that had pinpointed this weekend. The empty place setting at E's table seemed to confirm it. He wanted it to happen, wanted very much to put this one behind him. Most of all, he wanted to put it behind E and see her safe on the other side.

As usual before an operation, he lost any taste for food. Not even the perfectly rare pepper steak and thin, crisp *frites*. He picked at his meal to avoid attention, for why else would one come to Père Bise if not to eat? Only years of training allowed him to watch E without seeming to stare. He was aware of her every movement.

From his table beside an interior window, Nick saw the waiter clear their plates and hand them the dessert menu. He watched E glance at it, roll her eyes and pat her stomach. He heard her laughter dancing through the air and noticed he was not the only one to feel its warmth. Whatever E did, she did with her whole heart. Kaissaris knew what he had—and knew how to use it. The bastard. Manipulating that fine, free spirit.

Not at all like him. It was hard to take the moral high ground when one's own actions were so similar to those of the enemy. Nick was ashamed. Despite his vow to protect her, he knew how vulnerable she was. For he feared the truth about his plan, the entrapment—and her part in it—had not really sunk in. At that moment, he wanted to hold E, to shield her from what surely was coming.

He stiffened as E put down her menu, following Alexis's gaze toward an Asian woman entering the wood-beamed dining room. She wore a tailored gray suit and carried a dark brown briefcase.

As the new arrival was shown to their table, Alexis rose. "May, darling!" He extended his hand. She took it.

"Alexis," May said. A waiter pulled out the third chair and she sat.

E stared at her. *Chinese*, maybe? Or *Japanese*? The woman wore steel-rimmed glasses, thick black hair knotted at her neck. Despite the one touch of softness—a peach silk scarf tucked inside her jacket—there was something forbidding about her. Was she the customer? Somehow E had expected it would be a man.

"You received my message, Alexis? There was some last-minute business."

Alexis dismissed her apology with a genial wave of his hand. "As long as it wasn't with one of my competitors." He winked. "What matters is you're here. And we shall feed you. But first, you must meet my dear friend Evelyn Walker—E for short. E? My colleague Dr. May Min."

With guarded looks, the women shook hands. "Hello, Dr. Min." E forced a smile, trying not to look at the dark briefcase. *His* was still with hotel security, so it remained possible this was an ordinary encounter.

"You must be hungry, May," Alexis said. "What can I order for you?"

"I had some soup when I saw I was running late." She glanced around the flower-filled restaurant, with its earnest diners and rich smells. "Pity."

"I'm sorry you were delayed. The food is just wonderful. Alexis tells me this place is world-famous." E felt as if she were babbling, but the woman made her uncomfortable with her aloof air and strange accent. *And those steely eyes.*

Gunmetal eyes that glinted in the candlelight. "Alexis has exquisite taste."

He beamed. "You are too kind, May darling."

What exactly was their relationship? E wondered, gazing unfocused into the vase of white peonies. She'd spotted Nick's tight face through the terrace window earlier. But his presence was no longer reassuring. "Do you two work together?"

"We are involved in joint projects from time to time. Of course, May is a top physicist. I am just an idea man."

Reality punched E in the belly. Certain now that this was the contact, she felt a resurgence of the doubt she had experienced, then brushed away in Milan.

Then she knew: Milan was a whitewash. Either Nick had not told her the whole truth, or she had simply not grasped it—and he'd made no attempt to enlighten her. The risk was inescapable. People involved in nuclear espionage were not messing around. And that included Alexis.

"I've got a perfectly marvelous idea. Coffee and brandy in our suite."

May made a small movement of her head. "I would not wish to intrude."

E was trying to keep the panic off her face. *You'll be acting as a decoy to keep him busy.* But what did that mean—really? In this dangerous world she had so blithely entered, there were no ground rules, no rules at all. All she knew was it would end up in the bedroom. Damn you, Nick Ross! She had to struggle not to glare at him, to tell them all to go to hell. But it was a terrible threat, this atomic Mafia. E knew she could not walk away. She had her kid brother to think of, her parents. And she was committed. It was her duty. "Oh, please. We'll be more comfortable."

May looked impassively from one to the other... almond-shaped eyes rimmed by steel. "Thank you."

Alexis snapped his fingers and signed the bill without a glance. Then he got up and left, a woman on each arm... on his way to retrieve his briefcase from hotel security.

Nick watched, along with more than one other man in the restaurant, as they walked out. His emotion, though, was not envy—it was a nasty blend of tension and release. But at least it had begun. And, he hoped, it would soon be over. He glanced across the terrace at the two diners in dark suits eating with methodical precision.

After gesturing for his check, Nick finished his double espresso. He felt it go straight to his stomach, joining the acid already raging there. When the bill came, he left seven hundred francs and didn't wait for change. A nearly hundred-dollar dinner and he didn't taste a goddamn bite. He got up and headed for the stairway.

Nick climbed the steps to his room, feeling a rush of adrenaline. The operation was underway. He wasn't really worried about himself, but couldn't stop thinking about her. His agent, the beautiful brave woman from North Carolina. She was smart, but she'd never been trained for this. He sighed. It was up to her now.

The deadly transaction would go forward, and he wouldn't be there to protect her. Evelyn Walker was alone.

Chapter 12

The logs were already laid in the fireplace. As Alexis struck the match, E saw only the blueness near what Nick called the source of combustion. She felt the blue flame reaching out to her, drawing her in... closer to combustion.

As she stared into the fire, Alexis put on a CD of The Three Tenors while Dr. May Min sat quietly on the sofa beside her. E was trying to suppress her anger at being manipulated into this place. Being forced to play dumb. As if she didn't know their game. She gritted her teeth, desiring only to get it over with. "Your suit is lovely."

"I had it made in Hong Kong. Cheaper than Tokyo. If you know your fabric."

E had never known anyone who shopped in Hong Kong or Tokyo. "Do you live over there?"

"Korea," May said.

Alexis pulled up a chair and loosened his tie. "I really prefer Placido. How about you, E?"

"Oh, definitely." Did that mean North or South Korea? Her mouth dry, E took a sip of water then put the glass back down on the coffee table, telling herself that she had the upper hand, she had the secret knowledge.

They didn't know she knew about the briefcases—*his black, hers brown*—sitting on the desk across the room. According to Nick's theory the money would be in hers while his contained the "commodity." And whatever *that* was, they had to get it. Whatever it took.

"Shall I order up some coffee, May?" Alexis asked.

"It has been a long day. I had in mind something a bit more calming."

"Of course." He glanced toward the bar. "Some Rémy Martin perhaps? Or a nice, cool Pear Williams? I also have some marvelous Afghani hash."

May inclined her head. "Cognac, please."

Alexis looked at E. "And you, my dear?"

She couldn't meet his eye. What were they doing here, anyway? Nuclear espionage—or foreplay? Or both? However the thing played out, it was over between her and Alexis. E stared at the tall bottle of clear liqueur, still beaded with moisture from the minibar refrigerator. Back in her Little Miss Innocent role. "Is that a real pear in there?"

"They grow them this way—trees with bottles on every branch, each with a small pear growing inside. *Et voilà: eau de vie.*"

"Water of life?"

"Exactly." Alexis rose and moved to the bar, pouring E's liqueur and two cognacs. He served the drinks, then tipped his glass against each of theirs. "To friendship."

"Friendship." As E swallowed, the iciness on her tongue became a glowing heat in her upper chest. She blinked. "Oh, my."

Alexis looked at May, who replied with a quiet nod. Removing a pouch from his pocket, he took out a bit of hash and a small ivory pipe, then lit it and drew deeply. He exhaled a wispy puff and passed the pipe to May, relighting as she inhaled. The ball glowed dark red. She held her breath, then coughed delicately, a filmy cloud escaping her mouth. The frost in her steely eyes began to melt.

He turned to E, offering her the pipe. "And now, *ma belle*, for you—a small taste of a new pleasure."

E stared at the pipe, remembering her daddy telling her about drugs. *And patriotism.* That night in the rock star's limo, she had turned it down. Now she was obligated to take it. She felt her free will slipping away, and wondered if Mata Hari ever felt trapped. And what had she done about it?

"Do you not trust me?" Alexis looked at her with those persuasive blue eyes. "I promise you will find it pleasant." He put the pipe to E's lips.

After an inner sigh—and a quick *Dear God*—she inhaled. It was a scratchy, burning feeling. Awful. E felt the cough coming on and tried desperately to control herself, but it exploded. Her cheeks flamed red.

Alexis exchanged an indulgent smile with May, then patted E on the back and gave her some water. "Are you all right, my darling?" She took a sip and nodded, the blush fading. "Good. Now, try it again. You must hold that smoke in and wash it down with some nice cool *eau de vie*."

She inhaled again. The muscles in her throat tightened and screamed for relief, but E held her breath. He handed her the drink. It tasted so soothing and smooth going down. As her head went all light, silly laughter burst from her lips, followed by exhaled smoke dancing before her eyes. "Oh, my," she said again.

And with the smoke went the apprehensions. E felt clear-eyed and confident in her duty. She needed to get the pair to the other room—away from the briefcases so Nick could grab them. And if he was right, Alexis would be going to jail. "It is pleasant," she said with false ease. "Although I hate to tell you what my daddy would say."

"Well, then we must not tell him."

This was not really funny, but she laughed anyway. "You're the professor." She glanced at May—the North Korean physicist—stunned by the path her life had taken. Still, she could handle it.

May removed her glasses, followed by a few hairpins, then tossed her head freeing her long black hair. "A professor in pleasure, is that it? And where did you take this degree, Alexis?"

"I have pursued my studies at many higher institutions."

"And lower," she said with an amused look.

He nodded. "You would know."

E stared at the woman, all at once struck by her severe beauty… her penetrating yet impenetrable gaze.

May turned to meet her scrutiny. "As one who knows fabric, I would say this is fine." She touched E's shoulder. "Very fine. And soft. How pleasant it must feel on the body."

E cleared her throat. "Why, uhh, it's very comfortable." Then the woman trailed a finger down to the top of the bust dart. E shifted away, about to flee inside the bedroom to the connecting toilet.

At that moment, May rose to her feet. "If you will please excuse me."

As she walked away, Alexis cupped E's face in his hands. They heard the bedroom door close behind them. "I knew you two girls would get on."

E looked back at him, his features strong, commanding. Remembering Athens. She felt a wave of fear.

Alexis ran a thumb over her lower lip, his touch soft and seductive. "You know I want the best for you—don't you, *ma belle*?" The tone firm, the eyes unwavering.

"Yes," she whispered, steeling herself for what was to come. The fire crackled and sizzled.

"That's my good girl." Alexis stood, extending his palm. E rose slowly, allowing him to take her hand. Grabbing his cognac, he led her to the bedroom.

The tiny listening device was in place, its spiked end inserted in the fabric wall covering. Nick listened to the small speaker. The Italian arias muffled all but brief snatches of conversation and laughter from the adjacent suite. He shook his head in grudging admiration for Kaissaris. Two beautiful women and soft music. How does a guy get a job like that?

Your girl is in desperate jeopardy and you're making a joke? His eyes bored into the wall with fury. At himself as much as the fucking Greek criminal.

Nick pulled a chair closer to the speaker, but couldn't sit still. He kept shifting, thinking about E in there. He tried a soft armchair, but that didn't help. Finally he took out his fresh pack of Marlboros and stared in disgust. Shrugging, he gave in, opened it and lit one. He inhaled, hot steel wool scraping his throat. He got up and began to pace.

Waiting while your agent was in jeopardy was the worst. All that time, all those "what ifs?" So you made promises to God—deals—the ones you never kept. Because always there were new dangers to counter, new enemies to defeat. And new agents to be used to achieve those goals. Agents who didn't know what the hell they'd gotten into.

At least Nick knew that his operations had never been for career, only conscience. And duty. So somehow on the great scales of justice, it had balanced out correctly. But tonight—for the first time—he could see that one day that equation might change. And then it would *all* change. And that back door could hit him on the way out.

But for now, while he paced he made new promises to his God.

Chapter 13

E blinked as they entered the bedroom, lit only by a small table lamp glowing amber under May's silk scarf. May sat at the foot of the bed wearing a shimmery gray slip that revealed her broad shoulders and strong, rounded hips. Her face was shadowed but her gimlet eyes shone silver.

E swallowed, mesmerized by those glittering eyes as they drew closer and Alexis offered May his glass. All she knew was she needed to unlock the door for Nick, but how could she go without arousing suspicion. A fog was enveloping her brain and it was hard to think clearly. Why ever had she smoked that hash? Why was she even here? And what the hell did that bastard Nick mean by "piece of cake"?

Alexis eased her down beside May. He took the glass from May and pressed it to E's lips. Then it was his turn.

No words had yet been exchanged. The only sound was a lyrical aria drifting from the sitting room.

"I commend your taste in women, Alexis dear," May said.

They looked at E. She returned their stare, boldly, but her bravado soon fled and she grabbed the glass from him. After tossing down some more cognac, she stared into the golden liquid, searching her brain for a solution other than outright flight. Because then, it would be all over and she would have failed.

Lost in her unreal reality, she was aware of the growing pressure of Alex's hand on her right shoulder as May slowly unbuttoned his shirt and then removed his belt.

E was mortally embarrassed—and wanted to throw up. Unfortunately, the toilet offered no access to the front room.

May turned and for the first time smiled at E. The smile was an intimate one, as if they shared more than they really did.

E went somewhere in her mind, and when she returned May was still smiling. Helplessly, she smiled back, not even trying to mask the dread in her eyes. As May moved closer, E could feel the coolness of her skin... and Alex's leg pressed against her other thigh. She finished the drink.

Then she regained clarity. Transforming the dread in her eyes to promise, she stood up. "I think we need a little refill," she said, indicating the empty glass.

May ran a silky finger down E's arm. "You won't be long?"

"I am sure she'll be right back—won't you, *ma belle*?"

As he stared at her, E saw his dark side again. Mastering her fear, she kept her face composed. "I wouldn't want to miss anything—professor." Feeling their eyes on her back, she walked from the bedroom.

Heart pounding, E hurried to the suite's front door and opened it quietly. She looked back toward the bedroom and froze as she heard Alex's voice, relaxing only at the sound of May's throaty laughter. She let out her breath, then slipped the *Do Not Disturb* sign across the lock—between door and frame—to keep the latch from engaging. Done.

E refilled the brandy snifter, but would have no more to drink. From her purse, she removed a small black bottle of Joy perfume and dabbed the stopper behind her ear. Then her gaze was drawn back to the front door, every fiber in her being yearning to escape. But she knew she couldn't. E realized that sometimes you have to rise above the fear, or at least look at it straight on and acknowledge the truth of who you are. She had been raised to do the right thing and was proud of it. Even a soldier had to bow to the bigger picture. She felt sad at what was surely coming, but the time for feeling was gone.

Closing the door behind her, E re-entered the bedroom and saw them embracing at the foot of the bed. Turning, they stared at her. She saw his look. Did he suspect?

May opened her arms. "Come. Let me smell that perfume."

As E set the brandy glass on the table, she noticed the briefcase. Alex's black briefcase—with the commodity! May must have brought it in with her. But it was supposed to be out *there*. That was the plan, at least. Now what? What would Nick do? What could she do? What should she do? Slowly, she moved to May and was drawn into the circle of their arms... feeling the blue flame of their heat.

May brushed E's hair aside, pressing her cheek behind E's ear, inhaling. Alexis kissed her on the mouth as May stroked the back of her neck.

Tensing, E drew back, but there was nowhere to go–his arm firmly around her shoulders. She dug her nails in her palms.

May began to unbutton the front of her dress. A shiver ran through E's body. Beyond her control. Then May planted a delicate, almost chaste kiss on her neck... the other side of her neck. E bit back a sigh.

May touched the dimple on her chin. E swallowed and it sounded like thunder to her. Continuing down E's throat, May sank on the edge of the bed.

E forgot to breathe. Until this moment, she had simply been going along, playing the role of decoy. Then it all changed... as May's lips grazed her chest. E's breath came out as a gasp. Kisses like butterfly wings. Fluttering heart beats. E stood as if transfixed.

Alexis took her hand and kissed the inside of her palm. "Good, is it not?"

When May's warm lips reached her breast, E recoiled, a low moan escaping her mouth.

"You don't really want to go anywhere, do you, *ma belle?*"

She did, but she couldn't as Alexis held her in place for the butterfly wings.

In the next suite, Nick was still pacing and smoking, aware that the muffled voices and laughter had moved away–undoubtedly into the bedroom. By now he had relived his entire life and was acutely afraid of any further introspection.

He looked at his watch and tried to form a mental picture of what would be happening in the suite next door. *In the bedroom.* The logistics, at least. The rest, he didn't want to think about. They needed to be completely engaged before he could chance it. He decided to give E a little more time.

Her dress dropped to the floor. Locked in Alex's arms, she felt him pull her onto the bed. When the kiss ended, she was lying in the middle.

Stunned, E tried to catch her breath... find her brain... a way out. But his hold on her was firm and sure. May's fingertips explored her face... the tip of her chin, her jawbone, her ears, her eyes.

Her chest rose and fell. Fearful. Then May's mouth reached hers and she ceased to breathe. The kiss was slow and quiet. Warm. Alexis stroked her hair, soothing strokes, subduing. Amid the swooshes of silk, the sighs, he lowered the left strap of her chemise and put his lips to the intersection of throat and shoulder.

Boundaries retreated. E no longer knew where her body ended and another's began. And then there was no going back. She was falling somewhere–somewhere unknown, unexplored and possibly dangerous– but it was impossible to check her fall.

Now.

The hallway was clear. With a gloved hand, Nick turned the doorknob next to his and entered, hanging the *Do Not Disturb* sign back outside. His Colt poised, he closed the door silently behind him and surveyed the room, grateful now for Italian opera.

He moved to the brown briefcase–*May's*–and opened it, seeing stacks of yen, marks and dollars. Large bills, large sum. A quick search revealed this was the only briefcase here. He looked grimly at the bedroom door. *Oh Christ!*

Nick knew what it was to enter enemy territory. But one of his own people was in there. That made it even more treacherous.

Without further thought he slipped inside, holding his forty-five on the three people in bed, carefully professional. It happened all at once.... The screams, the scrambling to cover naked bodies–and his command: "Don't make a move!"

This was not his kind of scene, and he didn't even wish to look– especially with E there. But he had to look and there was no getting around the ugliness. Rumpled bedding, pieces of clothing–what had been erotic, now merely seedy.

"*Who*–?" Alexis demanded, sitting up sharply.

"Quiet." Nick viewed Kaissaris and the woman as threats to be controlled, but it was E whom he *saw*–crying, clinging to a sheet. He tried to send her a reassuring look, but her eyes were blank.

Mortified, E tried to put her mind somewhere else. Anywhere but here, this twisted reality. She felt degraded and ashamed, wondering if she had mishandled the situation. But what else could she have done?

"What do you want–money?" Then Alexis whipped around, darting daggers at May. "Or are you working with her?"

"Or *you*?" May spat back at him.

Nick held the weapon steady as he scanned the room. Where was the freaking briefcase? Then in an instant that contained a world, he saw it.

During his brief loss of focus, May pulled a Beretta from under the pillow. Quick, smooth and deadly as a cobra, she aimed the twenty-two across E's body at Kaissaris. "Die, betrayer." May pulled the trigger.

There was a scream and a gun blast. Feeling the heat of the bullet, E shrank into nothingness, eyes screwed shut.

So she did not know that the woman who had kissed her was now going to kill her.

As May turned the Beretta on E, Nick fired a clean shot into her heart.

The North Korean physicist died with a look of hatred on her face, too proud to cry out.

At the second shot, E's eyes popped open. She stared in horror at the bodies surrounding her, the blood. Whose? Did it matter? It was warm... sticky... red. *Their* blood. And bits of *them*. Bodies that had held her, their flesh and bones spattered on her arms, her stomach. And the smell. The foul stench slammed into her brain.

Tensely, Nick moved to the bed. He checked the bodies, then turned to her, voice flat. "You all right?"

She nodded mutely.

"Get dressed then."

E regarded herself in disbelief and then, dazed, began wiping the blood off with a sheet.

Nick grabbed the black briefcase. *Heavy!* He opened it, discovering it to be lead-lined and shielded. He saw the commodity: two stainless steel discs, each the size of a hockey puck–and each inscribed with the universal nuclear symbol. There was also a document from the All-Soviet Isotope Association in Moscow, certifying that they were 93-percent-pure plutonium-239. Weapons-grade plutonium! *Holy shit.* It took only about a kilo to make a good-sized bomb. Together, these discs came close. Gingerly, he shut the case.

E was now dressed, but disheveled. Uncaring, moving like a sleepwalker.

Holding the briefcase with its deadly contents, Nick stared at his agent. He smoothed her hair, then glanced at the red suitcase. "This yours?" She nodded dully. He picked it up, aware that she was in shock. "It's horrible, I know, E. But, please. You need to hang on till we reach the car."

Eyes vacant and shivering, she followed him into the living room.

After a final search, Nick paused at the brown briefcase. He didn't have to count the money to know that Kaissaris would have negotiated a nice profit on his three-hundred-thousand-dollar Russian "investment." The North Koreans were pros. Those bills would be untraceable. As E stared into the embers of the dying fire, he opened her bag, stuffed the payoff money inside, then handed it to her with her purse. Still gripping Alex's briefcase, he took her arm and guided her into the hall.

There they passed the two dark-suited businessmen from the restaurant below–Agency "sweepers" on their way to remove all traces of the operation.

Nick directed E toward the rear stairway. They were clear of the hotel room, but the air still smelled of cordite. And they were surrounded by death.

Chapter 14

The warm night breeze rushed over them, but E felt nothing. She did not notice as they passed Alexis's black Mercedes. And there was no one in the parking lot to notice them. Only a dog, and it was sleeping. Along with the guests in the dark, silent inn.

Nick's white Peugeot was as pale as the moon overhead. Pale as the fragile woman at his side. By now E was shaking as if from fever. He helped her into the car, then slipped behind the wheel. Once safely inside, E began to sob. Nick put his arms around her, holding her, rocking her like a baby, stroking her hair. This act of tenderness enabled him to feel human again. Then he caught himself—and the tenderness was replaced by anger. Self-contempt. *Human?* What kind of lowlife would put a girl like her in a situation like that? But he knew he couldn't go there now. He would, though. Later.

Nick eased away. "Time to go."

He started the engine and drove off. At the end of the lane he passed Alexis's briefcase to a man in a waiting Saab, then pulled onto the lakeside road, only now turning on his headlights. The Saab headed south, in the opposite direction.

E blinked, ran a hand across her face, gazing around at the blackness. "Go? Go where?"

He had some ideas, but they were about logistics. Nothing to do with broken hearts and wounded souls. So he just kept driving.

Gutted, she looked at herself, saw the blood on her arm. Her lover had been shot before her eyes, her world shattered along with his skull. "Where do I go? Do I go to the police? Or just hide-out in Washington?"

Nick was also shaken by the horror but the job wasn't over yet. He needed to keep her from spinning out. "No problem there, E. Tonight never happened. Those people were never in that room."

E was trembling again—this time from anger. "Great! You think to take care of them, but what about *me*?" She whirled toward him, her voice dripping scorn. "And what the hell did you mean in Milan by 'no danger'?"

Nick knew she was right, yet felt compelled to defend his actions. "E, I did everything I could to minimize the risk but I had to smoke out his contact. And get the damn briefcase! Who the hell would've thought she'd have a gun under her pillow?"

"*You*. That's who! You should have thought of everything. That's your job." Her eyes were blazing—at him, into him, through him. "I trusted you. And you—you manipulated me into some kind of… orgy!" Her next words tasted of acid. "Everlovin' E all right."

Nick twisted on that knife in his heart. He had violated an essential part of her being and taken advantage of her goodness. "I warned you about him being kinky." He knew he was being disingenuous. Just as he knew he'd had no choice.

"There's kinky—and there is *kinky*!" E turned away in disgust. "I feel dirty. Dirty and used. By you… and him… and her. By everyone." She closed her eyes, sickened. "And then watching them die. In my bed."

"I'd give anything to take that away from you, E. Just erase it."

"Really? But you'd do it all over again if you had to. Duty—right? God and country—right? Patriotism?" Arms tight across her stomach, E stared out the window. "What about decency? And respect?" She shook her head, appalled.

"You're a gutsy woman. I admire you, E. You made a tough call. You could have run, but you didn't. You stayed at great sacrifice. The way I see it you deserve a medal."

"You know what you can do with your medal, Nick?"

"I think I have some idea."

She opened the window and filled her lungs, then again, trying to replace all they had taken from her. Gradually the rage passed. "The truth is, yes, I went along. I made my own choice to continue even when I knew where it would lead. Maybe not the bodies, but the rest. You're right. I do bear that responsibility. Better than being passive and used, I guess."

Nick sighed, opened his mouth. Then closed it.

Several miles passed beneath them, then she closed the window. "I'm done, Nick. I won't be able to help you any more," E said calmly. "I need to be able to live inside my body and feel whole. To recognize the face in the mirror and respect that face. To not worry what lie to say to who. I just want to be Evelyn again." She studied her empty palm. "Whoever that is... or was."

"I've been there, E. Evelyn. You may not believe me, but you'll bounce back."

"Thanks for the vote of confidence. I just hope it was all worth it."

But he couldn't crack. He had done his duty and, yes, the awful truth remained: It was worth it. Nick gazed at that white line down the center of the road and retreated again into dry, cold professionalism. "E, for what it's worth? You know what was inside the briefcase? That's *plutonium* he was peddling. To North Korea. Almost enough for a nuclear device. You've done your country a very great service. The world."

"Can the rhetoric, Nick. It's over."

They bypassed Annecy on the way to Lyon, their silence broken only by another car, the unearthly howl of a cat. Then Nick's sigh. "We have taken advantage, E. And you—you have every right to be angry."

She grimaced. "You're a pathetic, mealy-mouthed slime."

"No defense." He knew how he looked, who he was. There was a very long pause. "What are your plans?"

She flared up again. "Plans? You bastard! You think I planned for this?"

But the fury was brief. Fatigue took over. It was over, finished. "I don't know. My boss Edie made me promise to tell her all about my grand European adventure. Cynthia, too. I just can't face any of that. Not now. So maybe I'll stay over here for awhile. Get a job—somewhere safe. Not Geneva. I don't care to see the inside of a Swiss jail, although I'm sure they're cleaner than the French ones." The laugh was not pleasant.

"On that, you've nothing to worry about. Switzerland, France—every trace of your connection with him is being removed by our sweepers. You're in no danger with the authorities—anywhere."

"That's reassuring."

"Your belongings will be returned. But what else can I do to help?"

"*Help?* Haven't you helped enough? First, it's a condo. Then travel, so I don't get bored. Clothes, money, jewels. Life couldn't be better when you're a pro for the CIA."

Like a slug to the gut. He took it. "We have funds for your resettlement."

"The payoff? Or are you setting me up with another 'consultancy fee'?" Her lips twisted in bitterness. "Thanks, but no thanks. It's over. I'm strangling on the strings attached to your generosity."

Nick didn't try to argue. He reached in his pocket and drew out a business card. "We'll be in Paris by morning. In case you decide to stay, here's the name of someone who might have a job. She runs a travel agency and they always need bilingual people."

"Another card," she murmured, dropping it in her purse. They drove on into the night.

Paris, France

Nick left E at the Plaza-Athénée. After she was shown to her hotel room, he placed a generous sum on her account, exchanging discreet nods with the man at the caisse. It was in the budget and he figured that was the least the taxpayers could do for her. As to the North Korean money–which she'd soon discover in her bag–that had nothing to with anything but his own guilt.

Washington, D.C.

Nick flew back to Washington, thankful for the pills that knocked him out on the plane. Later, their debriefing over, Jay took him for a stroll past the new west wing. It was muggy and both men were in shirtsleeves. "Maybe we'll get you to move in one of these days. Get your career back on track."

"Yeah, but–which track? Or whose?"

"The thing is, Nick? You can be so independent they forget your fucking name. The real action is here. Although," he winked, "who am I to tell you about action?"

Nick did not react.

"I love it. A kinky Korean! South, maybe–but *North*? Here we thought they were all so dull and dreary." Jay shook his head, tickled. "Of course, they're disavowing the woman, but our sources say she was a physicist at the Yongbyon nuclear research complex. Maybe just a case of 'fatal ambition'–trying to win points with the Great Leader. Or the tip of the iceberg. You'll be the first to hear about it, though. You did good, buddy boy."

"E didn't do too badly herself."

"Granted. But she's *your* agent and you ran her well. Besides, those kind of broads like the thrill."

"Thrill? She almost got killed! We used her."

Jay poked an index finger at Nick's chest. "You. You used her. She was *your* asset. It was your operation. The song she played was from *your* score."

Nick's eyes turned hard.

Jay smiled. "Hey. That's the name of the game. We paid for her and if we can't use what a whore has to offer? Then we're in the wrong business." He wiped his forehead. "Damn, it's hot today."

"She was called on to serve her country—and did—without question. If you'd been the one out there, would we have called you a whore—or hero? But that's different, isn't it? Easier being a pimp."

Jay looked at him with pity. "Don't be so naïve, Nick. Besides, I hear she's made out quite well—some very generous patrons. She certainly knows how to pick them." He grinned. "What about you, Nick? Has she screwed *you* yet—or aren't you rich enough?"

Nick smashed a right into his jaw. Off-guard, Jay fell to the ground. He lay there a moment, rubbing his chin in surprise, then got up slowly. The two men stared at each other. Nick was shocked and embarrassed, Jay amused.

"Feel better, pal? You like feeling holier-than-thou? Well, let me tell you something. It may feel good, but it sure as hell doesn't pay the mortgage." He shook his head. "Don't be a fool, Nick. That broad is not worth blowing your career over."

Without a further glance, Jay strode away, brushing himself off as he went. Stunned and immobile, Nick watched him go.

Paris, France

E didn't leave her hotel room that first week. She slept a lot and spent a lot of time in the bath. She ordered room service, but couldn't eat. Her suitcases arrived from Geneva, but she didn't open them. She was still reeling about the money in her bag. A dizzying amount of money, more than she could comprehend. That discovery had been followed by the arrival of an opulent fruit and wine basket from the concierge, with a little note of welcome and thanks for the generous advance on her bill. E crumpled the card in her hand and threw it at the wall. That damn Nick. Still trying to look after her.

Well, she didn't want him to look after her! She wanted to crawl into a hole and–if not die–then at least hibernate for a good long time.

But however much she wanted to escape, she couldn't stay in bed all the time. Needing to pass the hours between sleep, she watched French television and was surprised at how much she could understand. She ventured onto her balcony and took in the summer street life with its hazy light and horns and diesel fumes. It was not the poetic Paris that she saw but one of energy and intent. As the fashion parade continued apace, she recalled staring out from another hotel–the Watergate–where the rock star had brought her what seemed a lifetime ago.

It had been summer then, as now. Hot and humid with busy, stylish people all knowing where they were going, what they were doing. She had gone down to face that world–and landed on her feet. She had learned she was a survivor.

And so, vowing she wouldn't be beaten, Evelyn Walker got dressed and again went down to take a walk. Into the sunlight.

Part Three

The Lovers

Chapter 15

In a strange way, it was the best of times. Even though it was the worst of times. Charles Dickens had written about the Paris of another era, but E knew exactly what he meant.

She was alone–and to be alone in Paris is like no other loneliness. The city was achingly beautiful. Saddest of all, she couldn't imagine wanting someone to share it with. She had stared death in the eye and it had left her hollow inside. The girl she used to be was gone and the old truths didn't hold.

Yet Paris was Paris.

One moody night, E followed an enormous orange moon as it twisted through ancient cobbled streets. At times the moon seemed so near she could almost touch it. Then it would disappear around the corner, or behind a murky cloud. Compelled, she continued after it–as the moon rose higher and higher in the sky, moving further and further away. Stricken, E knew she'd lost something of immense value.

She was left with a new awareness of time... of her place in time. These streets had been here forever. Others had walked them before her, and would again after she was gone. Lives had unfolded in these very buildings. People had loved in them. People had died–sometimes in the blink of an eye.

The shadows moved in around her. She shivered and hurried back to the hotel.

As soon as she fell into bed, E drifted into the nightmare of blood and gunshots. The gunfire grew louder, assaulting her consciousness.

In terror, she awoke with a start. Alone. Daylight streaming through the curtains. No dead bodies, but the bombardment continued–outside. Agitated, E peered from her window and glimpsed a mass of uniformed men. Silver planes cut through the sky. Were they being invaded? The fear returned, a familiar emotion these days. Anything could trigger it–a car backfire–and certainly the roar of a jet engine. Not to mention a squadron of them.

E looked out again and saw the blue, red and white plumes of jet exhaust. She noticed all the people milling around–looking not frightened, but festive. Edgy at first, E joined them and was soon caught up in the Bastille Day celebrations. July 14. The French Fourth of July.

The crowd carried her along to the broad sidewalks of the Champs-Elysées, where it seemed the entire populace was turned out in blue, red and white. A huge military parade was sweeping down the great boulevard from Place de l'Etoile to Place de la Concorde. Tanks and motorcycles, low-flying fighters and whirring helicopters. Crisp, gold-braided bands playing rousing music. Dignitaries making patriotic speeches. Elderly heroes of the Great Wars marching tall, followed by straight-backed young men ready to defend the nation in future wars.

E joined the revelers surging through the city. Before she knew it, the day had passed. It was evening and with the opening burst of colored light, she felt like a child again, joyful for the first time since *that* night.

She found the best view on the *quai* below the Eiffel Tower. Across the Seine, great flowering displays of fireworks were erupting over the Palais de Chaillot. From the foot of the bridge, Pont d'Iéna, E watched the dazzling flashes and plumes of smoke. She heard the pops and hisses and this time did not flinch in fear.

But the scent of burnt explosives brought it all back and her mind became flooded with fearsome images… May's gun, smoke rising from the barrel. The charred flesh surrounding the hole in Alex's head. The hideous smell. E steadied herself against the railing for a moment, wobbly and woozy.

She became aware of a silver-haired officer glancing at her in concern. With a weak smile, she nodded that she was okay. He met her look with sympathy as if to say he understood. It was a moment of human connection, one she hadn't experienced in some time. She allowed it to happen and they watched the spectacle in companionable silence.

Then he opened his bottle of champagne and it went off with an explosion of pure white light. *"Vive la France!"* He handed her a glass and she drank with him.

Thus Evelyn Walker began her third week in Paris.

The next morning, she awoke ready to get on with life. She would be practical, swallow her pride and contact Nick's travel agent friend about a job. E dug out the card and was struck by a wave of revulsion. That bastard! Her anger at the way he had used her was soon swamped by deeper, darker feelings–haunting memories of the night Alexis died. How they'd all used her.

But that was history. She had survived and would look out for herself from now on. E squared her shoulders and made the call. *"Bonjour.* Madame Monique Julien?"

"Oui, bonjour. Hello. You may speak English, if you like."

"My name is Evelyn Walker. Nick Ross suggested I contact you. He thought you might have a job opening?"

"Not the best recommendation, Mademoiselle Walker, but…" E could almost hear that Gallic shrug over the phone. "We will see. I trust you are available for an interview?"

"I am." Fearing to poison the waters, E didn't pursue the subject of Nick. "When?"

"Are you free this afternoon? Perhaps around 3 p.m.?"

"I'll see you then."

The office was not far and E counted the hours until it was time to set off for the Champs-Elysées. Turning onto the narrow rue Pontheiu, she soon reached Voyages Monique.

The fashionable little travel boutique appeared a reflection of the owner herself. Monique was definitely *une Parisien,* chic but with a slightly hard edge. She had red-hennaed, chin-length hair and was in her late thirties or early forties. E couldn't really tell. She had probably looked the same ten years ago as she would ten years from today. Her black linen suit was well fitting, but not necessarily expensive. Two other employees were on the phone, a dark-skinned young man and a long-haired woman in an embroidered orange tunic.

"Bonjour, Madame Julien." E extended her hand.

Her glance unwavering, the woman weighed E. "Please call me Monique." Her handshake was firm.

"My friends call me E."

Monique studied the young American through serious, cinnamon-colored eyes. "I prefer Evelyn."

"*D'accord.*"

The Frenchwoman indicated a chair opposite her desk. "Please."

"Thank you for seeing me," E said, after they sat. "And thank you for offering to speak English, but I've studied French and would prefer to practice as much as I can."

"Until you become fluent, I do not mind the opportunity to polish my English," Monique replied in her warm, smoky voice.

"Oh, but your English is perfect."

"One can always improve. We have many international clients who speak only English. It's a pity, but there seem to be fewer people learning French these days."

"That's hard to imagine. And how sad. It's wonderful to visit a foreign city and know the language."

"How adventurous of you," Monique said, restacking some travel folders. "You have family here?"

E's eyes clouded over. "No."

"Well, I suppose you have many friends?"

"I've only recently arrived."

"I see. And how do you come to know Nick Ross?"

"It's a long story." And a closed one, E's expression said.

Monique did not pursue the subject. "Your timing is good, dear. This is our busy season." She furrowed her brow. "I must pull some strings to get you working papers, but I think I can handle it. I would like you to start tomorrow morning. If that is convenient?"

"Oh yes, very convenient." E wondered about Monique's connection with Nick and resolved that one day she'd ask. Just not yet.

The next day, while filling out documents for the work permit, Monique was shocked to discover that E was living at the hotel. "You Americans have never lived through a war, Evelyn. However, we French still know the value of *un sou*. I can not bear to see you waste your money *comme ça*. You must move immediately."

E had just received her weekly statement. There was enough on account to last a little while, but she would obviously have to start thinking of the future. She was determined not to touch what she considered the blood money except in a dire emergency. It was in the hotel safe, an albatross of sorts. "Of course I'd love to get settled."

Monique tapped her lips in thought. "I will see what I can do."

Within a few days, Monique came upon a promising lead. After work, they took a taxi across the Seine to Montparnasse, alive with brightly colored sundresses and animated conversations. The women walked around the corner to rue Delambre where people were darting in and out of the cheese shop, the baker and the butcher. Just past the Rosebud bar, they stopped before a five-story stone building.

A push of the buzzer brought forth a woman in an ancient floral housecoat who cracked open the door with a scowl of cigarette smoke. They were soon inside an old-fashioned wrought iron lift that delivered them to the top floor where the concierge, still smoking, took out a large antique key.

The apartment was a quirky, three-level place with a tiny attic bedroom and balcony, a romantic bath/dressing area in the middle and an airy downstairs living space that opened onto a second balcony. It was like some kind of artist's garret. Not a starving artist–but not a rich one, either–for it could be had at quite a reasonable rent.

"How can I thank you, Monique?"

"Just work very hard."

"Don't worry about that!"

Voyages Monique was open six days a week and E refused to take a day off, preferring to keep busy. And so she came to spend a great deal of time with her boss. Worldly yet practical, witty yet tough-minded, Monique was demanding but respectful of the other employees, a bespectacled young Moroccan intellectual and a black-haired bohemian with a passion for travel.

A divorcée with an active calendar, Monique began to show E around town, and before long she had her first dream in French. From time to time, Monique tried to introduce her to eligible bachelors, but E made it clear she was not interested.

Her response was more positive to another suggestion–*le shopping*. Most of Monique's favorites were on the Left Bank, chic little shops tucked into crooked lanes. However, she never bought anything too trendy, advising E that good classics were the best investment and would last forever. They skipped the department stores, but not the Marchés aux Puces, where they unearthed an old set of floral-painted china for E's new abode, along with some odd pieces of silver.

She wondered if she would have ever bought china and silver with Alexis, then banished the thought from her mind. Such thoughts always led to images of her former lover–the trickle of blood seeping from the wound, his sightless eyes staring at her. It remained painful to think about him.

E tried not to let memories run her life, but still jumped at sudden loud noises. She still had nightmares and eerie feelings that someone was following her. Sometimes there was a face that looked familiar–or dangerous. But she figured it was all in her mind. She just needed to wait for the ghosts of her past–real and imagined–to be put to rest.

E approached her twenty-first birthday with mixed emotions. She had lived so many lives already. How many more were there to come?

She and Monique celebrated with a girls' night out at the famed La Coupole brasserie, around the corner from her apartment. After they settled into one of the raised banquettes–better to see and be seen– Monique ordered champagne and *fruits de mer*.

"Fruit of the sea," E marveled at the icy platter of seafood. "You French are so poetic."

Monique shook her head. "We French are the *opposite* of poetic. We are practical and hard. Scratch even the most sophisticated Parisian, you will find a peasant with dirt under his fingernails. And proud of it!"

E squeezed lemon on an oyster and drank it down. Monique was unwavering in her opinions and there was no one like her. She knew everything and everyone. Especially men. Throughout dinner, many of her "old friends" dropped by the table–often with eyes on her new friend, the *charmante américaine*. E continued to distance them with a smile, insisting she had absolutely no desire to get involved.

"No desire?" Monique raised a carefully shaped eyebrow. "This is like denying the moon and the tides. Someday there will be no escape."

E sighed into her espresso cup. "Maybe. But from now on, I intend to make my own decisions about who, when and where."

"Of course."

As they set off into the lively Montparnasse evening, E felt something. Or thought she did. She glanced over her shoulder as they strolled to the taxi stand, en route to some trendy club. The well-dressed blond man she'd caught watching her inside was walking behind them. Maybe she'd seen him before, maybe not. Maybe they had met. Maybe he just wanted to meet her. Or was he following her? She brushed the fear aside and told herself it was nothing. The truth was that actually *a lot* of men looked at her. She frowned and scolded herself. Still paranoid.

She and Monique moved to the head of the queue, hailed a taxi and drove off. Yet E couldn't help turning again to look—and *thought* she saw the man enter the vehicle behind them.

E wrote Cynthia a censored version of recent events and invited her to come visit any time. Cynthia wrote back that she wished *she* could have been born under the same lucky star as E and would take her up on it one of these days. But for now she had a new boyfriend, so it might be a while. In the meantime, she'd sublet E's Georgetown condo and send her the rent checks.

E reread the letter, then frowned. What kind of "lucky star" would lead a person on such a painful path? And yet, that path had led here. *Paris.*

She took pleasure in the small, everyday moments. Early each Saturday morning she would take a basket to the Edgar-Quinet *marché* at the end of her street. Everything fresh and displayed so beautifully—all manner of produce, bread, cheese, herbs and flowers. It was evident the French had an extra *chic* gene.

The trees had it too, their simple grace even in the starkness of winter. But now with the coming of spring, they were preparing to flaunt their stuff... proud rows of lindens with their lime green buds. The aristocratic chestnuts making grand promises.

The past gradually receded. As May approached, it seemed as if everyone in Paris were either traveling or preparing to travel. One busy morning, E soothed an agitated American couple, who were having trouble with the French and wanted to go home.

"They're so rude, make me feel like a nobody," Mrs. Phillips frowned.

E gazed at them across her desk. "I understand completely. But one thing..." She lowered her voice conspiratorially. "The French are that way even with each other. It's nothing personal. So you must enjoy Paris and simply ignore the Parisians."

As they smiled in relief, she sold the couple an excursion to Versailles. "But don't forget the Eiffel Tower." She winked. "Once in a lifetime, you know."

Monique approved, despite their small commission on tours. "One would think you were always in this business."

E shrugged. "It's nothing. It can be frightening to be alone in a strange place."

"So sentimental, you Americans," she replied. "I do not begrudge you your good heart–nor do I envy it. But the stomach is also important. Is it not?"

"Those sacred French principles, *liberté, égalité, fraternité*–and *déjeuner!*" E grinned in pride at her own witticism.

"Not only beautiful, the girl can joke in French! For this, a special lunch. On me."

Monique and E walked onto the rue Ponthieu, now swarming with a purposeful crowd: the French internal clock had struck *midi*. As the sun flirted through hazy skies, Monique hailed a cab and told the driver to take them to the Parc de Bagatelle.

As they headed up the Champs-Elysées, E wondered again about her boss. "Monique? I hope you don't think I'm being too personal, but how do you know Nick?"

Monique stared straight ahead, expression fixed. "All I can say now, dear, is that it's not what you think."

"What do I think?"

"The man is attractive, which you have no doubt discovered. However there was never a romantic link between us. Once there was some business. *C'est tout.*"

"That's all, huh? All it was with us, too." E's face darkened. "Just business."

Monique patted a white-skirted knee. "Never mind. What woman does not have a thorn or two in her past? The idea is to move forward. And make better choices next time." She smiled. "I think we will both be in agreement about my choice for lunch. I have reserved for us a table at a charming little bistro in the heart of the Bois de Boulogne. Have you visited the park yet?"

"I know it's the former royal woods, but... no, I'm ashamed to say."

"Too busy working, yes?" Monique gave her a flicker of wink. "Now we are tourists ourselves."

Tucked inside the great swath of greenery west of town, Les Jardins de Bagatelle was an elegant bistro with large windows overlooking a secluded garden. E could see that it might have been romantic, but these days she was just happy to settle for a good meal. The women dined well, then decided to walk off their lunch… *une promenade*.

Great wrought iron gates opened onto a gravel path that led them through the ancient woodlands until the shrubbery parted to reveal the famous Roseraie. Open-mouthed, E stared at the rose garden with its profusion of color. Creamy white to red-violet. Roses rambling high and low. Everywhere more buds, more blossoms waiting to pop. An intoxicating springtime display under a soft blue-gray sky.

"It's a wonder! Why isn't *everyone* here?" E indicated a man buried in his newspaper on a park bench. "Do you think maybe they take it all for granted?"

"Some do." Monique shrugged. "It was Empress Josephine, you know, Napoleon's wife, who—" She spotted a slim, dark man in a brownish-gray suit moving in their direction. "Karim? Kari?"

He appeared startled, as if recalled from faraway. "Monique?"

"It is you. Darling." They kissed cheeks three times. "What a marvelous surprise."

Kari nodded. "A perfect delight. You ladies could be flowers yourselves."

Monique took hold of E's arm. "Where are my manners? Evelyn, I would like to present to you my friend Monsieur Karim Mansour. Kari–my colleague, Mademoiselle Evelyn Walker."

Their handshake was reserved, even hesitant. Feeling something, but easing around its edges. "Nice meeting you, monsieur," she continued in French.

"The pleasure is truly mine, Mademoiselle Walker. You are American?"

E nodded. "*Oui.*"

"I have some family in California."

"I've never been there, but would like to go some time."

"Have you been long in Paris?"

E smiled. "Almost a year."

He turned to Monique. "And where was *I* this past year?"

Monique gave him a look. "Busy breaking hearts. I've heard the reports, *mon cher.* But I did not know that you too are a rose enthusiast."

"Roses are my passion. I had a fine garden at home. In the spring I come here almost every day. But this lady? Her beauty overshadows all of nature's artistry."

E was aware of his doe-like brown eyes—eyes that admired her through velvety lashes. She wondered if this were another attempt by Monique to fix her up. And was he really a playboy? He was certainly handsome, his bearing graceful yet relaxed. He had an easy quality, his dark hair a little mussed, green silk tie slightly askew.

Monique wagged a finger. "You must beware, Evelyn. Persians are born flatterers."

"Iranians. Our name in our language."

"I stand corrected, *mon ami.*" Monique nodded, then checked her watch. "A pity, but we must be getting back. I have a rendezvous. A rather important one, scheduled long before this delightful day."

He stared at E. "A pity indeed."

E thought so, too, but, well… *C'est la vie.*

The women nodded their goodbyes and returned to the office.

About a week later, a new customer appeared at Voyages Monique. Karim Mansour, inquiring about flights to London. "And where have you been booking your tickets in the past, *mon ami?*"

"Here, there. I don't know. My secretary does it. But she's on holiday." His eye was searching out E's.

Monique shook her head. It was so obvious. "Why don't you help him, Evelyn, *ma chère.*"

E nodded. He was not the first in Monique's circle to pursue her. "And when do you wish to travel, monsieur?"

"Maybe sometime after lunch."

She smiled. "That is awfully short notice. For a flight, I mean."

"How about a taxi?"

"To *London?*"

"If this is a problem, I would settle for someplace closer. Perhaps the rose garden?" He studied her with boyish hopefulness.

E swallowed hard, feeling that old knot begin to tighten in her stomach. She liked him… too much. And it was too soon. She glanced at the papers on her desk.

Monique gestured them toward the street. "It is almost lunch time. But you owe me, my friend. Your business," she added, then reached for the telephone.

As Kari opened the door, E stared at Monique's unheeding back. There would be no reprieve.

Kari hailed a cab and helped E inside. With a deep breath, she settled into her seat. After he directed the driver, they sat quietly. Although she hadn't given him much thought–until now–there was, well, something about him. Something that made her awkward and tongue-tied.

"So you like Paris?"

"Oh, very much."

Silence.

"And Monique? She is a good employer?" he asked in English.

"The best." But it didn't help. E's social skills had deserted her. She wanted to respond in French, yet not one French word remained in her head.

They reached the rose garden just as the clouds parted to bathe the entrance in rays of golden light. "It is still early. So I thought I would offer you lunch–after a promenade." He gestured toward the sky. "The sun seems to have extended an invitation. Don't you agree, *mademoiselle?*"

She nodded in silence, realizing she wasn't herself. Certainly not my-friends-call-me-E-self. But there was nothing she could do about it.

As they strolled through the maze of flowerbeds, Kari told her about the history of roses, how they had originated in the ancient heartlands of Asia, spreading through trade and conquest to the other great civilizations–including his own Persia. "For a time, roses fell out of favor in Europe until the Crusaders rediscovered them in the Middle East. Later, the Spaniards carried them to the New World."

E was entranced by these tales of bygone days. But he too seemed from another day, another time. Kari was a romantic figure with his quiet resonant voice and musical accent, his dashing yet gentle manner. He was not young, not old, but somehow just right. She made an effort to gather her wits. "How long have you lived in Paris?"

"Many lonely years."

"That's not what Monique said." She half-smiled, but was still wondering about the playboy comment.

He raised a palm and shook it. "One hears things, but not always the truth." They followed the gravel path as it led them to two large shrubs bent heavy with pale color. His face softened. "My dear friends from home. 'Omar Khayyam' and 'Ispahan.'"

"Nice to meet you," E addressed the roses with a twinkle, studying their delicate blossoms, luminous pink with a hint of gold at the center.

"Like a ballerina's tutu." Then she buried her nose in one. "Mmm. If heaven had a smell."

"We Persians say Paradise is a garden."

"Better than floating around in boring white clouds."

He cocked his head. "Interesting point. Quite broad-minded of you."

"Well, it's a big world. Lots to learn. For example, I never thought much about roses before. Especially the old ones." Her eyes crinkled, suddenly very happy. "I always thought a rose is a rose…"

"…is a rose." With an appreciative nod, Kari completed Gertrude Stein's famous line. Their eyes connected. "Think of all you have been missing, *mademoiselle*."

There were other visitors close by, but they could have been alone. As they resumed their stroll, they were so aware of each other–aware of the space between them–and the tension to keep that space intact.

"Tell me about your home," E asked.

Kari looked at her. "Another time."

She saw a sadness in his eyes that reminded her of her own losses.

His face lit up as he spotted a sprawling mass of red. "This lovely lady started life in China until an admirer carried her off to Calcutta where she became known as 'Bengal Rose.' Then an English ship captain brought her to London. There she was called 'Slater's Crimson China'–after his boss." He shook his head. "No one remembers the name of that poor sea captain."

E stared. "Have you ever been to China?"

He stiffened. "So many questions about where I've been. Does it really matter?"

She felt his discomfort. "It's just, you know things I've never even thought about."

"Some of them, perhaps it is better you never did."

She glanced away. "I know what you mean."

"I have too much history in my head. I studied philosophy at the Sorbonne. But such a wondrous spring day is no time for pedantry. I do not wish to bore you."

"The contrary. I'm fascinated by your stories, Kari. And your beautiful imagery."

He turned to her. "It is your beauty that inspires me, Mademoiselle Walker… May I call you Evelyn?"

She felt her cheeks warming into an uncontrollable blush as their eyes met. And held. "Yes. You may."

Still gazing at her, he took her hand and kissed it, then didn't let go. "We Iranians have a word in our language... *kismet*. Fate."

E knew this was all going too fast. Yet she didn't want to put on the brakes. Maybe even couldn't.

Chapter 16

Fog was still rising white off the river that early Saturday morning. When E emerged from the Cité métro, Kari was waiting beside a lamppost entwined with brass leaves. They regarded each other in brief hesitation. A three-cheek embrace that might be normal between acquaintances felt somehow premature. She extended her hand and they shook.

E had warned herself to be cautious. No matter what Kari said–and with such beautiful words–Monique had called him a playboy. Nonetheless, she felt girlish and fluttery. And again charmed by the poetry of this man. To meet at a flower market in the middle of the Seine!

"I must send all my tourists here," she said.

"And then again on Sunday when the flowers become birds."

"I've been to the bird market. Very lively, although not quite as peaceful." She indicated the flowers and plants, the refined shoppers.

His face fell. "I wished to show it to you, Evelyn."

"Oh. I'm… sorry." He'd caught her off-guard again, his manner so open and vulnerable. She could not fail to be touched.

Then his face brightened. "Never mind. It will be different when we go together."

They moved on to a cozy bistro at the Place des Vosges, an arcaded square with a small garden where children played. After lunch, they listened to the Spanish guitar of a soulful, long-haired musician, then Kari tossed a pocketful of change in the boy's open case. The couple strolled past pale stone buildings, their slate roofs rising into the cloud-bright sky. Leery of the romance in the air, E was careful not to invite him to take her arm.

She sought distance too in their conversation… something cerebral, far from the personal. "I'm glad I'm not a writer, trying to find new words to describe this city."

"This is the Old World, so people have been trying a long time, Evelyn. Especially here, the oldest square in Paris."

"I'm from the New World, a quiet little town where everyone knows everyone."

"And here, only the buildings know each other."

She smiled.

"But what I like about this place," he said, surveying the square, "is the symmetry, the sense of order and permanence. It takes me back to another age when things were as they always were." He glanced at the children, then back at her, his look resolutely personal. "I prefer the old ways."

It was too soon. Or was it too late? E looked away, more desperate than ever to put on the brakes. The freedoms she had known had brought nothing but pain and confusion. Wounded and wary, she had come to Paris to put that life behind her. She could now see the possibility of another kind of life, one of stability and enduring values—the "old ways." But who was this man, really, and how did she know she could trust him?

Kari confronted her caution with an old-fashioned courtship. He didn't know about clubs or trendy restaurants, preferring quiet bistros and walks in the park. And when it rained, he sheltered her under his big black umbrella. He never asked about her past; he seemed not to care. She still had the anger inside her, but gradually began to rely on him. He was respectful and polite and made her feel safe.

During the long days-into-evenings of summer, E and Kari wandered the streets seeing old sights through new eyes. They approached the Pont-Neuf one dusk as the sky was warming into a rosy wash.

"Whenever I come here," E said, "I try to imagine Paris before this bridge linked the two banks. How did they ever manage before?"

"My sentiment exactly," Kari replied gravely. "How did I manage to conduct my life before you?"

She stared at him, realizing he had slipped through her defenses. It was hard now to imagine life without him.

On her birthday that September he took her to a Persian restaurant for a meal of grilled kebobs and eggplant, mounds of golden rice and stacks of hot buttery lavosh.

"Nothing like French cuisine, of course, but I hope something you will enjoy." He looked at her. "Perhaps even wish to cook? *My* food."

E nodded. "I would like that, Kari."

Would you? he asked with his eyes.

Outside the restaurant, he hailed a taxi which took them to his apartment in an old vine-covered townhouse on a quiet street.

After the courtyard, all E remembered were the high ceilings and thick Persian carpets and then she was in his arms... his fingers stroking her forehead, his mouth finding hers. They didn't want the kiss to end, and when they finally drew apart, they were breathing the same air. She placed her hand on his heart, felt its wild beating, and allowed herself to trust.

They felt they had been lovers forever and were soon speaking of marriage. When? Where? How many children? He had a small import-export business that would support them well, although she enjoyed her work at Voyages Monique and intended to remain there. Believing the promise of the future, Evelyn finally forgot her past.

Gstaad, Switzerland

To celebrate the holidays Kari took her skiing. They started on the Eggli—a perfect novice slope with a good restaurant midway down. Within three days they moved on to the more challenging Wasserngrat where she put her snowplow to good use and even dared long moments of parallel.

As they rode the final chair up the mountain that afternoon, there were but a few skiers on the lift, fewer still on the slopes. "We've outlasted all of them," E said with a pleasant sense of fatigue. "Not bad, for a southern girl."

"You even fall with ease." The corners of his eyes creased in a fond smile.

"You don't even fall! Who'd have thought a desert land would produce such a good skier?"

"But I have always skied. We have magnificent mountains north of Tehran. In fact, my company is named for our highest peak—Demavand."

"And yet, you never returned. Why?"

"Why?" he repeated slowly, staring ahead. "Sometimes life takes us on a path."

Tell me about it, she thought.

"I was an eager student, idealistic, and came to study philosophy at the Sorbonne. When the anti-Shah demonstrations began at home, my father, a respected diplomat, was taken to Evin Prison and 'questioned' by SAVAK, the secret police." He scowled. "He of course denied I was a communist." His voice became hard and flat. "I never saw him again. My scholarly, rose-loving papa."

His grip tightened around her shoulder. "There are no words to describe Evin–the 'special section.' They always let a few survive to spread the tales of terror and sow fear in our hearts. I was powerless to save my father. If I returned I too would be arrested."

"Your mother?" E asked softly.

His body stiffened. "Alone, with our family split. My sister, married to an anti-Shah activist, had gone underground in Qom. On the royalist side, my mother's uncle took his family to Los Angeles, as did my father's two brothers. Having already lost her parents, my mother lost her will to live. All I had left was my rage. So I stayed in Paris and joined the resistance against the Shah and his corruption." His hand relaxed. "Our current government is far from perfect–but anything is better than *that*!"

"You've never talked about any of this."

They were nearing the top of the mountain. "Sometimes the sorrows are buried so deeply." Kari shrugged, then suddenly smiled. "You have sent them packing!"

E nodded. "I know the feeling, Kari. We're good for each other."

"We are, aren't we? We are blessed and I will always care for you."

He wrapped her in his arms and they were still embracing as they reached the summit–separating just in time to ski off the lift. Then they laughed and resumed their kiss… blocking the path of a man on a chair behind them. Clad in a white Fila jumpsuit, the ashen skier swerved hard to avoid a collision, his gold-rimmed sunglasses dropping with an icy crunch alongside the run.

"Sorry," E said. "*Désolée*."

As if he hadn't heard, the man pulled down his knit cap and turned in search of his dark glasses, then skied off to collect them, kneeling to readjust his bindings.

Although his back was to them, the man seemed fine, so they dug in their poles and pushed off downhill. Amid evergreens dusted white, soaring over deep powder.

Suddenly Kari caught the tip of his upper ski and fell. E glanced back over her shoulder, but he waved her on. "I'll catch up."

Reluctantly, she slowed to a cautious snowplow and continued down the trail. Pausing to check back, she saw a plump skier in red stop to give Kari a hand. After a brief exchange, the man skied away.

Kari brushed himself off and headed toward her.

E watched him approach, then stop on a dime. "You all right?"

"Fine. I guess my thoughts were still far away."

Slipping her wrist from the pole-strap, E squeezed his hand as they watched the empty slope soften into gold and pink. Below, village lights were beginning to wink in the deepening blue.

"Now, something to warm us."

E grinned. Without a further word, the couple glided off and soon reached the bottom, red-cheeked and elated. Skis over their shoulders, they staggered to the hotel in loosened boots. The mood in the village was festive, Christmas only two days away.

They thawed out over a rum tea that felt like fire going down. As they were leaving the Palace's tea room, a man greeted Kari. They shook hands and Kari introduced E to Eli Becker, an Israeli acquaintance, and his red-haired wife, Miriam.

"You will join us for dinner this evening?" Kari asked.

"Why not?"

"The Sans Cravate?"

The plump Israeli grinned at his wife. "Grilled food, oh excellent—I've been ordered to watch my cholesterol these days."

"But no business," Miriam insisted.

He gestured at her with affection. "The boss. Well, perhaps only a little."

His wife rolled her eyes. "Another false promise."

In fact, there was little talk of business at dinner. The conversation revolved mainly around skiing and shopping. E mentioned that Kari had grown up on skis. "In Iran."

Eli feigned surprise. "And I thought he was a Frenchman, born and bred."

Kari groaned. "Heaven forbid."

That reminded Eli of a joke about a Frenchman and his dog and the streets of heaven. The Israeli was a wealth of stories and Miriam his equal in wit, but Kari and E were glad to return to their cozy hotel room.

They spent the rest of their holiday alternating between the mountain and bed.

And with the New Year, they were reborn.

Chapter 17

Paris, France

Back home, the grayness of Paris never entered E's spirit. She was busy cooking Persian food and sending people off to the Seychelle Islands or the Swiss Alps. One dark March day, bogged down in ticketing, E decided to walk to the corner café for a quick bite. It was colder than she'd expected, yet not worth going back for her fur. The "mysterious lynx"—as Monique called it, wondering who was the man attached. *Why do you think there's a man? Ma chère, there is* always *a man.* What was attached in E's mind was the pain, but that was private. Along with her old life—and Nick. And the blood.

E shrugged deeper inside her sweater, turning her thoughts to lunch. Either a sandwich or some *soupe à l'oignon*, dripping with cheese.

Suddenly a beige Citroen with darkened windows pulled up at the curb. Its rear door swung open. A fair-haired man in dark glasses got out, grabbed her arm and pushed her in. He slipped in beside her and slammed the door. The car sped off. It all happened so quickly; E was sinking into the cushiony seat without even a moment to think—to protest, to fight back.

The vehicle whipped around corners and down narrow streets. Outraged, she glared at the man, unruffled in his crisp, beige raincoat. "What is this? Who are you?!"

A polished exterior was all she saw, his sallow face closed and silent. She stared. There was something familiar about him. "Who *are* you?" She felt the onset of hysteria and steeled herself, needing to remain calm.

More silence.

Then after a desperate search of her memory, E remembered. And was now truly frightened. He was the pallid man at the top of the Gstaad chairlift. The man in white who'd almost collided into them—and dropped these very sunglasses. Images flashed before her mind, as she recalled she had seen him before, too—*here* in Paris. And now he was kidnapping her!

"*Merde.*" The grizzled driver cursed as he turned onto avenue George V. The circulation had slowed to a near halt. He honked, but there was nowhere to go.

E had been waiting for this moment. She grabbed the door handle. Locked! She glanced wildly about—seeking an answer, an angle. *Anything.* All she could see of the driver was the back of his neck—no hope of contact. Her captor stared straight ahead in blank silence. The car itself was a sort of void, which threatened to swallow her into its soft leather and deep cushions. She perched at the edge of the seat, arms crossed, trying to hold back the queasy feeling. Trying to remain alert for a way out.

The Citroen inched forward, finally reaching the end of avenue George V, the place de l'Alma. There, at the foot of the bridge, it stopped.

E reached for the door again—and this time it opened. She rushed out, defiant, ready to flee. She looked for an escape route, but what she saw made her bones turn cold and froze her to the spot....

A tall man in a windbreaker, leaning against a wrought iron lamppost. *Nick!*

She stared, stunned. Her heart stopped.

But then a wave of anger struck—hard—so hard it knocked the breath out of her. She could barely whisper. "You *promised.*"

He took a step closer. "I happened to be in town and was wondering about lunch?"

"You have some nerve—scaring me like this. You think this cloak and dagger shit is funny?"

"I knew you wouldn't talk to me any other way."

"You were right about that!" Her eyes blazed.

"What I'd really like is a hot dog, but I'll settle for a *sandwich gruyère.* How about you?"

"I have lost my appetite. And don't think I owe you anything because of that money—that *blood* money you stashed in my bag."

"No thanks expected."

As Nick reached for her arm, E shook him off. "The entrance to the sewers is just across the bridge. Funny. I can smell them from here."

He looked at her quietly. "We need to talk." Her expression was harsh, not giving him anything. Nick moved down the path toward the river, then turned. He looked at her again and nodded.

Mouth set, keeping her distance, she followed. Down cold stone steps to the Seine.

They reached the departure quay for the Bateaux Mouches sightseeing barges. One was waiting, nearly full. Nick knew he had to get her onboard–and keep her there. There would be no other way to hold this conversation.

"After you."

Brushing icily past, she moved up the gangplank. He followed, elbowing his way through the crush of passengers to the second deck, then to an empty spot in the bow.

"*Well?*"

Nick studied her. Hands on her hips, fiery eyes, alive and beautiful. "Paris becomes you, E. How are you doing?"

"Great–till you showed up!"

The boat embarked with a lurch. Loudspeakers began blaring a multilingual commentary. "In case you've been too busy for sightseeing," Nick offered.

He was trying to soften her up. E didn't respond, armoring herself against a trap.

"Not gonna go easy on me, are you?"

Pointedly, she turned, staring straight ahead–oblivious to the granite vista of sky and river, oblivious to the mist rushing over her, the damp air. He placed his jacket on her shoulders, but she didn't acknowledge the gesture. It was obvious he'd gone to a lot of trouble to arrange this "meeting" and equally obvious he'd "forgotten" his promise to leave her alone.

Nick sighed. Best just begin. No way to sugarcoat it. "You're right. I kidnapped you. I broke my promise to stay out of your life. And, yes, I am bad news." He looked down at his hands on the railing. The water below was black. "Really bad news."

"You had me followed. That awful man?" E inclined her head toward shore.

"Henri? Once you get to know him–"

"*Why?* Why are you doing this to me, Nick?"

"Ironic, isn't it? We finally slew the dragon, and now we find ourselves in a jungle full of snakes–poisonous and well-camouflaged." Taking a deep breath, he looked up and felt the chill wind in his face. His heart. "Karim's import/export company is a front. He runs Iran's Paris Logistics Center. His mission is to get around the trade sanctions against his country—to acquire restricted technology, military materiel. Worse."

"I thought *you* were the guys doing that!" E glared past him at the great clock on the old d'Orsay train station, now her favorite museum. "Iran-Contra—right? Arms for hostages?"

"Something like that."

"So we can sell to Iran? Is that it?"

"It's a messy part of the world—what can I say?"

She nodded grimly. "Pretty two-faced, don't you think?"

Nick shrugged. "After Irangate—and Saddam—there was a lot of soul-searching back home. Then came the inevitable crackdown. Mansour fell into a Treasury sting."

Sting? her face asked.

"Maybe he was in the wrong place at the wrong time. Maybe one of his friends wasn't really a friend." Nick narrowed his eyes. "These are not nice people, E."

"You should talk."

"Whatever. The fact is, the United States has an embargo against military and high-tech exports to Iran. Karim Mansour has been indicted in a conspiracy to violate that embargo."

Dead silence. *Indicted?* E was too stunned to react.

"You met one of his associates—Eli Becker—in Gstaad?"

"Who?"

"Your dinner companion? The one who 'bumped' into him on the slopes."

"How do you—? Oh, right. Your pasty-faced *friend*." E didn't try to disguise her scorn.

"That's just the Israeli connection, but there are others. We need to find out about the rest of the network. We'd like you to help us get him someplace quiet—say a vacation in the Mediterranean?—so we can talk to him."

"You *bastard*," E erupted, as an impeccably dressed, middle-aged Japanese couple looked up in surprise.

"E? This is not just spare parts, not ordinary contraband. We're talking *nasty* stuff—warheads packed with biotoxins or deadly chemical cocktails. Nerve gas. Poisons Saddam used against us—our troops—in the Gulf War. Now Tehran wants them. Even things up a little, I guess."

She shook her head in denial.

"It's for his own good. If he cooperates–gives us some useful intelligence regarding events in Iran–we may be able to cut a deal, protect him from less *kindly* elements of our government." The real enforcers worked out of the Treasury's Office of Foreign Assets Control.

Her face twisted in disgust. "Yeah. I give him to you and you give him to them."

"Wrong. A deal is a deal."

She stared. A deal? Nick?

He looked down into the murky, rushing Seine. The silence was broken only by the recorded travelogue. They were now passing Notre Dame, all Gothic towers and gargoyles–and then the Mémorial des Martyrs de la Déportation, a former morgue.

"But how did you know about me and Kari?" A big piece of the puzzle fell into place. She turned to him–utterly repelled, her eyes dark slits–and slapped him hard across the face. The dignified Japanese couple averted their gaze.

He took it, not trying to deflect the blow. It was the least he deserved.

E regarded him in utter horror. "It's Monique–isn't it?" Her words were like knives. Stilettos. "*Isn't it?*"

Nick met her look–the truth hung silently in the air between them.

She shook her head in disbelief. "You set me up to work for her. And she works for you! My God. Where were you when they passed out consciences?"

Nick looked back down at his fingernails. "I'm sorry, E, but this is a case involving national security."

Bitterly. "Aren't they all?" It was like a body blow. E could not comprehend how he could have done this to her. And *Monique?*

He could feel the revulsion in E's stare burning into his skull. Nick gazed blankly at the passing riverbank, stone gray buildings under leaden skies, a solitary fisherman hunched over a pole. Finally, there was no escape; he was compelled to look back at her–and felt the full force of her rage.

"Have you ever *not* lied to me?" Her expression changed, the smile devoid of humor. "I know you don't think much of my intelligence." She saw his wince, didn't care. "But I'm no bimbo. I *do* read the papers–and even read between the lines. You screwed up in the Gulf and need a new scapegoat. Or at least, the good-old *old* one. Right?"

E wiped the mist off her face. She didn't know why she was talking to him, other than being trapped on the damn boat. Yet for some crazy reason, she still cared what he thought. "You're wrong. It's just a typical American prejudice that all Iranians are terrorists or criminals. Not Kari. He's kind and respectful. Doesn't use me—like some other men." Her fury had again risen. "And hell will freeze over before I have anything to do with you or your... national security—ever again!"

As she paused for a breath, Nick looked at her matter-of-factly, his tone flat. "E—everyone's after him. Including the French, for customs violations. We'd like to debrief him first." He smiled bleakly. "They may want to cut their own deal, and the French are not known for sharing their intelligence."

Then Nick touched her arm gingerly, trying to avoid another slug. "I want you to know—*I* didn't set you up with him." His gaze was earnest and direct. "When Karim's name popped up in the investigation, my boss contacted Monique privately—and put the tail on you. He only told me after the indictment. That's when he came up with the idea of using the charges to turn Karim, so we could find out about his organization."

"But *you* set me up with her."

"You didn't have to call."

She narrowed her eyes. How low could you get? "After you conveniently dropped me in Paris? Alone, on the verge of a nervous breakdown?"

He had no answer. No defense. "Sure, Monique's one of our French assets—and I did ask her to help you out, but that was it."

"But I *told* you I didn't want you taking care of me any more."

Nick sighed, only too aware of his obligation to take care of her. His personal obligation. His *moral* obligation. No matter what she said. Still, he wanted—if not forgiveness—at least, understanding. "The chief knew he was looking at a major intelligence scoop—and a serious career move—if he could recruit one of the 'big guns' in this technology theft ring. Maybe work out a long term relationship?"

"Sure. Use Kari like you used me."

He pressed on. "My boss leaned on me—hard—saying he needed my help to get your help. Thought I was the only one you'd listen to." His voice trailed off.

E tossed him his jacket. "He was wrong about that, wasn't he?" The hurt from this betrayal was devastating. Her anger served to dull the ache, but not dissipate it. Nothing could. Nick had done her in, playing with her head and her heart, polluting her ability to trust. She had thought he was a human being, but he wasn't.

Bitter in her contempt E lashed out, her words possessing the savagery of an arctic winter. "Now who do I have to *fuck* to get off this boat?"

Nick saw the ice floating on her eyes... transparent, brittle, painfully sharp. He could feel the throbbing below the surface. Her anguish was a palpable, physical thing. She got to him in a way he had never been reached before. And he was ashamed beyond words.

If E had looked at him, she would have seen the rawness of his emotions reflected on his face. He was naked for the world to see. For her to see. But she did not care to look. She was out of there.

Empty, Nick watched her turn and stride down the deck. Wondering if any salary–any pension–was worth it.

For that matter–any "ideal."

Chapter 18

From the Pont de l'Alma, it was only minutes to Kari's office on avenue Marceau. The gray streets were lined with bent-over people and gaunt trees. As the taxi drew nearer, E thought of the Plaza-Athénée, a few blocks away. How long ago that now seemed, her life before Voyages Monique.

Monique. She paled, her insides shriveling.

Everything seemed dark and cold, including the curving iron staircase. She raced up the stone steps, two at a time, to the fourth floor landing and stopped before a heavy oak door. Drawing a breath, E ran her fingers over the engraved brass plaque, *Demavand, S.A. Société Anonyme.* Anonymous society. All of a sudden that seemed ominous. Then she frowned at the insanity of her thoughts. Some kind of big Logistics Center? Here?

Yet as she entered the empty reception area, E regarded the office through new eyes. The secretary's wooden desk was neat as a pin, a clean sheet of paper in the typewriter. The room had large windows overlooking a quiet courtyard. Kari's had no view at all, but he said he preferred the lack of distraction. If he were doing something illegal, he would naturally prefer the privacy. E became furious with herself at the very idea. Damn Nick!

She continued into Kari's office. Other than the computer and telephone, it would have appeared much the same a century ago, with its fine antiques, carpets and Persian miniatures.

"*Chinois...*" she heard.

Kari was giving dictation to Marie-Christine, his longtime secretary, a tiny woman who always wore black, brown or navy. On that day, it was a plain black suit and turtleneck, brown flats, brown chignon. She glanced at E, then returned to her notes.

It was the first time E had appeared unexpectedly and Kari gave her a startled look. Then his face softened. "What a marvelous surprise, darling. You had an errand in the neighborhood?" He gestured her to the sofa, eyes already drifting back to the papers on his desk.

E struggled to remain calm, her words quiet and measured. "I need to talk to you."

"Perhaps a drink later?" he suggested vaguely. "Fouquet's or Alexandre's, if you wish—a more quiet *ambiance*?"

"Kari," she insisted.

He stared at her. "Please take care of the Dutch purchase order, Marie-Christine, and hold all calls."

The secretary closed her folder and rose in one efficient movement, then left.

Kari moved to the sofa next to E. "What is the matter?"

Her eyes wide with terror and dismay, she stared at him, hands twisting in her lap. "The CIA," she whispered.

His gaze was steady.

"They want me to get you to the Mediterranean so they can question you. And then probably arrest you—you're under some kind of U.S. indictment." The very word sounded final, inevitable. Terminal. "They said if I refused—which I *did*—the French would get you anyway, on their own charges."

He watched her, emotionless. "How do you know—those people?"

E took his hand and held it tightly for courage. She studied his palm, then his quiet face, knowing how traditional he was, how deeply hurt he'd be by her revelations. E feared he'd think she lied by not telling him sooner. That he would lose respect for her.

But she had no choice.

Her eyes returned to his palm. "I knew a man when I lived in Washington. The CIA came to me and said he was a Russian spy. They asked me to help arrest him. I didn't want to, but finally agreed. Patriotism, I guess." She sighed deeply. "Later they came to me again and wanted to introduce me to a Greek businessman who traded in scientific secrets. To make a long story short, I got in the middle–and he was shot before my eyes." Still looking down. "After that, I told them to leave me alone. Then I came to Paris, to begin a new life." She finally raised her eyes to meet his. "And then I met you."

His expression reassured her that, yes, he still loved her. The tenderness in his gaze gave her the courage to continue. Now her eyes turned stormy. "We didn't meet by accident. I'm sure Monique is their agent."

"I understand." Kari took the hand holding his and kissed it. "Now it is my turn." He paused a moment, as if choosing his own words. "You know how I love my country, our great heritage. You also know that, along with most honorable people, I opposed the Shah's corrupt regime. Like you, I had reservations about 'government service'… but I answered their call, obliged by patriotism–like you."

E watched him, unblinking.

"My people have made many mistakes. Holding American hostages was wrong–and foolish. As a result, we have few friends in the world." He gave her an almost pleading look. "But Iraq invaded us."

She nodded. "I guess you were the only ones who knew about Saddam Hussein."

"Before Kuwait." He grimaced, then shrugged. "One must survive. Since I was already established here, I was asked to set up a procurement office for technological supplies. I, who had been a philosophy student, a man of peace." His eyebrows lowered in a frown. "Suddenly I was in a new world–a world of black secrets and black markets–forced there by the U.S. and their trade embargoes. Embargoes that may be broken only when it is in their interest. Forced by honor and love of country to deal with those who had no honor–those who profited from the horrors of war–the dealers of death."

E listened, attempting to reconcile the contradictions, yet she did understand being a pawn in someone else's game. "But–germ warfare? Chemical weapons?"

"*C'est fou!* Crazy! I would never do such a thing. How could you think that of me–and who would say it?"

E's lips tightened, just thinking of Nick.

"Spare parts, yes–even armaments. But after our war with Iraq ended, I told them no more weapons–no more military. Now I deal only in raw materials, factory tools, medical supplies. Chemicals? Yes, but for plastics, vitamins. My desire is to rebuild lives, not take them. You must believe me."

"Of course I do, Kari."

"And no poison gases. No biotoxins. This to me is immoral. Of course Iraq already has them. But it didn't matter when Saddam used mustard gas against us. In fact, your side rushed to supply him. You know where that led." He gazed at her. "It seems that I too was set up. One of those men without honor—one of my 'colleagues.' A man whom I suspect is also a U.S. informant, cleverly working both sides of the street—or, shall I say?—the Atlantic." His smile was bitter.

E shared his bitterness. "They want you to become an informant, too, an agent."

"Never. I cannot do such things. Betray my country? Not for them. They use people—they used you." He drummed his fingers on the sofa arm, then turned to her. "Now I will care for you. We must flee Paris."

E felt the strength of his commitment, yet there was still the doubt Nick had planted. "One thing, Kari. They said you had secret meetings in Gstaad, that Eli is your Israeli contact."

His dark eyes flashed. "I conduct my business wherever and whenever I can—Moscow, Beijing. It is my duty. Business with Israel must naturally remain secret. The truth is they are one of our suppliers."

She sat up and stared. "Israel?"

He shrugged. "After all, Iraq is their deadly enemy. As the saying goes, the enemy of my enemy is my friend. And we are linked also—Iranians and Israelis—by being non-Arabs, Middle East outsiders."

"Is Eli Mossad?"

Kari burst into laughter. "Is the Pope Catholic?"

E blinked. It was too much to take in all at once. And still so much she did not understand. One thing she knew, though: he would never hurt her. He had no agenda but love. "Now what?"

With a brisk movement, he brushed aside the past. "*On y va.* We go."

Kari returned to his desk and faced his computer, a gray Minitel provided by the French PTT, Postes, Téléphones et Télécommunications. He logged on to the Vénus messagerie and left a prearranged message, borrowed from Omar Khayyam:

Layla, Iram indeed is gone, With all his rose. Rostam

After logging out, he looked up at E. "It is done. We face a dangerous time now, but at least we are together. I must ask your complete trust in all that proceeds."

"I do trust you, Kari." She had questions, of course, but would save them for later.

He went to his safe and removed a small document case. "Now we wait ten minutes exactly."

The time seemed to pass slowly, but pass it did. He took her arm and led her out the door, barely pausing in the outer office. "I am called away, Marie-Christine. I will contact you later for messages." His demeanor was cool.

Once outside, Kari scanned the street. The sky was heavy with leaden gray-purple clouds, the air damp and chill. Pulling up the collar of her sweater, he hailed a taxi then followed E inside, telling the driver to take them to the Gare Saint-Lazare métro via rue du Rocher.

"*Comme vous-voulez.*" With a drag on his Gitane, the driver jammed on the gas.

The afternoon traffic was dense, but no more than usual. It had not yet started to rain, so Kari's view out the rear window was unhindered.

He nudged E, indicating a dark-windowed beige Citroen that followed two vehicles behind. She nodded grimly. Citroens were common in Paris, but she had no doubt.

After about fifteen minutes, the taxi turned onto the narrow rue du Rocher, the Citroen still on their tail. There was a post office ahead, where the road seemed to come to a dead end. But as they drew closer, E saw that it continued after a jog to the left.

Just as they began their turn, a PTT postal van pulled out from the curb, then stopped in front of the post office. All traffic was blocked– including the beige Citroen, which beeped its horn. Once and then again.

A final glimpse before rounding the corner showed the Citroen hemmed in by the car behind it, a black Renault that seemed to have developed car trouble. E enjoyed an evil smile. Their pursuers were now immobilized.

She hoped it was Nick stuck in that car. E looked at Kari who only shrugged. He directed the driver to take a right on rue de Rome, which brought them to the Saint-Lazare entrance.

The rain was just starting to fall. They hurried down the steps–winding through long, crowded yellow corridors past the train entrances–then back up another set of stairs onto rue d'Intérieure, fronting the station.

Kari bypassed the taxi stand, making straight for a double-parked taxi further down the street. He opened the rear door and followed E in, while the suit-clad passenger slid out the opposite side and got in front. Without a word exchanged, the leather-jacketed driver sped away.

The taxi turned onto rue de Clichy, which led straight to the Périphérique, the ring road encircling Paris. They headed south, skirting the Bois de Boulogne. E and Kari exchanged a glance, sharing the memory of their meeting. But then he returned his attention to the road and the threats around them.

The rain was now coming down in dark sheets. He squeezed her hand, but there was no conversation in the car. Although they saw no suspicious vehicles, visibility was limited and their grim driver doubled back on himself more than once.

E was trying not to think about what was happening to her life. She had vowed to trust Kari no matter what—and she did—but could not deny her alarm at the rush of events.

On the outskirts of Paris, the taxi reached a deserted industrial area and entered an trashbin-lined alley nearly obscured under the downpour. Enfolding E under his arm, Kari hurried her into a waiting blue Peugeot. Before they even slammed the door, the vehicle sped out the other end of the alley.

There were two different but equally wary men inside the car. As E shook off the water, she noticed a large gun barely concealed under the arm of the bearded young man up front. Disconcerted, she looked outside. A blurry sign directed them toward Versailles.

Kari studied the dripping windows for a few silent moments, then turned to E and wiped a raindrop off her cheek. "I hope you don't have your heart set on an elaborate wedding."

Her breath caught in her throat. It had been a day of staggering events, but—? "*Kari?* Is that some kind of proposal?"

"This is not the way I envisioned it, but yes, it is. Will you marry me, Evelyn?"

"I… will." She swallowed, suddenly terrified.

Kari leaned closer, positioning his shoulder for a bit of privacy. "I would not pressure you, my love," he murmured, "but if you can find it in your heart—it is best if you convert to Islam." He paused. "I know this is a lot to ask, but it is only a technicality for the marriage certificate."

Convert. Marriage certificate. Things were moving too quickly! This was no sudden outrush of passion but a carefully designed plan. Why would it be "best"? She felt a tightness in her belly.

E looked away, seeing only sheets of rain and blurred headlights. *Islam?* She had seen Kari pray at certain times during the day. He never spoke of his faith, but it seemed to give him a sense of peace. She would like to share that peace, yet… it was a lot to ask.

Or was it? *Sometimes life takes you on a path.* He had said that to her on the Gstaad chairlift. Did it really matter how you prayed to God? "What does that mean?" she asked slowly. "What would I do?"

"My religion is a simple one. To belong, you merely have to profess your belief. Only one sentence: *There is no God but God and Muhammad is the Messenger of God,*" he said in English.

E stared at him, wondering about any conflict of heavenly interest. She didn't think Jesus would be offended—Muhammad was the Messenger, not the Son. And God, of course, was God. "I think I maybe can handle that." The words trickled out and then she was committed. But the tightness in her belly remained.

"It is called the *shahada.* The mullah will ask you to say those words." Kari repeated the phrase as she rehearsed it in her mind. He kissed her fingertips, then produced two small Cartier boxes—the rings.

It was dusk when they stopped before a white domed building on the outskirts of Neauphle-le-Chateau. By now the rain had stopped, but the air was still moist and the sky muddled. The village road was slick and deserted.

Kari spoke a few words to the bearded young bodyguard. The man nodded, laid his M-10 machine pistol on the seat, then strode toward a nearby stucco house. The driver, Omar, picked up the weapon, got out and leaned against the hood of the car, eyes alert. He was joined by two others, also in their twenties—dark-haired, and armed with Skorpions.

Kari helped E from the car and gestured to the domed building. "The mullah here is a cultured man, a man of books. In Iran, he is also a notary public licensed to unite couples in both religious and civil rites. He will perform the rites."

E had seen a mullah once at the Paris mosque, on a quiet street not far from the Sorbonne. She and Kari had sipped sweet mint tea by fig trees and a fountain in its courtyard garden. And now, she was to be married in a mosque.

"We have a tradition that during the ceremony the bride stands behind a partition."

That gave her pause. She drew back toward the car and shivered in the damp air. "I don't know, Kari. It's what you hear about—the second-class thing."

"It is just a tradition. I will be right there," he assured her.

E still hesitated, shaking her head. The sky pressed down on her, the falling darkness, the sense of closing doors. She felt claustrophobic and wanted to flee.

"These are the old ways that we carry with us to give order to the modern world. This practice is merely symbolic of a man's desire to protect his wife. Do you think you might come to see it that way?"

What she saw was the vulnerability in his eyes, the open look of fear that she might reject him. She knew she could never do that. "I know that you are committed to protect me."

"Thank you, Evelyn." His shoulders slumped in relief. "All right then. When the mullah asks if you wish to marry me, you must not reply until the third time... Another tradition. Something to do with feminine modesty."

She nodded, as new questions were born. The knot expanded in her belly.

Then the bearded bodyguard reappeared with a plain gray headscarf, averting his eyes from her face.

"*Merci*, Javad," Kari said, taking the scarf.

Javad reclaimed his weapon from Omar. They exchanged nods with the two local guards and strode toward the mosque. Javad stationed himself at the arched entrance, while the others went inside.

Kari draped the scarf over E's head and shoulders, tucking in a few loose curls. "Are you ready, *mon amour?*"

She lifted her chin, but felt her brain grow fuzzy. They entered the tiled entrance portal and removed their shoes. E followed him to a marble basin, splashing water on face, hands and feet. Now purified, they followed a short passage into a starkly furnished space of whitewashed brick and piled rugs, the doors manned by the two local youths. Light filtered through small windows circling the base of the dome.

Kari indicated a carved wooden screen to their right. E stared, struck anew by the changes about to enter her life. She hesitated again, then turned back to him. She had been betrayed before. It was a risk putting herself in his hands. Was she sure she could trust him? "Don't be afraid. I am with you."

As she disappeared behind the three-panel partition, E was swamped with panic. Walls closing around her. How had she ended up here, *trapped*? Her mind flooded with conflicting emotions, she saw rays of fractured light cut through the carving. Images... Kari, still looking toward her. She saw his concern. And love. The wooden screen smelled freshly of cedar, and she felt the knot loosen.

A low linen-covered table sat in the center of the room, covered with bread, eggs, sweets, gold coins, candlesticks and the Quran—symbols of health, good fortune and faith. As Kari approached, Omar and Javad followed a few paces behind.

A white-turbaned mullah in a long black cloak entered through a side door. He paused, taking it all in, then frowned at the sight of so many weapons.

Karim apologized with a quiet look. Yet some things had to be. He needed two witnesses for the ceremony, as well as the security these men provided. The town, once Khomeini's refuge, tolerated the mosque, which served many immigrants—from wealthy Iranian expatriates to students and laborers. However, he now knew they would always be viewed as outsiders in this society—strangers and therefore suspect—and therefore never truly safe. The proof was E's warning that the French authorities were after him. He had done business with them, but was not one *of* them. If a sacrificial lamb was needed, it would be he. He who had lived here half his life. Of course he needed protection.

Sayyed Araf Sadra, the silver-bearded cleric, smoothed the folds of his loose black aba, sheer woven mohair over a long, gray cassock. "I see you have brought your two witnesses, Karim," he said in French, with a glance at the bodyguards. "But where is the bride's *wali*? A marriage is not valid without the father or other male relative."

"She is alone in life," Kari said. "An American far from home."

The mullah sighed in reflection. "In the absence of the wali, a prominent Muslim can stand in." He studied the far wall. "I will act as wali," he said, glancing at the cedar screen. "And does she wish to convert?"

"She does." Kari looked in E's direction. "Her name is Evelyn Walker."

E listened as they spoke for her. She recalled thinking of herself as an accidental tourist. Or maybe as Kari had often insisted, it was fate that had brought them together... here. But she had vowed to be an agent of her own fate. What was she doing?

"One final request." Kari opened his palms in further apology. "We do not have much time."

"Of course." The mullah cleared his throat and turned again to the screen. "It is my honor to ask you, Evelyn Walker, to proclaim the shahada—the Muslim declaration of faith. You may speak in English."

E took a deep breath. Suddenly her mouth was dust-dry. She swallowed, took another breath, then: *"There is no God but God and Muhammad is the Messenger of God."* Her heart was pounding. She felt faint, thinking of what her Pop would say, but steadied herself, focusing on the patterns of light that emerged through the carved cedarwood.

The mullah nodded, then began reciting the timeless words: "Almighty Allah created humanity, male and female, each in need of the other, and established the institution of marriage as a means of uniting the souls in the blessed bond of love, leading to their pleasure and happiness in a way advantageous to mankind.

"At this precious and auspicious moment, in obedience to the guidance of our Creator and in obedience to the practice of the beloved Prophet—Peace be upon His Name—we unite in the bond of marriage our brother Karim Mansour and sister Evelyn Walker who have decided to live together as husband and wife, sheltered with the blessing of Almighty Allah and His Divine Benevolence. May He fill their life with joy, and may He grant them peace, health and prosperity.

"And now, we will listen to the wali of the bride and the bridegroom creating this contractual and solemn bond. We are all witnesses to this blissful event. May the Almighty Allah make us worthy."

Shifting to his role as wali, Mullah Sadra addressed the groom, "In the Name of Allah, the Compassionate and Merciful... I give to you Evelyn Walker, whom I represent in accordance with the Islamic Shari'ah and the tradition of the Messenger of Allah."

Resuming his official role, he asked, "Do you choose this girl to be your wife?"

"Yes," Kari said.

The mullah turned to the two witnesses. "Do you so hear?"

Familiar with the ceremony, they replied, *"Oui."*

Mullah Sadra looked toward the partition. "Do you choose this man to be your husband?" Silence. He repeated the question.

Hands clasped over her belly, E remained silent, still focused on the rays of light. After the third query, she cast her eyes toward heaven and replied, "Yes. *Oui*."

The mullah asked the two witnesses if they heard. *Oui*, they repeated.

Then he turned back to the bride, Evelyn Walker. "May Allah make it a blessing for you and a blessing to you. And bring you together with all that is good. May He make us worthy, *Insh'Allah*, of being witness to this marriage."

Kari moved behind the screen to claim her. "My beloved bride."

She entered his embrace and felt a tightness in her throat. The tears welled up and her chest began to heave. He was her husband.

"Shh," he murmured, soft soothing sounds. "Now, nothing to fear. And I swear on my life you will come to no harm–ever."

His hand on her head, stroking her hair. His sweet, gentle words. She sniffled and sighed, then looked at him, eyes shining. "Where's my ring?"

Laughing, he placed her hand in the crook of his elbow and as if in a processional, led her back around the screen. They signed the marriage certificate with black fountain pens. Then with much ceremony Kari slipped the three interlocked Cartier bands on her finger. As she presented him with the matching three-gold ring, E wondered how long ago he had purchased these rings.

"In our tradition, we would now celebrate with food and gifts–the *walimah*." His face creased in distress. "But there is no time. I hope this will suffice." He picked up a honeyed sweet and fed it to her. Following his lead, E selected and fed one to him.

The two witnesses, Omar and Javad–guards once again–escorted the bridal pair to the rear door. Skorpion over his arm, one of the local youths rushed to join them, carrying a jacket-wrapped bundle. Grabbing some candies and gold coins from the table, he tossed them at the couple. "For luck."

The guards smiled at the youth and made joking comments, bachelor comments. Blushing, he untied the sleeves of his jacket and handed everyone their shoes. Mullah Sadra followed as the other local guard opened the door to the central courtyard.

It was like entering the eye of a hurricane. Howling winds whipped their hair and clothing–almost tearing off E's scarf. At first, she thought it was the storm returning with a vengeance. The roaring turbulence intensified. Clapping her hands over her ears, E looked up to see a helicopter descending from the sky–landing in the courtyard.

Kari grabbed her arm. They rushed aboard, followed by Javad and Omar. Within minutes, they were safely aloft. The mullah and two remaining guards watched them go, staring into the purple sky, smelling of fresh rain mixed with exhaust fumes.

The Mediterranean Sea

Two hours later, they flew over the Marseille harbor and this time into a real storm. They were tossed about unmercifully, and E felt her stomach dropping into the choppy seas below. She clung to the arms of her seat, unable to decide whether it was better to keep her eyes open or shut—both were equally awful and her head was spinning no matter what she did. At least she didn't embarrass herself by throwing up.

Before long they saw a large container ship, ablaze with lights to guide their landing. The instant the helicopter touched down, the guards said farewell and helped the newlyweds out the door. The deck rose to meet their feet—pitching and rolling—and very slick. They clung to each other, attempting to gain their footing, while assaulted by the pounding rain—and the great whirl of wind from the aircraft that was already lifting off.

Shielded against Kari's body, E watched it rise into the roiling sky. She shook her head, utterly overwhelmed by the day's events. From a tour boat in the Seine to a cargo ship in the Mediterranean.

Then there was no more time for reflection. Oblivious to the downpour, rocking deck and crewmembers who looked discreetly away, Kari took her and held her. And kissed every inch of her face.

"*Je t'aime, Madame Mansour.*"

"And I love you, Mr. Mansour."

The storm surrounding them raged and intensified.

Chapter 19

Tunis, Tunisia

The wind and rain buffeted the ship unmercifully. The couple spent their wedding night in the captain's cabin, locked in each other's arms. Then, the heavens spent, the morning dawned fresh and clean. The ship docked outside the ancient city of Carthage, now a suburb of Tunis. They took a small motor launch ashore. E's sweater, finally dry, was no longer necessary. It was hot, the sea a blazing clear blue. Most everything else was stark white—the sand, the buildings—even the sun. E was reminded of Greece—and Alexis. She felt a chill, despite the heat.

Kari hustled her into the waiting green Toyota. He spoke a few words to the wiry, olive-skinned driver, who wore a white shirt buttoned to his wrists. The man set off for the port's large medieval kasbah and then parked, disappearing into one of its winding alleys. As they waited, Kari asked how she felt.

"I guess it's every girl's fantasy to be whisked away by a tall, dark and handsome man." Her smile faded. "Okay. The truth is I'm still stunned, Kari. You turned my world upside down today. I mean, yesterday."

"You've turned mine right-side up, Evelyn." He put his arm around her.

"You always know just what to say." She put her head on his shoulder. "The other truth is, every day with you is a gift."

"It is a joy to be flattered by one's beautiful—wife." He pulled her closer.

She closed her eyes and felt his chest rise and fall. "Now what?"

"*Insh'Allah*—we will live happily ever after."

"Insh'Allah?"

"Allah—God willing."

"I sure hope He is." E sat up. "Otherwise what will we do?"

"I gave you my vow that I will always protect you. So there is nothing to fear."

She placed a hand on his cheek. "I believe you, Kari. I never thought I would trust another human being in this life, but I do trust you."

He looked in her glistening eyes and then out the window at the vast expanse of sea and sky. "The very same color. I believe God was smiling when you were born and a glimmer of His smile lives in your eyes."

The wiry driver returned bearing dates, oranges, croissants, as well as some thick bread and cheese. He also had a small newspaper-wrapped parcel, which he handed to Kari. Devouring the food, they continued along the Gulf of Tunis. The hillside was dotted with white stone houses, olive trees and ancient ruins.

After a short drive, they arrived at the airport, boarded the waiting plane and took their seats near the front. An Arabic prayer for safe flight came over the intercom and then the Egypt Air jet took off.

A little later, Kari unwrapped the parcel, removing a piece of thick black fabric. "Evelyn, my beloved, I must ask that you wear this on our arrival. It is called a *chador*."

He explained how to wrap the large, half-moon-shaped cloth over her head and body. How she must hold it in place at the chin area, just over the mouth. E glanced around. Although some of the female passengers wore jeans and lacy headscarves, many were already covered. Several regarded her curiously. At least, appeared to—since their eyes were barely visible. What did they think of her? Maybe she was exotic to them, too. "I feel like I'm entering the *Arabian Nights*."

"Not Arab—Iranian," he corrected her gently. "The chador is for the protection of women. It is our form of veil and will shield you from undue attention at the airport."

"What airport, Kari?" She finally had to ask, finally able to think beyond surviving the next moment.

"Why, Tehran, of course." As if that were the most obvious thing in the world.

Tehran. Of course. And then, in this airborne pause, it struck her: They were fugitives from the law. She who had always been so respectful of the government was now defying it–and she didn't even care. Her respect for people in authority was long gone. They were the ones guilty of breach of trust, not her. So now, her sole trust would be in this man, the only one who had behaved toward her with honor and decency. But he was going home, while she was leaving every shred of her past behind. In the most dramatic way possible, she was beginning a new life with her new husband.

E carried the chador to the toilet and unfolded it. The black material was not what she expected. Rather than fluid and silky, it was stiff and heavy, some kind of synthetic blend. It wouldn't show the dirt, that was sure. Probably wouldn't wrinkle, either. Beyond her control came an image of Dr. May Min, who had been so interested in fine fabric. She saw the blood again and, dizzy, lowered herself onto the toilet.

The moment passed, but E was still shaken by the memory. She stood and draped the chador over her head and body, trying to cover the lower part of her face as well. But even in these close quarters with little room for movement, it didn't stay that way. She found that you had to hold the edges in place–and keep holding. What they really needed here was velcro! She figured she'd get used to it, though, just a matter of practice.

His eyes locked onto hers as she returned–and an erotic shiver rushed through her body.

By midday they were approaching the jagged, snow-covered Elburz Mountains surrounding Tehran. Kari pointed out a solitary peak to the northeast of the city. "Below is the Demavand, an ancient volcano as high as Kilimanjaro."

"Next winter you can take me skiing."

"In fact, the Chemchak resort has skiing through mid-April. Although we may be too busy settling in this year. Many adjustments face us." He rubbed a hand over his stubbled cheeks. "Different customs. For example, a clean-shaven look is not the fashion."

She smiled. "I know–chadors are the latest style."

"More like a classic."

"That's what Monique used to tell me: good classics last forever."

"Actually, I was thinking more of men's fashion. These days, it seems, ties are out–and beards are in."

"I hate ties. I like beards. I love you," she said, dancing the veil over her eyes.

"Good, my wife. You are already learning the Iranian way."

And then, mountains to the north, desert to the south, the plane began its sharp descent into Mehrabad Airport.

Washington, D.C.

At about the same time, Nick realized the couple had slipped through his net, which now seemed more like a sieve. Henri had phoned from the Citroen yesterday after losing their trail, but Nick told him not to worry. "Just head for Mansour's apartment and don't blink." Another man staked out E's place. However, there was no activity at either location, coming or going. The next morning, a shamefaced Henri reported the full details of their efficient getaway. Nick telephoned Monique, who said E had not shown up for work yet–and that she had neither seen nor heard from her since before lunch yesterday.

"But do not worry, *chéri*. She left her beautiful lynx here at the office, so she will no doubt return."

Maybe Monique would return for a fur, but E was a different breed. Nick's heart sunk. His security sucked–there was no way to get around it. With hindsight, he realized part of the reason for his negligence was delusion. He hadn't wanted to believe the plain fact that E's love for Karim had put her beyond him–and his concern, and his manipulation–and his own deep feelings. Now he could never make it right to her. His agent had truly split. And he would miss her like hell.

Nick knew that his boss would have to activate one of their few remaining Iranian assets to follow through on the case, and he'd never hear the end of it.

Well, to hell with him. To hell with all of them. By now Nick could give a shit. Especially when he realized that yesterday was the Ides of March, and he could no longer stomach the role of Brutus, even one more time.

Maybe he'd take a walk himself.

Tehran, Iran

Kari and E were waiting at the cabin door as it opened. "*Il fait beau*," he said, turning his face into a warm gust of air–no longer bitter cold, not yet searing hot.

Maybe a nice day for him, E thought, enshrouded in the voluminous chador.

With but a brief opening for her eyes, she had barely made it down the aisle. Struggling to see and keep properly covered, wanting to reach out to steady herself, realizing that her hands were not free. It was like learning to walk all over again. As she stepped out the door, E caught her foot on a heavy fold of fabric and almost tripped down the stairs—and would have, had not Kari grabbed her in time.

As he hovered at her side, they crossed the tarmac to an airport bus. E felt weighted down, forced to compensate for her lack of peripheral vision by moving with slow caution. From toddler to old woman... The chador started to fall and she had to grab it—fast. Thus absorbed, she found herself falling behind Kari—exactly like all the other shrouded women trailing after their men. Only most of them had veils clamped between their teeth, as they carried the bags, too.

The bus pulled up in front of a large, shed-like building, and the Mansours joined the milling crowd inside the terminal's stuffy arrival area. They took their place in the passport control line behind a Japanese businessman, an Arab in robe and headdress, several men in loose pajama-type garments and a few veiled women. One of them, wrapped in a floral chador, kept retying the headscarf on her frisky daughter.

E tried to determine the nationality of a leathery-faced laborer who wore a Western suit jacket over some kind of skirt. Then struck by an awful thought, she clapped a hand over her mouth, letting go of the chador. "Kari, my passport!" she blurted in English. Seeing his horrified stare, she immediately re-covered her head, but for that brief moment, her golden hair seemed to magnetize the room.

Kari's eyes darted around to see who had heard her. He patted his pocket. "It's all right, darling, I have it," he whispered in French, with a warning glance. "I kept it after Gstaad—just in case."

She stared at him, astonished at the thoroughness of his escape plans, which must have included the Cartier rings.

"And your money, of course, is accessible—wherever you are."

E hadn't even thought of all that until now. Her clothes didn't matter, but at least she had resources. After she had asked Karim for help with a "unexpected inheritance," he'd suggested the Swiss bank account. Just where Alexis would have wanted it. She realized the immensity of the secret she could never share with her husband. Then wondered, *Did he have secrets from her?*

They finally reached the immigration official. Kari handed the man their papers, including the marriage certificate, which affirmed her conversion to Islam. E could see his distaste when handling her U.S. passport. He was staring at her strangely, in a way that made her uncomfortable. She pulled her chador more closely around her face.

"*Amrika?*" The sullen official asked Kari, while appearing fixated by her hands.

American? was what it sounded like. Kari replied evenly, but E heard his clipped tone of voice.

Upper lip curled in distate, the man tossed a kerosene-soaked rag on the table in front of E, indicating her fingernails. "*Haram.*"

"*Interdit,*" Kari whispered. Forbidden.

E didn't need a translation to feel the hostility. She took the rag from Kari. But how did she use it and still keep the chador on? Stunned by the turn of events, she gripped the veil in her teeth and scrubbed off her polish as the official watched, stroking his mustache.

"I am so sorry," Kari murmured. "Some people think nail varnish is a polluting thing." Believing that his position should speak for itself, he was offended—and embarrassed for E—but tried to remain calm. Soon they would be home.

Finished, E dropped the rag on the table. She wanted to give the man a dirty look, but felt intimidated. Even a little afraid. She heard him ask something about dollars.

Kari shook his head.

The official held up an imperious palm, then eyed her again. Taking her passport, he moved to a small cubicle and conferred with two colleagues, a uniformed man with stars on his shoulders, the other in a plain buttoned-up shirt, no tie. Then turning his back on the Mansours, the immigration man made a phone call. A long one.

Kari suspected he was checking with one of the *komitehs*, the revolutionary committees that still wielded such power, operating under a wing of the interior ministry. His old friend and brother-in-law, Hassan Ghotbi, worked at the ministry and would be shocked to hear of the reception accorded them. Then they would laugh about these petty bureaucrats—and Hassan might even want the the fellow's name. Kari drew himself up; he understood hierarchies. He knew where he stood in this society. And from there, he could look down on the little man.

While they waited, E glanced about the bustling terminal. All manner of posters were taped to walls and pillars, including a photograph of the late Ayatollah Khomeini with his hawk-like gaze and scholarly hands. She surveyed the crowds, searching for signs of nailpolish or lipstick. None. Poor Mr. Revlon. At the far end of the hall, she noticed a special area where people were kneeling in prayer. She caught Kari's eye and pointed.

He pushed her hand down. "Yes, naturally, every airport has a prayer area."

Aware they were both tired, she decided to keep her silence.

Then the official returned, addressing a space somewhere over Kari's shoulder. After examining their papers again, he began to stamp them with exaggerated precision, finally handing them over.

Kari made a short reply, then clamped his mouth shut.

As he steered her toward the exit, E saw a handwritten sign outside the Melli Bank: *Dear Guests. God is the Greatest. Welcome to the Islamic Republic of Iran.* She glanced back and saw the immigration man watching them.

They both sighed with relief when they got outside. The sky was cloudy and the air thick with dust and diesel fumes, but they were free of officialdom.

After a look around, Kari directed E to an empty orange taxi, a domestically manufactured Paykon. Kari and the paunchy driver shared a heated exchange, but finally reached an agreement. They had barely settled into the backseat when the driver honked his horn, grabbed his bejeweled gearshift knob and set out into the maze of traffic–oblivious to the sharp banging of his muffler against the concrete street.

"Normally these taxis are shared between many people, always stopping and starting. So for the privacy, this thief held me up for ransom. But after all, it is our honeymoon. And homecoming." He smiled.

They drove around the Shahyad Tower, rising high above its four arches, sparkling with turquoise mosaics. "The Shah's delusions of grandeur," he said.

Leaving the expressway, they passed a shiny Mercedes with new whitewalls, its bearded driver accompanied by two veiled women, five children, three hens and a silver samovar. "That looks suspiciously like two wives in the car," E joked.

"Of course."

She stared at her husband. Of course? Two wives? He didn't seem to think it funny–or unusual.

The orange Paykon continued amid congested city streets. The air was chalky pale from smog, desert dust and exhaust haze, which obscured even the huge mountain backdrop. Honking cars jockeyed for position, refusing to signal or obey traffic lights.

Then the beat-up Honda in front of them made an abrupt stop. Amid a squeal of brakes, E lurched forward and grabbed Kari's hand. The car's bearded driver got out, removed a bleating sheep from his trunk and handed it to an old man standing at the curb. The man began examining the animal's teeth, ears and hooves, then paid the driver, who returned to his Honda. Neither gave so much as a glance at a wall-poster of the Shah's head attached to a curving bikini-clad body. The bikini had been painted out in black. The only one who noticed was E.

The taxi driver shook his fist, then leaned on the horn and slammed down the accelerator. The engine almost flooded, but finally it caught and the taxi zoomed right through a red light. Still dragging its muffler behind.

E rolled her eyes. "Looks like green means go–and red? Go faster."

Kari made a wry smile. "They are on their good behavior today." He gazed out the window, taking in the changes along Revolution–formerly Shah Reza–Avenue. Then he pointed to their left. "That's where I studied before the Sorbonne. Tehran University."

After passing the block-long campus, the driver turned onto Takht-e Jamshid, an avenue of once-elegant shops–and the former U.S. Government compound, with its tall iron gates and brick walls. "This was the American Embassy."

"Where the hostages were held?"

"I'm afraid so. The source of all our problems. If not for that four-hundred-forty-four-day melodrama, there would be no U.S. embargoes. No U.S. embargoes to break."

"And we'd still be in Paris."

"You were but a girl then. Fifteen years ago." Kari sighed. "I was already in France. I often ask myself what I would have done had I been here."

"And?"

He lifted a shoulder. "I would have probably been in there–in the 'nest.'" He met her gaze and explained, "The nest of spies, the students called it."

E stared at a painting of the Statue of Liberty with a skull where her face should have been. "And now you're married to one. American, I mean. Joke."

Kari glanced at the driver, who was listening to what sounded like a sermon on the radio. "People change."

"That's for sure." E remembered TV images of blindfolded hostages, jeering Iranians, burning American flags. "It was terrible, though."

"Terrible," he agreed. "A tragic turn of events." He didn't think it necessary to translate the freshly painted graffiti, *Marg bar Amrika*. Death to America.

"But there is more that you should understand." Kari explained the element of national pride, erupting after years of Western domination. In the fifties, the CIA had rigged a coup to overthrow a popular prime minister who had nationalized Iran's oil industry. Could she blame them for finally saying enough?

Knowing a little something about CIA manipulation, E wouldn't at all put it past them to try manipulating an entire country for the "national interest." It was something to think about, though, being in enemy territory. Not that she saw Iranians as her enemy, but there were some here who might consider her *theirs*. The immigration official, for one.

E tossed her head. There were small-minded people everywhere. What mattered was, they had made it. Safe and sound. With that, she was seized with fatigue, and wanted only to let go. "How about if I take this thing off now, Kari? It's hot."

With another glance at the driver, he shook his head. "Only at home." Then he added gently, "And I hope you don't mind, my love, but I think it best if you call me Karim from now on."

"Why?"

"In this country my name is Karim."

She gave him a puzzled look, but he was already staring out his window. E turned to the other side and regarded her new home, teeming with veiled figures just like herself.

Skirting the old city, the driver turned left, heading north on Shemiran Avenue, up into the foothills of the Elburz range. Lining the lower end of the road was a section of garages, with mechanics working outdoors. Then they entered an area of new development—modern apartment buildings with shops at street level and satellite dishes on top. As the taxi continued uphill, they reached the older, wealthier neighborhoods, their rooftops dotted with more dishes. The road wound past large tree-filled compounds—some government, such as the radio broadcasting facility—

and others private villas, partly hidden behind small village-like shops providing food and services.

The sky became bluer, the street borders more green. Narrow, concrete-lined streams flowed along the base of tall poplars that sheltered courtyard walls. Karim told E that these joubs used to deliver mountain water to the city via underground canals, called *qanats*, which fed cisterns beneath the houses. Water was piped in these days, but nonetheless the *joubs* remained a prized tradition–a babbling creek on every street. The trees were also precious. In the old days, workmen would dust their leaves daily.

The Iranian love of gardens seemed a private affair, though. E noticed that there was no such thing as a front yard here. Other than the scattered shops, all properties were closed off, their facades blank except for faded revolutionary posters of soldiers with guns and roses.

She stared at a crumbled wall with a sprawling garden behind it. "I wonder why they tore down that wall."

He regarded her in amazement. "They didn't tear it down, Evelyn. It was bombed."

"A bomb? Here?"

"There was a war, if you recall." He gazed back at the overgrown courtyard. "Wonderful, is it not? In Iran we always have flowing water and gardens–never mind war, never mind revolution."

"Wonderful. I guess."

The taxi stopped in front of a high stone wall with trees peeking over the top. Karim opened the wooden door and they entered the gatehouse–on their right the former gatekeeper's room, on their left the old stable, now stacked with firewood. Soon after his father's death, his two younger brothers–Karim's uncles–had emigrated to California. Before it all fell apart–before the revolution–they had been a close-knit family.

The couple continued into a grassy courtyard, enclosed by the house's white stucco walls. At once, the air became cooler, sweeter. Water bubbled down four tiled channels radiating from a square marble pool. Each quadrangle was planted with fruit tree borders, budding roses and bright spring bulbs. Birds chattered.

"*A spot where roses bloom, and sparkling fountains murmur.*" Karim clasped her hand, leading her to the nearest waterway. A goldfish flashed through the stillness. He turned a knob and a fountain spurted up in the central pool.

It looked delicious. The two dusty travelers could no longer restrain themselves. E kicked off her shoes and and soon they were sitting beside the gurgling watercourse, bathing their feet, exhaustion sweeping over them.

After a moment, he took one of her feet in his hands. "In our tradition, I am supposed to remove your shoes and wash your feet after the wedding. Then I say: *O Allah, bless me with her affection, love and her acceptance of me; and make me pleased with her, and bring us together in the best form of union and in absolute harmony.*"

"When do I wash yours?"

"Now, it is for me to care for you."

Then it all started to sink in. All of it. They stared at each other, struck by the enormity of the events of these past twenty-four hours. It was not to be believed, yet this was real. E put her hand in the cool water, trying to come back to herself. She recognized nothing around her in this strange new world… its only constant, her husband, Kari–who was now to be called Karim.

Pushing the chador down onto her shoulders, he embraced her, then lifted her to her feet. "Welcome, Mrs. Mansour–to your new life, new home–and new bed."

Her doubts slipped away with the chador and her lips relaxed in a shy smile. E shivered at the romance of having such a man–a man she would follow to the ends of the earth.

Had followed.

Two elderly people burst from the house in surprised delight. Thin with a hawk-nose and white hair, the man was wearing floppy gardening clothes, his wife a long skirt and no chador. Emotion trembled from her; she appeared on the verge of laughter or tears.

After clasping them in his arms, Karim introduced Rostam and Fatima to his bride. The childless couple had been with the Mansours long before his birth. Since the death of his parents, they had tended the house awaiting his return. Other than his sister who lived across town, they were all that remained of his family.

Fatima eyed E with timid curiosity, while the men spoke. Then the old servant sprinkled them with rosewater in traditional welcome. Impulsively, E hugged her, and Fatima beamed, a silver tooth sparkling along with her eyes. "Welcome, *madame*."

That night they prepared a banquet for the newlyweds. A carpet was spread on the *talar*, the covered porch connecting house with courtyard. Candles flickered in wall niches. The newlyweds reclined against thick cushions, gazing out at the moonlit garden with its mysterious shadows and dazzling whiteness.

Now wearing a patterned household chador, Fatima served platters of salads, lamb kebabs, rice, warm flat bread, nuts and fruit. The feast was washed down by pomegranate juice—and *doogh*, a carbonated yogurt drink for digestion.

"Better than Paris," E said, devouring the food, her first since their croissant breakfast in Tunis… and before that Parisian croissants, yesterday morning. *Yesterday?*

Amid the fragrance of jasmine and orange blossoms, Kari showed her how to sip tea the Iranian way with a sugar cube tucked into her cheek.

"And much sweeter," she said.

"Much."

Paris, France

Nick was smoking. *Again.* His relationship with E was definitely not good for his health. He shook his head. There was no relationship. Evelyn Walker was his agent. Retired. Then reactivated. Until she flipped them all the bird and disappeared. With the Iranian arms dealer she was supposed to turn. Who turned her head, instead.

As a result, his boss was on his butt. Big time.

He stared down at the muddy-gray Seine from a window of the Company's Île St-Louis apartment. It was good for discreet business, and sometimes functioned as a safe house. Sometimes it was just a perk for the brass.

The phone rang several times before he heard it. He grabbed it. Still hoping.

"Have you found Evelyn?" Monique's voice was agitated.

"She's gone."

"Where?"

"Where do you think?" His retort was harsh, not really a question. By now, Nick was sure.

"*Iran?* With Kari?" Her voice was incredulous. "But her fur."

"Why don't you just keep it for her, Monique? If she doesn't return, I'm sure you'll find a use for it. Services rendered. Right up your alley."

"You sound angry, *mon vieux*. Or bitter. This girl means something to you, I think." After he did not reply, Monique sighed. "Whatever your feelings, I must tell you. That boy loves her." More silence. "And she loves him. Perhaps they will be happy."

"In Tehran? Get real, Monique. They eat Americans for dinner over there. And women? They lock 'em up and throw away the key."

Tehran, Iran

The defense ministry in downtown Tehran was located in an ornate prerevolutionary building. In stark contrast, the komiteh offices inside were austere revolutionary, its occupants militant... unyielding... unforgiving. Nothing escaped their view.

The members of the komiteh were all tieless and bearded or unshaven. Wearing facial hair was considered *sunnat*–a desirable, although not mandatory, act that followed the ways of the Prophet. In the Islamic Republic of Iran, it had become a fashion at once religious and political. Like the chador. The men sat around the table and listened to the shocking report that detailed Karim's recent activities. That he had activated his escape route and left Paris. That he had arrived in Tehran with his new wife. An American.

The scholarly leader fingered his amber prayer beads. "And what of the Paris Logistics Center? Our special program?"

Hassan, the sharp-eyed bureaucrat who delivered the report, shrugged. "It no longer functions." He returned the cleric's gaze. "Could it be a coincidence that the one who seduced him from his duties is an American?"

"Karim has done much for us over the years. Perhaps he knows nothing of her duplicity?" The mullah perceived Hassan to have special insight into the matters at hand.

Hassan's expression was one of dismay. His words seemed to slip out reluctantly. "Or perhaps not."

The mullah nodded slowly, but did not answer. No answer was required. Everyone present knew the three most important facts: This Evelyn Walker was a woman. She was an American. And therefore she was the enemy. Of course she was a spy.

Chapter 20

Behind the gate, it was paradise. But the outer world still existed, and there would be no escaping their new reality. The first week was busy as both sought to find their way in an unfamiliar environment, E at home and Karim at his government office. Then things began winding down with the approach of *Nau-Ruz*. The Iranian New Year, a traditional pre-Islamic rite of spring, was a time to be with family, buy new clothes—and clean house.

Fatima was occupied with scrubbing and dusting and let it be known, in her limited but firm English, that the young couple would be happier outdoors. Buoyed by the holiday mood, Karim looked forward to introducing Evelyn to his sister's family tomorrow—and today, her new neighborhood. E too bubbled with excitement at the prospect of a "date" with her husband, especially on such a fine afternoon. Before they left the courtyard, he checked that she was properly covered.

E had been practicing with the chador and moved with a little more ease. She wore cat's-eye sunglasses and red lipstick that gave her a lift, even if no one could see it. The rawness of her experience at the airport had faded. Nonetheless, she took pains to keep her mouth covered. Karim was wearing a white shirt buttoned at the neck, no tie—and his new mustache, which E found very attractive.

As they turned down the leafy suburban road, E had the funny feeling she was emerging from a hospital confinement. Everything was so new and bright, noises and smells assaulting her. Although fairly comfortable in her basic black, she couldn't deny the sense of being disconnected from her surroundings. Inside your home and garden, you didn't have the wear a chador—a good way, it occurred to her, to keep women off the streets. But then she brushed aside all negative thoughts, determined to enjoy the day.

Karim was eager to see old familiar sights, pointing out his primary school, the local mosque, his mother's favorites shops. The food stores were especially crowded as exuberant Tehranis prepared for the festivities. It was a happy time, hopeful.

However, E could also see further bomb damage. And even in this wealthy district, there were beggars. But there were also teenagers in Nikes and baseball caps. A girl in a U.S. Army jacket over her long-sleeved tunic. Another wearing Walkman earphones over her headscarf.

With a wistful expression, Karim regarded a group of kids hanging out in the park. Three boys on a bench flirting with a pair of chador-clad girls who sat sipping Cokes and giggling nearby. "They're so normal. It's almost like when I was young."

E turned and reached for his hand. Releasing the clasp, he indicated the old cinema house. It was deserted except for a one-armed man sweeping in front. Two women dressed in black housecoat-like garments and high heels paused in front of the theater's *Closed* notice, then moved on.

"What are they wearing?"

"*Manteaux.*"

"Isn't that French for coats?"

Karim nodded. "They were introduced after the Revolution as an alternative for women, supposedly more modern. But Fatima thinks the chador will provide you better protection."

As they continued along, the two woman joined a queue in front of a bakery. Drawn by the sweet, smoky fragrance, E peeked in. There were four bakers weighing, rolling, stretching and slapping their dough against the blackened oven walls. Customers grabbed the hot bread with a piece of veil to avoid being burnt.

E rejoined Karim. "Shall we buy some?"

"Fatima was already here. She usually comes early—to have fresh bread for breakfast."

Next door to the bakery was a pizzeria, the sign *Observe Islamic Dress* posted over the door. "Fatima puts in a long day for an old woman. Why don't we go out to dinner tonight? Give her a break."

He nodded slowly. "I have heard the international hotels are a good place to go."

"Are you saying you can't be seen with me in a local restaurant?"

"To be honest, I don't know. Everything is always shifting in our country."

"Politics?" Karim shrugged. "Who's up, who's down. One day President Rafsanjani is a hero, the next they try to assassinate him. Coca-Cola and Pepsi come in, then radicals protest them as 'un-Islamic.' But you saw the kids at the park–drinking Coke. Even Khomeini had to withdraw his ban on musical instruments and chess. How could one ban chess?" He smiled. "This is our life: A chess game. Every move must be thought out, and every move has consequences." His smile faded. "So we must be cautious for now. But never mind them. I have everything I need, don't you?"

With an intimate look, he moved closer. Lost in his eyes, E loosened her grip on the chador. She forgot all the rules and just felt happy.

Red lips. Radiant smile. Tenderly, Kari adjusted her veil.

Just then, a green Toyota Land Cruiser screeched to a halt. Three grim black crows leaped out–*zeynab* sisters on patrol. They descended on E, scolding, shaking their fingers, tugging at the hair that had escaped.

"Haram!" they shouted as they scrubbed her lips, yanked off her glasses and pulled the chador tightly around her face. E was too stunned to protest.

"What is the meaning of this?" Karim stared, incredulous.

One of the three, the youngest, tossed the sunglasses into the joub. Eyes flashing darkly, she watched the current carry them away. "She is no longer in the land of the Great Satan. Pay heed!"

The sisters hustled back into their vehicle and drove off in search of lace stockings and loose hair and handholding. Karim stared after them, more stunned by their parting comment than anything else. *The Great Satan?* How did they know his wife was American? He looked at E, speechless, as she stood there, ashen–hand to her pale lips.

She spoke first. "I don't understand. Who are they?"

"These women are a kind of morality police. They are poor people, uneducated. Angry." He shook his head. "This is what I was talking about. I should know these things, but I don't. It is too long since I've been home."

He told her about the *baseej*, walking wounded of the war. They were bearded young men in black shirts and plastic sandals–men who should have been working, but there were no jobs. Instead, they roamed the streets, on the alert for careless rich people who had forgotten the Islamic way.

E was indignant, in no mood for sociological explanations. And sweaty, even on this mild day. She felt confined by the chador, her world beyond the garden wall. Irritated by how it limited her freedom of movement, she tugged at the garment–all eight heavy yards. "And will I ever get used to this? I can hardly see–and it's hot as hell!"

Karim looked at her in astonishment. "How could you be hot? It is quite pleasant today."

"Yeah–for you."

Noting the curious glances coming their way, he pulled her off into an alley. "You must not speak to your husband this way, especially not in public–and especially not in English. This is most dangerous."

E stiffened, blinking in surprise at his tone of voice, his brusque manner.

Then his face softened, eyes shadowed with shame. "Forgive me, my love. I know our ways must seem unreasonable–even offensive. But we will adjust. We must."

E remained silent, her furrowed brow hidden beneath the chador.

"It is not easy, my darling, even for me. I can only imagine how difficult it must be for you. But our freedoms would be in greater jeopardy–even our lives–in the outside."

Troubled, they walked the rest of the way home in silence. Immediately upon reentering the garden, E flung off her chador. Free again, she ran her fingers through her damp hair and took a breath of precious air. "And what if I don't want to adjust?"

Karim regarded her in stunned silence. "There is no question. If you are not happy, we will leave–somehow." He took a tentative step closer. "My only desire is to make your life a paradise garden."

She sighed, feeling her anger melt. "Before you... there was no life."

He reached for her hand and they stepped over the discarded black chador. Leaving their shoes at the entrance, they made their way to the bed.

The perfect way to celebrate the Eve of New Year's Eve.

But there were those who chose to mark the occasion by other means.

Just before dusk–just as E was slipping into Karim's embrace–a car bomb exploded in central Tehran. The little Fiat, packed with fifty pounds of explosives, was parked in Ferdowsi Square amid happy crowds engaged in the last minute, pre-holiday bustle. The blast damaged nearby buses, cars and motorcycles. Windows shattered and filled the air with flying glass. Twenty died. Many more revelers were wounded.

As word spread, so too did the rumors—Iraqis, Afghan refugees, Iranian monarchists, Kurds, Bahais, Zionists. But the authorities had a different theory in their official report.

The blast was the work of American agents.

Chapter 21

Rostam told them of the bombing incident over breakfast the next morning. Karim translated the news to E. The juicy melon and fresh bread lost their appeal. Karim wondered who did it.

The old man leaned forward so they could hear his whisper. "They say it was agents of America."

Amrika.

This word E understood. The attack was upsetting enough, but now she felt quite shaken. She gave Karim a look.

He frowned. "Never mind. They always say that."

"Always say *what?*"

"These kinds of incidents. Bomb blasts. They always blame the Americans. We have many enemies. Even among our own people. So it's easier to blame the convenient scapegoat." Even as he uttered these soothing words, Karim felt a chill run through him. He picked up his tea glass to warm his hands. The tea was already cold.

By that evening, their festive mood had returned in anticipation of the New Year's celebration they would share with his sister, Nasreen, and her husband, Hassan Ghotbi, Karim's old schoolmate, an anti-Shah activist who had risen in the interior ministry.

Wearing green paisley chiffon, Nasreen greeted embraced E with a three-cheek kiss in the French manner. "Welcome, my sister." Then she turned to Hassan, a slim man with a neatly trimmed beard. "My husband and I are honored to invite you to our home."

"Nice to meet you." E extended her hand, but he only stared at it, unmoving.

Nasreen moved swiftly, clasping E's hand between hers. "Let me help you off with your wrap." An auburn beauty with skin the color of milky coffee, she added it to the rack of chadors, manteaux and scarves. "What a chic outfit," she said, taking in E's pale blue tunic and pants. "It must be from Paris."

E shook her head. "In fact, it's from right here. Tehran." For all that remained of her Paris wardrobe were her wool "getaway" clothes. Nothing to wear under a chador.

"You must tell me the name of the boutique."

She smiled. "We'll have to ask Fatima." The morning after their arrival, Karim had dispatched her to buy E some clothing. E wasn't mad for the polyester fabric, but otherwise felt quite presentable. "I *am* looking forward to going shopping, though. Maybe we could go together sometime?"

"It would be a great pleasure," Nasreen replied with a glance at her husband, who was speaking with Karim and their two children.

Karim said something to young Layla in Farsi, then opened his hands a few inches apart. Layla blushed.

He turned to Adil, punching with his fists. The tall, robust thirteen-year-old punched back.

"Candles are traditional tonight," Hassan remarked to E in English, his black eyes directed over her shoulder. "I hope you don't miss electricity."

"It's more cozy this way," E said. "Your home is lovely."

Nasreen beamed. "How did you two meet? Where do you come from, Evelyn? And what have you been doing, my dearest brother—so *important?*—to keep you away this long? I want to hear everything. You simply must stay the night."

After an annoyed look at his wife, Hassan turned to Karim. "I can understand why you might prefer to return home tonight. That fine house of yours up in the hills. How fortunate it has been waiting all these years. A pity it is so far from us in southern Tehran."

"We thank you both for your gracious invitation. But we are only just now getting settled. We look forward to another visit. Soon, I hope," Karim added fondly to his sister.

"Soon, for sure," Nasreen said, gaze lowered.

With that, she hustled them to the table, covered with embroidered linens, flowers and too many platters to count. E was proud of her newly developed skills in the Iranian manner of eating. The spoon was the main utensil, used to cut the meat or scoop the rice, with the fork held in the left hand, European style. The flat bread was used as a third "utensil." E raved about the meal and the bountiful presentation.

"We are sorry we have no Coca-Cola to offer you," Hassan said, still looking past her.

"Don't be silly." E noted the exchange of glances between Karim and Nasreen.

"And no Salman Rushdie, either," Hassan said with a thin smile.

"I've heard of him," E replied. "But I've never read his books. Have you?"

Hassan stiffened. "I have not seen them."

"But we love to read, Evelyn," Nasreen assured her. "Has Karim introduced you to any of our wonderful Persian poets?"

"Yes, he has. He has taught me so much about your great culture."

"Sometimes I think my brother should have become a teacher," Nasreen said.

"I've often had the same thought." Karim sighed, proud of his wife's grace and charm in this foreign culture, yet ashamed at all she did not know. For although Ayatollah Khomeini was dead, his *fatwa* against Rushdie lived on. "And now you shall learn more. You have no doubt admired this lovely table, but it is much more."

He proceeded to explain to E the significance of the items on display. The centerpiece was a mirror set with several items, including a Quran, two candles—for the number of children in the home—and a tray with the *haft sin*, seven symbolic foods whose names began with "S." Another tray held a small mirror with a colored egg.

"Later, we must watch this egg with great care." Nasreen nodded at her children.

E gave them an encouraging look. "Would you like to tell me about the egg?"

"I know they would like to," Nasreen replied apologetically. "They understand some English, but do not speak it so well. So I will explain this custom. According to our ancient myth, the Earth rests on one horn of a bull. At the beginning of each year, he shifts it to the other horn. And at that exact instant, the egg on the mirror will move."

"Perhaps it is the moment when the sun crosses the equator," Karim said. "When we were young—"

Nasreen burst in. "You would hold your eyes open so as not to blink."

"Please excuse the interruption, Karim," Hassan said. "Perhaps, Nasreen, you would like to let your older brother finish his words."

She bowed her head. "Oh, Karim, I am so sorry. Please forgive me."

"It's nothing," he said. "Nothing at all."

Mollified, Hassan nodded. "It is true. We love our old Persian myths and poetry, our great heritage. Our culture has influenced the world. We were writing epics while the Arabs were but camel herders. A small people, with small minds."

Feeling the subtle disdain with which Hassan treated his wife, E could only wonder at his behavior when there were no guests present. Nasreen reminded her somehow of a little bird whose wings had been broken.

"I thought you don't use the word 'Persian' any more," E asked Hassan.

"We are Iranians, " he replied. "But Persian–Farsi–has always been, and will always be our cherished language, ancient, unique. A language you must soon learn to appreciate, like sugar. This leads me to the important matter of *chai*. And dessert."

Any tension that existed was dissolved by the children's glee at the appearance of sherbet and baklava so sweet that E felt she could run a marathon. This the children understood and they all laughed.

Then Layla's face fell. She said something to her mother, who translated, "She asks how could you run in your chador?"

E stared helplessly at the child, unable to reply.

"Things are changing, my precious." Nasreen patted her daughter's hand. "They are talking of special 'women's hours' in the park. So who knows—maybe you can run someday. Or swim. Or even shoot."

Hassan raised an eyebrow. "In the meantime, there are many other activities, little one. Cooking, sewing. Your mother is very talented in this area."

Nasreen blushed. "Yes, sewing can be a very creative activity. In fact, Evelyn, I will show you some beautiful textiles I have made into pillows. At the same time we can continue our tea and chat."

She led E to a cozy divan where they could relax amid the bolsters while Layla and Adil settled on the carpet nearby, playing a little game with different sized balls.

E noticed a pout on the girl's face and asked Nasreen if it had anything to do with all the adult chitchat. "Oh, nothing like that. This is the night for *Santa Barbara* on Star-TV–and she is upset to miss it."

"What's *Santa Barbara?*"

Nasreen regarded her in astonishment. "You have been too long in Paris, my dear. This is a wonderful American serial. With the most beautiful clothing. What a beautiful life they have, the Americans—no matter *what* some people say. Even your own people say these things. I have seen Oprah," she added meaningfully.

Oprah? E turned to meet Layla's wide-eyed stare, hoping that soon they would become friends. "And Adil? Is he also a fan of *Santa Barbara?*"

Nasreen darted a glance at her husband, intent in his conversation. "Worse. He likes this... I don't know. How do you call it? 'Metal' music?" She frowned. "This is a bad thing for our youth. It leads them down the wrong path."

"I don't think you have to worry," E said. "Kids need to rebel a little. It's normal."

"For you, maybe. For us? It is too dangerous. Fortunately, my husband does not know these things." She shook her head. "My daughter is the age to wear full *hijab* now."

"You mean, chador? She's just a little girl!"

"You may not realize, but Layla is now ten—the legal age for marriage." As E gasped, a dark expression crossed Nasreen's face. "He would never do such a thing." She lowered her voice. "But he could. Sometimes he says I am too liberal a mother. I want my daughter to breathe free—my son, too—but then, he is a boy." She studied her tea glass. "Hassan only wants to protect us. He says we should also wear the *magneh*—you know, some kind of hood with a hole for the face."

E winced. "You mean, under the chador?"

Nasreen nodded. "Some ayatollahs say women should wear gloves, as well. So, you see, we are lucky." She put a delicate—unvarnished—finger to her lips. "Let this conversation be our little secret."

All over Tehran, people were celebrating. Yet Karim's servants passed a quiet evening at home. The old couple had been loyal to the family for years. They took their responsibility seriously and did not waver. There were things one had to do.

Rostam stood outside the bedroom door while Fatma slipped inside. Fatma had purchased—and laundered—the new wife's clothes, so naturally she had been there before. She knew nothing was in these drawers and told him that. Still, he ordered her to search, so she must look again.

Intrigue was every Iranian's middle name. It was in their DNA. It was normal. Male intrigue was of the highest order, though. Ignoring the whispers and secret smiles going on across the Ghotbi living room, the men were huddled in another corner, discussing their own secret dealings. Karim's precipitous move had compromised his position; even some longtime suppliers were no longer returning his calls or answering his letters and faxes. Yet the embargoes were still in place and the black market still thrived. Karim was determined to undercut the profiteers by providing fairly priced consumer and high-tech goods. But legitimate trading partners were in short supply.

Over chai, Karim told his old schoolmate that he had been contacted by Amir Hashemi, an expatriate Iranian who had brokered some small deals for him in the past and now promised new sources of trade. He frowned. "They say he is ex-SAVAK."

"Perhaps, but it is your duty to pursue every channel of supply. Besides, I know this man. He long ago redeemed himself by informing the Ayatollah of a plot against his life by treasonous air force officers."

"In which *he* himself had participated?"

Hassan gave him an amused look. "This only proves his cleverness."

Karim nodded dubiously.

"But naturally you will protect yourself. There are many factions here. Among them, those who would distrust one with an American wife. Especially in light of yesterday's bombing."

Surprise, then anger, then awareness filled Karim's mind. How naïve of him not to have understood the reason for the distance he'd encountered at work. The lowered voices as he passed. The quiet phone.

"Who do you think planted that bomb?"

"They say it was the Americans."

"I mean, really?"

"There are those trying to bring down our revolution. Conspiring against us." Hassan continued his warning. "In fact, I have heard murmurings of suspicion. You have spent many years in the West."

"But that's—!"

Hassan raised a hand. "Reality. And the reality, my dear brother-in-law, is that we must all tread softly. Your wife is very beautiful. Yet what do you know of her background? Truly? And how did she come to be living in Paris?"

Karim's eyes blazed. "I find this discussion offensive."

"But what a lucky coincidence the two of you found each other," Hassan replied.

"I prefer to call it fate. I am a blessed man."

"Indeed. I mean no offense, my old friend. However I do have my family to consider." Hassan nodded at the women. "Your wife should be happy here. Things have relaxed quite a bit, as you have no doubt gathered. And there is no more threat of jail if a woman laughs too loudly in public. Of course, this offends the traditionalists. Some forbid their women to join in prayers—at least without putting a stone or two in their mouths. You know, to distort the sound. But I find that a bit extreme. Don't you?"

Karim stared, horrified. Speechless.

"Better they not speak at all." Hassan smiled affably. "To be honest, I thought your wife was mocking me about the evil Rushdie book." His smile continued, but his eyes turned cold. "Until I realized such things require a certain mental ability, something few women possess. I decided to excuse her, knowing she will have time to learn."

Karim reined himself in. "A lifetime."

"You must explain to her this writer has insulted Islam, the Prophet and the Quran. Naturally, there was a fatwa against him. The people of Iran understand it is a matter of respect. And power."

"A death sentence—against a *writer*? Really, this is just too much."

Hassan regarded him with dismay. "How can you speak this way? Your wife may not know better but you do." He sipped his chai. "We must all be on guard against spiritual pollution. You have led a privileged life, Karim, but there are things you must know."

Hassan spoke for several minutes. Times were hard. Iran was a great power, but their enemies wanted to keep them down. Enemies both within and without. Satellite dishes were popping up on every rooftop, sowing confusion. People did not know what to believe anymore. "With such turmoil, it is no wonder the intelligence ministry has tightened its grip. They have many in their service." Hassan gave him a look.

Karim frowned.

Across the room, Nasreen shook her head with mock despair. "Those men. Always so serious."

E rolled her eyes, a mischievous look on her face. "Maybe it's better they don't hear our conversation." The two women had connected in an easy manner, their conversation ranging from chadors to where to find the best silk in town, the best dressmakers—even lingerie and other feminine necessities.

Nasreen laughed, then covered her mouth with her hand. In a whisper, she confided to E about a humiliating experience at the hands of the baseej—too unspeakable to reveal to anyone. Until now.

Two of them had stopped her and her son on the street, asking why they were walking together. One had accused her of being a prostitute and *Adil* her client! They released them only after she produced an identity card proving she was his mother. She had been too ashamed to tell even her husband, who probably would have scolded her—as if it were her fault. Adil had since refused to do his daily prayers. And she was also afraid to tell her husband that.

E told Nasreen about her own run-in with the zeynab sisters. How they had scrubbed off her lipstick and made her feel like dirt.

"Terrible they should treat you this way." The dam burst open and suddenly Nasreen was spilling out her life to E… how inspired they had all been during those early days, protesting the rottenness of the old regime. But after the Revolution, she had been forced to take the veil—and Hassan became more conservative. She was grateful to have been able to give him a fine son, so there was that security against divorce.

Then she shrugged. "But this is all political and Insh'Allah, it will pass." Nasreen poured some fresh tea and resettled herself in the cushions. "Now tell me about Paris." Her eyes gleamed. "You know, I have traveled with our father. Cairo and Beirut. Even to Paris! I miss this, the travel, the openness, the fun. Almost everything, really." The light in her eyes faded. "Not that I would wish to turn back the clock. The Shah's evil people murdered our father." She reached for E's hand. "Oh, you must please excuse me. I have no wish to spoil your evening. Now it is your turn to tell me about your life."

"Let's begin at the beginning: Fashion." E winked, telling Nasreen about Saint-Germain and the Marais. The best places for croissants and hot chocolate. The new film about Charlie Chaplin. Seeking to feed her hunger, E went on and on with tales of high and low society, a delicious blend of politics, artistic trends and gossip.

"This is one thing we know," Nasreen said. "Gossip and lady's talk. And for this activity I have a wonderful suggestion—a day out at the *salmani*."

They'd pamper themselves with haircuts, manicures, pedicures and facials. All female beauticians, of course. "So we can really let our hair down."

E was glad to see the sparkle return to Nasreen's eyes—and not just from the joke. "I'd love to, Nasreen. Anytime."

The family drank tea long into the night. After Leela spotted the egg roll across the mirror, they all rejoiced. Then the Mansours left, full of hopes for the New Year.

Chapter 22

It was a few days into Nau-Ruz, still early in the morning, still fresh and green. As Karim drove downtown to work, gazing at the familiar sights around him, he realized that for Evelyn none of this was familiar. He was reminded again of the great sacrifice she had made for him, tearing herself up by the roots, leaving it all behind.

He could do nothing comparable—only care for her. Protect her. Hassan would not be the only one who might distrust his American wife. Then, too, there was the matter of the comfortable life Karim had led in Paris, during a period of great suffering for the Iranian people. That was all cause for their resentment. Even suspicion.

Nonetheless, he did not underrate his value to the nation, his specialized skills, breadth of contacts and knowledge of the world. The outside world.

As he approached the sprawling ministry complex, his thoughts turned to the day ahead. When forced to flee Paris, he had been in the middle of a project to obtain American chemicals for the production of plastics and paints. Although the deal was jeopardized, he'd managed to get it back on track through some fancy footwork. The Dubai middleman, happy with his increased commission, had placed the order with a German company, which then specified delivery to Spain. In fact, the Norwegian ship would depart Houston, bypass Barcelona, and deliver the cargo in Bandar Khomeini. It was a good plan, but a waste of time and expense. All this for a fresh coat of paint on their homes and schools.

No wonder this place was so rundown, Karim thought again as he entered the once-grand defense ministry. His own office was a faded yellow, patchy, with some watermarks on the high ceiling. It was located at the end of a corridor in an out-of-the-way wing, with a small window that looked out on another wall. It had occurred to him that perhaps they thought he was contagious.

Nonetheless, he had the necessities—an assistant, telephone, fax machine and fan. He would rebuild his life.

At the behest of his government's Petrochemical Commercial Company—PCC—Karim had begun negotiating a joint venture with that same accommodating Norwegian shipper, which would provide parcel tankers fitted with separate tanks to export petrochemicals refined in Iran. The destination was East Asia. The end-product polyester fiber and film. Benign products—and benign activities that merely required a few people to turn the other way. Yet these benign activities provided bread on Iran's dinner table.

Washington, D.C.

Nick crumpled the paper and threw it in the trash. Then he got up and retrieved it. The report was *Eyes Only* and, therefore, food for the shredder. Although he didn't quite want to let it go—yet. Somehow this printout represented his only link with E and he needed to preserve the connection. He sat down at his desk again, smoothed out the paper and closed his eyes.

She was there. In Tehran. Married to a goddamn arms dealer.

There was a brief tap at his Georgetown office door. Jay Stiles grinned. "I'm sure she's okay. Just one more invisible female bundled up in a few hundred yards of fabric."

"What are you doing off the reservation?"

"Slumming." Jay's eyes went icy. "I want to remind you that you owe me on this." He indicated the paper on Nick's desk. "We're down to our last decent source there—"

"Since you burned his predecessor."

Jay didn't acknowledge the interruption or implied critique. "It was hell getting that report out. I would have preferred to save him for a true crisis."

"I've heard that song before," Nick said, not asking him to sit.

"Before I'm through, you'll be singing the tune in your sleep."

"We can't leave her there."

"She's happy. Isn't that what Monique told you? Never mind. I'm working on another angle. We have a man in Frankfurt, Amir Hashemi, an Iranian exile who smiles out of both sides of his mouth—if you know what I mean. He'll keep his eyes open for us."

"For *us*—or for E?"

"Let's look at the positive side. We have a new player in Iran. A great agent, if I can trust your evaluation of her other assignments."

"Don't you dare. Don't you fucking dare."

"I won't go near that one with a ten-foot pole." He winked. "Of course, your reports were based on her work, weren't they?"

Nick shot up from his chair, eyes blazing. They would not put her in jeopardy again. He wouldn't let them.

"Just a thought." Jay moved to leave, then turned back. "Not a bad one, though. Remember: we have a lot invested in your girl. On Wall Street, they look for a high 'return on assets.' No pun intended." He grinned. "It's all about the bottom line." His grin faded. "Ours is national security."

The door slammed. Nick felt like he was going to gag. He took a deep breath, then picked up the phone.

Tehran, Iran

E gradually made peace with the chador.

One afternoon, Karim entered the gatehouse to see a black veiled arm beckoning through the wooden door to his right. Following that arm, he entered the empty gatekeeper's room and saw a figure concealed behind filmy black chiffon. As he moved closer, she backed away. He stared as she slowly lowered her veil… to reveal sea-green eyes rimmed with black kohl.

He took a step. The eyes disappeared behind the fabric. He paused. Then the fabric shifted to reveal a mouth the color of wine. He wanted to drink from that mouth, but it disappeared into blackness. A sliver of creamy throat appeared, followed by a tantalizing glimpse of breast.

Hypnotized by the moment, he watched the veil open to reveal her naked body, inviting him. Blood pounding, he pressed her against the wall, kissing her eyes behind the silk, then parting it to find the mouth he sought. His hands caressed her as they slipped to the cool stone floor, lips never leaving lips, bodies flowing together.

Karim knew he was the fortunate of men. He had his precious wife, his home, his homeland. His faith. He had always prayed in France, five times a day as required, but felt isolated there. Here he was connected to something greater than himself; he was part of the community of believers.

One warm spring morning, Karim took a taxi to the Friday prayer service at Tehran University. Traffic was backed up, so he got out a few blocks away, joining the immense crowd swarming down Revolution Avenue. A crowd so dense, as they said in Persian, that a needle could not pass through. For a brief moment he felt hemmed in and wanted to flee, but was then swept up by the people's spirit and sense of unity.

He knew that Evelyn, though, might find this overwhelming. All these people, so close. And what would they think of her? Karim immediately suppressed that unsettling thought. Happy she was safe at home, he turned right on a wide side street, lined on both sides with plane trees and clean flowing joubs. One side of the pavement was for men, the other for women, each leading to separate gates.

When he found an opening beside the waterway, Karim put down his prayer rug and joined in the ritual wash. Once purified, he continued on until he reached the mosque area and took off his shoes, joining them with thousands of others. Then he entered the courtyard, surveying the neat lines of prayer rugs. He found a place and as the call to prayer began, unrolled his mat.

Shoulder to shoulder with his fellow worshippers, he listened to the sermon. According to the mullah, the Prophet Muhammad had predicted that the Iranians would be "pioneers of Islam at a time when the world had deviated from the faith."

As Karim looked around the sea of proud faces, he saw they understood the cleric's words. The quarrel went back centuries. The Sunni Arabs had betrayed Muhammad, whereas the minority Shia–the Iranian Shia–had bravely defended His honor, withstanding Arab attempts to suppress their identity and culture.

From Arab imperialism, the mullah moved on to that of the Great Satan who had conspired with Iraq–and the Zionists–to crush their revolution. But they would never be crushed. They would defeat all their enemies. "Remember! The path laid down by Imam Khomeini passes through a sea of blood in order to reach the coast of salvation. Islam is nourished with blood."

The emotions of the crowd soared wildly.

At the same time, Karim's mood of spiritual elevation began to wane. He was disturbed by the fierce anger surrounding him. Much of it emanated from the baseej—the Mobilization of the Meek—the revolution's hardcore young supporters. Very militant, a law almost unto themselves.

Troubled, Karim checked his watch. It was a little before two and the service would be soon over. He rolled up his mat and headed for an exit, where he was relieved to spot his brother-in-law. "What is this nonsense, Hassan? Don't you think the 'Great Satan' business is a bit tired by now?"

Hassan looked shocked—and nervous. His eyes darted about. "Do you realize who is speaking today? This is the successor to Khomeini. The head of our government. You must not talk this way. Certainly not here. These people will eat you up and spit you out."

"Is this the result of our revolution? To breed fear and suspicion, even among ourselves?"

Hassan stared. "Perhaps you have been too long in the West. You are out of touch with our realities. The world is against us. Only through our common strength can we survive."

"But the war is over. We lost. At least, we did not win. We have to get on with it. Be pragmatic."

Hassan shot him a warning look. "Some would construe your words as treason."

"Those people would be fools!" Karim lashed out. "No thinking person could doubt my loyalty and contribution to our struggle."

"Intelligence is not the highest criterion these days, but rather faith. And we must never question our leaders."

Karim replied with a calm smile. "My faith and intelligence are not in conflict."

Hassan nodded coolly. "I must return to my prayers, Karim. We should continue these discussions another time. We shall take tea together, soon." He walked away.

Karim watched him melt into the rapt crowd, unable to suppress a vague premonition.

Suddenly, he felt a sharp blow to his kidneys. Then a kick to the back of his knees. Karim stumbled and fell. As he was trying to get up, someone grabbed his hair and pushed his head into the ground. He must have blacked out, because by the time he rolled over to confront his attackers, there was no one there. No one, but several thousand worshippers kneeling toward Mecca.

Chapter 23

Karim did not dare tell his wife of the attack, which had left no physical marks. He needed to protect her from the fear such knowledge would inevitably create.

He had his own concerns. In the political minefield that was Tehran, he was attempting to make his way amid a myriad of intrigues, sharpened tongues like knives. As Hassan had warned, there were power struggles between every faction. Between clerics and secularists, traditionalists and modernists, free-marketers and black-marketers. And always the komitehs and the baseej, ever vigilant in the defense of Islam.

Were they so vigilant as to see *him* as a threat? To assault him? He thought back to the immigration official, the airport komiteh, their contempt. Shocking at the time, not so shocking now. He had enemies.

Although watchful at work, he picked up no hints that anyone was aware of the attack. In fact, most people seemed unaware of his very existence, especially given the remote location of his office. Unless they were avoiding him.

A few mornings after the prayer service, his small, droopy-eyed aide, Abdul Reza, entered with some papers and an apologetic shrug. "Pharmaceutical requisitions."

"So be it," Karim said with a sarcastic snap of his fingers over the unfilled requisitions stacked on his desk.

"You have done much good so far, sir," Abdul said, handing him the papers.

"Insh'Allah. But is it really God's will to threaten a writer with death?"

With a brief anxious look, Abdul closed the door. "If you permit me, sir. It is said that one must spend his words like gold."

"What we are spending is the lives of our children," Karim replied, heavy-hearted. "If our nation is to survive, we have no choice but to repeal the fatwa against Rushdie and negotiate an end to the trade sanctions."

Abdul rubbed his brushy moustache. "I know nothing of such things, sir."

"I fear I have made life difficult for you, Abdul."

"We all love our nation."

"Of course." Karim nodded his dismissal and picked up the new requisitions.

His thoughts kept returning to the Iranian go-between Amir Hashemi, who had offered the prospect of renewed trade with the United States. Hashemi held the key to the important first step of that trade–opening dialogue with the American companies he represented. Karim knew the man was no philanthropist, but that didn't matter.

What mattered, as Hashemi had insisted, was the good that could come from these contacts. Iran was a market of sixty-three million and there were many U.S. firms unwilling to concede the business to Europe and Japan. Even some in Washington supported a loosening of the export ban. Consumer goods, raw materials....

Technology was what Iran really needed. Karim now saw the opportunity to redeem himself with the leadership. He must pursue the opening to the West. After all, his brother-in-law had advised him to "pursue every channel of supply."

One night at dinner, he mentioned to E the possibility of traveling to Hamburg. There was a man he needed to meet, an Iranian consultant who offered the possibility of rapprochement with America. At least, trade contacts. And who knew where they might lead?

E almost choked on her rice. "Why can't he come here?"

"He used to work for SAVAK."

She swallowed, spoon in mid-air. "They killed your father! Why would you even talk to him?"

"My business requires me to talk to all sorts of disreputable people."

"If he wants your business, let him come to you," she repeated doggedly.

Karim shrugged. "The man has many enemies in Iran."

"I don't doubt that." She glared at her spoon, lowering it back to the table.

"It would be a short trip. A great deal of good might come out of it for our country."

"What about me?" E felt a creeping panic.

"You'll be at home. Safe," he tried to reassure her—and himself.

"And if something happened to you, and I was trapped here. Unable to help? Unable to do anything?"

"What could happen?"

She shook her head. "Well, for starters, you could be arrested! I'm sure the CIA has your name—our name—on every airport watch list in the West."

Karim regarded her calmly. "I have a 'French' passport, Evelyn—an excellent forgery, which I obtained some time ago." He didn't mention that he considered the greater risk to be upon his return home. In his mind, it would be a patriotic mission, but he knew others might view it differently. Or use it against him. His enemies among the baseej?

E stared at her husband, fighting back hysteria. "You can't go, Karim. Please." Then overcome, she burst into tears.

He leaned closer and kissed her tearful face. "You have nothing to worry about, my beloved. And nothing can ever happen to us."

Almost believing those reassuring words himself, he carried her into the bedroom and together they escaped their fears.

At least, until morning.

When the sun dawned, though, they were still in Iran. And E was still trapped behind "enemy lines." It was a terrible thought, which she had never voiced to Karim, but there was truth to it.

She had a sick feeling in the pit of her stomach. After he left for work, E realized he had not actually agreed *not* to go. How could he even consider leaving her alone?

Later, she got into words with Fatima, whose over-solicitous behavior made her feel like an intruder in her own house. E adored her husband, but in truth it was becoming difficult to fill her days. She read, practiced the piano and was learning about Persian cooking and rose gardens. Yet there was an aimlessness about it all. She missed her independent, productive life in Paris and could now see now why women had babies. Children gave you a purpose.

That was what she was lacking, a purpose. Until they decided to start a family, she yearned to explore her new world. She needed to fly from her cage, however gilded, and breathe different air from time to time. E did not wish to lose the use of her wings like poor Nasreen, who had faced her husband's disapproval after their trip to the hairdresser. She had been saddened–but not surprised–when her sister-in-law suggested they postpone their next visit.

As an independent woman, E was already chafing at the restrictions considered so normal in Iran. Somehow, she needed to find her own way in this culture, a path between respect for them–and herself. To do so, she'd have to make friends with her worst enemy, the chador. With its help, E would learn to navigate this divide.

For her plan to work, though, she had to repair relations with Fatima.

It was French onion soup that broke the ice. So delicious that Fatima asked for a recipe–a face-saving request for a truce. She invited E to visit the forgotten basement room with the narrow, blue-tiled pool, once fed by an underground qanat. It was a quiet space, with only dim light slipping through small latticework openings. In the old days, they would escape the summer heat there, then sleep on the roof at night. Those had been good times, Fatima told her, when the family was still together. In those long ago days, they would cool melons in the garden water channels and collect ice for sherbet in the mountains.

"You must know our customs to pass them to your children." Fatima looked at her pointedly. It was time the master had an heir.

"Soon."

The young woman and the old woman smiled at other, each pleased to be advancing her own agenda.

As the pile of unfilled requisitions grew, Karim continued to focus on the opening to the West. Out of respect for his wife–who, after all, had never asked for anything–he decided he would not travel to Hamburg. He telephoned Hashemi, who had been in contact with several U.S. companies, some of which expressed cautious interest in re-entering this lucrative market. "*If* they can see a green light from their government."

"That is a big 'if,' is it not?" Karim replied with caution.

Hashemi's voice had a smile in it. "Which is why you must hire me! Look at me as a sort of marriage broker–or at least, divorce counselor."

"Interesting analogy."

"More than interesting. I have reason to believe that certain of these companies are close to the current administration in Washington. They are pressing the issue of the growing trade imbalance. And the value of having an ally next door to Saddam Hussein."

Karim had never felt more hopeful. The trade contacts might lead to restored political relations. And if he were involved in legitimate dealings with the United States, he might be able to negotiate away his indictment. Then he and E could live their life as they wished–where they wished. Without fear.

He still did not trust Amir Hashemi, but his offer to act as a liaison between Iran and America was tempting beyond belief. There lay the crux of the problem: Could he believe it? And could he propose it–officially?

Choosing to ignore the recent unpleasantness between them, he called Hassan whose work at the interior ministry would give him a perspective on official views. Besides, they had a relationship that went back to childhood and was deepened by the closest of family ties. Surely that would sustain them.

They met at a quiet table in the rear courtyard of the Café Firuz surrounded by evergreens and honeysuckle vines. "Thank you for joining me, Hassan," Karim said as chai was served.

"My dear brother-in-law, you will please forgive my behavior at our last meeting," Hassan replied. "But you were out of line, especially at a prayer service. One thing you must understand is that for the mass of Iranians, life is not just eating, sleeping and indulging in luxury. To them, achieving a pure Islamic society is more important."

"As long as it's not a dictatorship of the righteous."

Hassan put down his tea glass. "These are difficult times. One must choose his words with care, certainly in public–and often in private as well."

Karim recalled a similar warning from Abdul. He sighed. "Sometimes I think we have traded one form of tyranny for another."

"I am honored you speak so freely before me, but I must urge you not to." Hassan directed a warning look his way.

"I have to speak to someone. I'm troubled. My colleagues are trying to isolate me. To be quite truthful, I don't care what they think of me or my work. What concerns me is my duty to my country. Our people. For our defense, I have obtained what is necessary. Technology, raw materials, whatever has been requested of me. I did so willingly, despite my distaste for the black market." He paused as the waiter brought a plate of sweets.

After the waiter left, Karim continued, "I now have the hope that my work may become legitimate. I may be able to supply all our needed resources. Openly. It is possible that Amir Hashemi holds the key. For he does seem to have someone's voice. Somewhere."

He explained his hopes for restored U.S.-Iranian commercial relations. Such a breakthrough would prove his point that communications with the West might benefit everyone. With a sign of official approval—and a minimal budget allocation—he would proceed with the Hashemi deal.

As Karim drew silent, Hassan rubbed his chin, tugging a strand of his beard. "I understand your position. I will think about it and see what I can uncover. In the meantime, we will let the Americans simmer."

Chapter 24

E understood that her new life would entail compromises, but what marriage didn't? Nonetheless, she was determined to make a space for herself here, however invisible. With the help of the chador, she would begin with the bazaar.

Her alliance with Fatima was bearing fruit. The old woman had begun teaching her to cook the treasured Persian classic, crusty rice. There were several steps, each very precise, including how to rinse and pick through the grains for any impurity. Once clean, two cups of rice would be put in a saucepan, salted and covered with one thumb-length of extra water, then brought to a boil and simmered for five minutes. After draining the rice, the liquid would be reserved and half a small tea glass of it used to soften a thread of saffron for five minutes. This saffron water would be added to a bowl of two cups yogurt and a little more salt with the rice then stirred in just enough to coat it.

At any point, Fatima might stop E for further critique before allowing her to continue. One afternoon there was no critique and E labored in silence under Fatima's proud eyes.

With growing confidence, E melted a chunk of butter in a deep skillet, then mounded the rice just-so, poked seven holes in it and covered the pan. She carefully rotated it over the burner for ten minutes, the key to even cooking. Then she reduced the heat to low, watching for the water to absorb and adding the reserved liquid little by little until done. With a nervous glance at Fatima, she inverted the rice onto a plate revealing the golden brown crust, fragrant and still sizzling.

"Quickly. Now you must serve," Fatima commanded. "Master waiting."

Karim practically fainted from joy when E appeared at the table, placing the platter before him and taking her seat. After his first taste, he proclaimed it perfect. "Do you know, some men pick their wife based on her skills with this dish?"

"It is pretty good, isn't it," E acknowledged with pride–and relief. "Fatima is a stern taskmaster and has had me sweating over the oven for days. She finally proclaimed it suitable for the master."

"I am honored, my wife."

E lowered her gaze, the way she had seen Nasreen look at her husband. "Next, Fatima wants to teach me to navigate the Tehran bazaar," she said, trying to keep the subterfuge out of her voice.

He put down his spoon and shook his head patiently. "Why go out into the heat and noise? Let Fatima take care of it. Whatever it is you want."

"But what I want is to get out. I like shopping. I want to buy some fabric. And learn how to bargain."

"You know, it is difficult to find a taxi–and then..." Karim frowned. "Well, you surely haven't forgotten our encounter with the baseej." He had a sudden terrifying image of his wife being set upon and beaten in some dark alley. Or worse.

E stared. "I can't just stay locked up in here, Karim."

Locked up? He looked at her, troubled. He did not wish to worry E with the shifting political sands on which he stood, but the last thing he needed was having to fear for her safety as she wandered around the city.

His brother-in-law had come back with encouraging words about Hashemi's proposal. Nonetheless, Karim's early euphoria had given way to a deepened sense of the risks involved. He was aware he had enemies who would mistrust his contacts with the West. Who did not want improved relations. If he were to land on the wrong side of some faction, it could be very dangerous–for them both. It would be better if his American wife remained out of sight, protected by the garden wall.

"Are you not happy, Evelyn?"

Seeing the complex wave of emotions pass over his face, E felt it best to drop the matter for now. "Of course I'm happy, my love."

"I can take you to the bazaar."

It wouldn't be the same as roaming freely, but she didn't want to hurt him by saying so. "When you have time."

E knew he was very busy these days. He had spoken of his hopes for a potential breakthrough in U.S.-Iranian relations, although she had her doubts about the Hamburg consultant. Ex-SAVAK? She sensed there was more going on that Karim wouldn't, or couldn't, talk about. But what did any of that have to do with a little trip to the bazaar? She would simply bide her time until the right moment. And then, after she returned home safe and sound, he could hardly object.

Early one warm morning, she was practicing the piano when Karim entered, ready to leave for work. Sensing his presence, she stopped. "I learned it as a little girl. It's sweet, isn't it? A simple piece."

"Simply beautiful."

"What? The Mozart?"

"You." He leaned over and kissed her earlobe.

E smiled, resuming her music. "Go now... before I show you my new plans for the gatehouse."

A few moments after he left, E stopped again. Hearing Fatima's familiar bustle, she turned. "Fatima. Come here, please."

"Yes, *madame.*"

"Today we go to the bazaar."

Fatima looked shocked. "But master say–"

"He'll never know."

"You go with Nasreen. She take you."

Nasreen was a kind, lovely woman, but E would not want to cause her further trouble. If she would even be *allowed* to accompany her. She knew Hassan did not approve of her. After much thought, she had decided that in the face of Karim's resistance, it would be best to go with Fatima. "No, Fatima. You must take me."

The servant's wrinkled face was a study of despair. Fatima saw no harm in accompanying her to town–as long as she was properly covered– yet hated to act without her master's permission. Then she shrugged. It was a matter between females, a secret knowledge about spices and various kinds of rice and dried fruit and who would put a finger on the scale to try to cheat you and who was honest. It was normal for Tehrani women to go to the bazaar. "Yes, okay, we go. Quickly."

Before leaving the house–before even entering the courtyard and putting on their shoes–Fatima insisted E cover herself thoroughly. "Hijab," she emphasized. "Complete."

E was wearing a long-sleeved, calf-length black tunic and pants. Now, she must add a headscarf. Fatima studied E sternly, then tucked in a stray curl. "Not one little hair." She continued her visual inspection, frowning at the wrinkles in E's thick dark socks that might allow a glimpse of leg if the chador happened to open. Fatima pulled up her socks, then handed E the chador, watching carefully as she wrapped it.

"What about a manteau?" E asked. "I see them everywhere."

Fatima shook her head no. "Those are Iranian ladies. You are foreigner. And no talking, no English speaking."

E backed off. "I know you're just trying to protect me, although in this disguise who could ever recognize me?"

Fatima stared. "Many. Too many." Then she sighed. "Insh'Allah, we will be home soon." Brow furrowed, she moved toward the garden gate.

The two women left their protected world and emerged into the real one, the one that was treacherous and required so many skills to navigate. At least, they found a taxi quickly.

From the quiet, green Shemiran foothills, it was a long, stifling drive downtown. The streets were jammed. Heavy clouds hung low in the gray sky and E could almost feel their weight, especially in her now-clammy chador. There was so much to see, though. She felt like a tourist again—but this time it was not an accident.

At last, the taxi pulled up at the main entrance to the Great Bazaar. Before getting out, Fatima rechecked E, then opened the door and stepped onto Buzarjomehri Avenue in the center of Old Tehran. E bounded out behind her, at least as much as one could bound in a chador.

A moment later, a thin, wispy-bearded youth in a black shirt emerged from a dingy white Paykon sedan. Dark eyes smoldering, he followed.

The two women moved down steep stone steps... entering an immense cavernous world. E felt enveloped in darkness. She squinted up at the tall vaulted roof and tiny windows, which allowed only feeble beams of light to reach the murky floor. Motes of dust floated through the humid air. Gradually, her eyes adjusted and she began to take it in. The narrow, arcaded lanes were overflowing with goods, overcharged with energy. It was a festive place, alive with flashy lights, bright colors and rich aromas.

"Everyting here. Ten kilometer," Fatima whispered. "Only necessary enough rials for paying." She glanced at the masses of gold and silver jewelry surrounding them. "Some do not have enough. Some must sell family treasure to eat. But some can always buy."

Then grabbing E's arm, Fatima elbowed her way into the bustling flow. They were immediately absorbed, identical to most of the other veiled bargain hunters—except to the intense, black-shirted baseeji trailing behind.

The old bazaar was a traditional place, but some women wore bright raincoats with leggings and high heels, while others had black cowl-like magnehs draped over head and shoulders—but no chador. E saw jean jackets—even a flash of jeans under a chador. The layered look was in—many layers—*too* many. It was definitely a man's world for no man would willingly subject himself to gadding about in the heat wrapped up like some kind of mummy.

Soon, however, E forgot her rebellious thoughts. All kinds of exotic music wafted from the shops—and the smells! Sights she'd never seen before. The lanes moved off at different angles, each devoted to a single category—pottery, copperware, spices, sweets, even soccer balls—each hazy with dust. Vendors kept pouring water in front of their stalls to damp it down, but the dust kept rising.

On the ladies' clothing street, E spotted a ruffled red negligee and giggled at Fatima through the tiny opening of her chador. She could see the scolding look in the old lady's eyes. Despite the heat and dribbles of sweat down her legs, E was enjoying her adventure, although glad Fatima was there to guide her through the crowded labyrinth.

And to demonstrate the art of bargaining. E couldn't understand the words, but the drama was quite evident as Fatima and a fabric dealer went at it over some dusty bolts of silk. E watched as the two pros haggled over the price, their attitudes and the inflection of their voices positively Shakespearean.

As they left—Fatima gloating with satisfaction—they walked past eager rug merchants, then onto the street of metalworkers. Fatima pointed out suitcases made from flattened tin cans still bearing their brand labels.

E was impressed with their practicality, the way nothing went to waste. She thought of America's throwaway society and admired the Iranian way of coping. Their cleverness.

Then she noticed a small boy emerging from a teashop carrying a round tray of tea-filled glasses. She was struck by an idea. A surprise for Karim. She would buy him a nice new—or rather, a nice *old*—tea service. She grabbed Fatima's arm. "Chai."

"Chai? Tirsty?" Fatima glanced in the teashop, where its male patrons were sipping, chatting and fiddling with prayer beads. She shook her head, her eyes telling E it was not possible to enter. *Only men.*

"No," E explained in an undertone. "Tea set. Silver." She pointed at Fatima's shiny front tooth.

Fatima smiled. "Ahh. Tea set for chai."

The old servant led her to the street of silver. As they were browsing through the stalls, E and Fatima were almost knocked over by a delivery boy on a motorbike, a Walkman plugged into his ears. He dropped a folder. Sheets of papers flew out. Without thinking, E gathered some up and handed them to him. Fatima grabbed her, then shook her fist at the boy, scolding him loudly. She hurried to readjust E's chador and headscarf, tucking in some bright golden curls.

A few shops down, the wispy-bearded baseeji pocketed his camera, then ran his finger across a dusty samovar.

As Fatima turned away from E, she noticed him. The young man seemed familiar. Suddenly she recalled she had seen him earlier that day. And more than once. Near the jewelry. Even the ladies' clothing. Her skin began to crawl. This had always been a city of suspicion. During the reign of the Shah, there were spies in every corner, behind every door. In some ways, nothing had changed. Still spies, still fear. Not that she would wish a return of the past after what they did to the old master! Yet the baseej were everywhere–and everywhere was danger. Especially for the foreign mistress.

Her heart grew still, but she was only a woman and all she could do was pray.

Chapter 25

It was the end of spring, the beginning of relentless days of dry, blistering heat and swirling dust storms. The monotone haze was broken only by magnificent orange and purple sunsets brought on by the devastating smog.

Barely aware of the fan's cooling breeze, Karim was going over the draft proposal for the joint venture between the Norwegian shipping company and Iran's Petrochemical Commercial Company. PCC would supply the cargo, the Norwegians the ships, and they would split the profits fifty-fifty. It was not a bad deal, but if his people were in a stronger position, they could simply hire the tankers.

Karim thought of his past dealings. And all the complex transshipments—Germany to Switzerland to Hong Kong to Iran. Or via Singapore, to be offloaded onto an Iranian ship, sailing under a false flag, its name blacked out until it reached international waters. Captains had to use code words when referring to embargoed ports. Instead of Iran being a proud name, it was one to be ashamed of, hidden. Blacked out. Iran was a pariah nation, the lowest of the low. And to be a patriot, one had to slink around the back alleys of the world. It was all false—the cargo documents, invoices and export licenses, the end-user certificates for "dual use" technology.

So many schemes. And scams.

And wasted resources. The price they had paid. The crippling cost. To the nation. To himself.

It was a dishonorable life that Karim led, yet he followed it out of honor. And in a perverse way, he recognized the scale of his achievements, the international network he had set up. A United Nations of sorts. United in the desire for oil and money.

After a brief knock, Abdul Reza entered. Although his eyes were still sorrowful, a corner of his mouth tilted up. "From Bombay–regarding the pharmaceutical order."

Karim put down his pen. "You have details?"

"The shipment arrived at the Shatif Trading Company in Dubai and is already reloaded on a Danish ship. It is due in Bander Abbas within the week. Insh'Allah."

"Insh'Allah," Karim agreed, grateful that there would be a renewed supply of antibiotics for children. Insulin for diabetics. Maybe even some aspirin. He could use it.

A serious boy, just old enough to be unshaven in the current style, entered the office. He stared at Karim, the merest hint of arrogance in his manner. "The ministry komiteh requests your attendance at the National Security Council this afternoon."

Karim raised an eyebrow, then rose, well aware that he must not refuse this "invitation." Noting Abdul's worried frown, he left.

The meeting was held in another wing of the ministry compound. Karim entered the stuffy office and stared at the men facing him across the long table–all bearded or stubbled–all in nondescript suits, long-sleeved shirts buttoned at the neck, no ties. All reflecting an austere purity that cast a cold shadow on their guest.

Karim could feel their distrust, his years of service seemingly forgotten. He was surprised to see his brother-in-law present. Hassan, seated to the right of Sayyed Ahmad Basti, was busy with some papers and did not meet his look.

Presiding from the center of the table, the scholarly Sayyed Basti peered at Karim through thin steel-rimmed glasses. Before him was a manila folder on which his amber *tassbeads* rested, the prayer beads that moved ceaselessly between his thin fingers. "It is kind of you to join us."

"It is my pleasure and my duty."

Leaning back in his chair, Sayyed Basti stroked his neat silver beard, his face a chiseled mask. "Your duty was to our Paris Logistics Center. Of course, we understand your situation. But your lack of discretion–"

"Excuse me." Karim forced back a frown. "Since when has my personal life–?"

"Since now. Since you left us with a big hole in our binary chemicals program."

"I had to leave. The Americans were after me. And the French." Then it hit him. "*What* binary chemicals?"

"How refreshing your innocence, Karim. Perhaps even the basis of your success. You arrange export licenses, barter deals, third-party trades—"

"But the chemicals were for the production of plastics. Paints—"

"—And don't even know. Or don't want to know."

"I do know, everything. In times of war? I will do whatever necessary. But now I wish only to concentrate on healing, rebuilding."

"Exactly. Building blocks. Think of it as a matter of one plus one equals a great deal more than two. A man of your special skills obtains one innocent chemical here—another there. We mix them together—and pouf... A weapon of great power and efficacy."

"You've lied to me." Karim stared. The betrayal was a bitter stake to his heart, but that pain was only the start. Chemical weapons? The implication slowly set in. He was horrified to have participated—however unknowingly—in such an evil enterprise. The CIA had been right!

"You should be proud, Karim, of your contribution to our national defense. We are surrounded by enemies and must remain strong. At such close range, the nuclear option is a bit risky, but these binary weapons provide a believable threat. Without them, we shall surely face Iraqi attack. Again. And they have all the poison gas and biotoxins they need—thanks to your friends, the Americans."

Karim shook his head, devastated. He was overcome by guilt at his responsibility in releasing such weapons on the world. He could see people writhing in agony as they died a horrible death. Iraqis perhaps, but human beings. Women, children. Even other so-called enemies. His nieces and nephews in California? *Evelyn.*

"Now. Now. You are a dedicated man. A creative man. This we know. How you forged ahead with your mission, despite the dangers. The risk of losing your self to the superficial and dazzling self of the West. It must be difficult to withstand its false lure."

"I know that world too well to be misled."

Sayyed Basti continued fingering the beads, an instinctual form of prayer. He smiled thinly. "Your strength of will is admirable. And brave of you to marry a woman of the nationality of our enemy. I trust she is well?"

The air hung heavy with heat and hostility–and menace. Shaken, Karim forced himself to remain calm. "Quite well. Insh'Allah."

"Insh'Allah. Some information has come to us." Sayyed Basti moved his prayer beads from atop the folder. "Information that may interest you." He opened the file, took out a photo and showed it to Karim. A photo of E passing some papers to a man in the bazaar.

Karim was shaken, all his vague premonitions of danger fulfilled. Evelyn in the bazaar? Passing papers? "There must be some mistake." He glanced at Hassan, desperate for help–some corroboration that this was not what it seemed.

Hassan remained silent, his face expressionless.

Sayyed Basti put the picture back in the folder, then shut it. "Your wife is a spy."

"I can assure you there is some innocent explanation for that photo."

"That is difficult to imagine–given her background."

Karim regarded him with scorn. "You are referring to my wife's past? We all know the CIA has tentacles everywhere. They did not leave her untouched. And she hates them. It was she who warned me. Saved me."

A burly man in his thirties, Ali Emadi, broke in. "She is tainted by this past, and would bring you down with her."

"She is now a quiet married lady."

"She is a whore!" cried Muhammad Khalili, a stark ascetic with blazing eyes.

Livid, Karim rushed toward him, only to be halted by Sayyed Basti. "Karim. Muhammad. You must stop this. We are brothers here. And as a brother I advise you, Karim: there are greater things, and there are lesser things. Think of your people. Then, think of your duty. And trust no one but Allah–*only* Allah. Not your American wife."

Karim stared, too angry for words. Stonily, they stared back. As Muhammad and Ali shared a dark look, Karim turned and walked out, hands clenched in rage.

Revolted by the accusations and threats, he strode down the long lime-green corridor. His mind reeling in an attempt to make sense of it, he hurried out to the dusty street. Karim heard his name, called faintly through the incessant din, then again. As he turned, he saw Hassan waiting at the entrance to a narrow alleyway.

Fighting to contain himself, Karim moved toward his brother-in-law, then finally exploded. "Have you no shame? My wife? A spy?"

"She will be detained." Hassan's face was closed. "Perhaps in the 'special section' at Evin."

Karim shook his head in horror. "The prison where my father perished? If it has truly come to this, then we are all lost."

"You may still be able to prove yourself."

He stiffened. "And thus they hope to force my cooperation?"

Hassan glanced around, his voice now barely audible. "Perhaps. Perhaps your precious chemical compounds are all that stand between your wife and her life—perhaps, even your own."

Incredulous, Karim searched Hassan's eyes and saw only a dark wall. He could not accept the blind stupidity of such thinking. That they would kill him? A man of his knowledge, his achievements? Then something struck him. "Where did you get that photo? And when?"

"This very day. We have the technology—thanks to you." Hassan gave him a hard smile. "Do you know what your wife does while you are gone?"

"Absurd. To attempt to smear us this way."

"A picture is worth a thousand words. I believe that is the saying."

"And my efforts to reopen trade with the United States?"

"It appears to be premature—and politically unsafe—for any of us to be seen dealing with the Great Satan."

"But Hashemi?"

"He can take care of himself." Hassan pinned Karim with a look.

At that moment, Karim knew: His old friend was no longer a friend. At least not his. Although maybe Hashemi's? "But you know the truth."

"What is the truth, and what does it matter? The reality is they see you as an agent of Washington," Hassan said. "Some have whispered that it was you—or those close to you—behind the New Year's bomb blast. There have been other attacks, too—ones not made known to the public. Perhaps you have heard of the attempt on our defense research center in Mashhad?"

"My years of loyalty? They count for nothing?"

"Of course they do. The men who beat you after the prayer service? They have been severely chastised. No one has laid a hand on your American wife. Thus far."

Karim's heart constricted, a chill seeping into his bones, freezing his speech.

"I say 'thus far' for a reason. You may still negotiate your survival. If you can see it in yourself to bend. If not..." Hassan shrugged. "I can only repeat the warning of Sayyed Basti: *Trust no one.* As your brother-in-law, I have warned you of these things. But you were too important, a French gentleman deigning to assist our Revolution. The fact is that no one is too important. Even one's own family. So now, for my security—and that of my wife—we can walk together no longer. If it is God's will, we will meet again." He did not wait for a reply, but turned and hurried away.

Karim watched him go, sickened with fear. Desperate over E's safety, he rushed to his car. It was late afternoon and traffic was heavy. He drove impatiently—aggressively—oblivious to the angered responses from other drivers. A unity existed between the bleakness of his spirit and the smoky haze enveloping the city.

What if she was not there? What if they had already arrested her? He could not bear the thought of what they would do to her—a suspected CIA agent—an American, a woman. He had to protect her. He would do anything.

Karim finally reached his home. Closing the gate behind him, he paused and wanted to weep from relief. E was sitting beside the water channel, chador at her feet, unaware of his arrival. Safe. He stared, at once realizing all that she meant to him—how empty his life would be without her—and knowing what he must do.

She turned and smiled, rising and speaking at the same time. She had done it. She had traveled through the city and returned home safely, a small but important victory. "Kari. You're early. Guess what? Fatima and I went to the bazaar and—"

"Did I not forbid you to go out alone?" Furious, he lashed out at her. "And did I not forbid you to call me Kari?"

Hurt, her smile faded, her open arms dropped. Her body tensed with rising anger. "My lord and master—*Karim*—is that who you think you are? Well, no. I am not your slave—nor your concubine—caged in your velvet harem."

Karim was dismayed. How could he speak to her that way? After just now realizing the unfathomed depth of his love. It was inexcusable. "Evelyn, my love. Forgive me—please. I was crazy from worry. You must listen." He reached out to touch her cheek.

E backed off, regarding him warily. He had no right to speak to her that way. She knew what it was. Being home had changed him. This damn backward, primitive country.

"Madness beyond belief! My precious one, my beloved. You are in grave danger. They think you are a spy—a CIA spy."

"That's a joke!"

His face was deathly pale. "No. It is no joke. They said you were passing papers in the bazaar." Searching her face. Ashamed, yet needing to know. For sure.

Her eyes widened. "Some kid nearly ran into us by accident. He dropped a bunch of papers and I helped him."

"Accident?" He sighed. "Of course, you would help him." Karim smiled sadly. "Would anyone doubt that?"

She stared at him, waiting for what was to come.

His expression turned grim. "That New Year's bomb blast downtown? And others. They think we were connected."

Her jaw dropped. She shook her head in disbelief.

He raised a palm. "It gets worse. Do you remember when your CIA accused me of chemical weapons work?"

"How could I forget? That's what got us here."

"I am almost ashamed to admit it. But I must. I was betrayed. My people were manipulating me. The CIA was right. I was doing that work, unknowingly. And now, they are trying to blackmail me to continue doing it–with your life. The threat is real. You must flee the country. I will find a way for you to go."

"I can't leave you. I won't." E planted her feet, mouth set. "Just forget it. We'll figure something out." An unformed, yet somehow potent feeling began to stir inside her.

He met her gaze. "And how can I bear to face even a single dawn without you? But we have no choice."

"Oh, yeah?" She drew a deep breath. Then let it out. The vague feeling began to take shape. "We can leave together. Why not?"

"Impossible. If it is not their will."

E was growing angry again, but not at him. "Well, it's my will." She would not be at *their* mercy again. No more a pawn in someone else's game. She was playing for herself now. For honor and self-respect. And love. "We won't bow to them." She was an American, after all. She didn't grow up being afraid. "Maybe I haven't learned much about being an obedient wife, Karim–"

"Kari... Please... And you are the wife of my life."

"But something I have learned. These bastards will squash you, if you let them." Her eyes flashed. "But you don't have to let them." Another thing she'd learned: If they deal you a bad hand of cards–you just deal 'em right back. In their face! She and Karim had resources; they were not powerless and they did not have to lie down and take it. They could shape their own fate. And to hell with all of them–American or Iranian.

Karim stared at his wife. Whatever she was thinking, his world was not her world and it could not be so simple. He knew he could not go with her, that he must remain–at least until she had reached safety. He knew also that because of her loyalty, her wonderful optimism, he must conceal his intentions. He would do whatever it took to ensure her freedom. No matter what happened to him. He nodded, saddened at the secrets that must now lie between them.

Flooded with hope–and courage–she smiled, knowing there was a way. "Now tell me again about Ramazan."

"It is the ninth month of our calendar, the holiest month. People fast all day and celebrate all night."

Her eyes gleamed. "It begins when?"

"With this week's new moon."

She looked at her chador lying on the ground, then back at him. "We don't have much time."

Chapter 26

"Are you sure you won't be in any danger?" Wrapped in a gray chador, E followed Karim out the gate into the warm, starless night. There were sounds in the distance, but here it was quiet. Only a shadowy cat stalking some prey.

"No danger at all. I will join you as soon as I get word that you are safe." He glanced around the dim street, then back into her eyes. "I know this country, I know its ways. And I know the way out," he said with calm certainty. "We will be together again soon and plant the seeds of a new life. Come now. It is time." He attempted a smile. "Besides, I have been fasting all day and am famished!"

There was no turning back. E gave a final look toward the house that had become her home. She reached out her palm and touched the gate. Then once again set forth into the future.

Under the new moon. A time of darkness and a time of beginnings.

The previous evening had marked the start of the holy month of Ramazan, known elsewhere as Ramadan. The period in which the Quran was "sent down" to the Prophet Muhammad, it is a time of worship and purification, a time to abstain from food, drink and sexual relations from dawn to sunset. As tradition dictated, the Ramazan fast had begun that morning at dawn when religious officials were first able to distinguish a black thread from a white one held at arm's length.

Now following a glorious sunset, people were gathering to break the fast and celebrate. There was a carnival atmosphere in the park as Karim and E arrived, strings of colored lights, lanterns and bright paper flags.

Food vendors lined the lanes, their carts and wheelbarrows piled with fresh bread, melons, apricots, pistachios and dates.

"The first day's hunger is always the worst," Karim told her after breaking his fast with some bread and dates, which she declined. "Everyone is happy now."

Almost everyone. E could not bear to eat and both she and Karim were tense as they moved through the crowds, their eyes alert, his smile brittle.

Under her veil, at least, she didn't have to pretend to smile. But she had had to pretend to believe him when he insisted there was no risk at his end. As he had pointed out time and again, they were a team, each playing a part for the benefit of the other. She would make him proud of her. She would be strong. And not cry.

There were two others not busy eating. Two slim, dark youth in black shirts… who trailed the Mansour couple, matching their pace, keeping a short distance behind. One was the wispy-bearded baseeji who had followed E in the bazaar, his gaze unwavering. Having taken no food since before dawn, he was light-headed, yet clear in his focus and purpose. It was a wondrous thing to be so high-minded and pure.

His companion, however, was less elevated. He felt the hunger pangs, smelled the bread and saw the people eating. This made him even more ill-tempered, more indignant against the enemies of the people.

As they reached an arched passageway off the main square, E followed Karim inside, then the couple reappeared and continued down the street.

The two young militants stared into the shadowy arcade but saw no suspicious activity, nothing to divert their attention from the traitorous pair.

The Mansours continued to mingle with the festive crowds, shopping, chatting, buying food—even eating. The general good spirits were contagious and Karim's mood seemed to pick up.

The two black-shirted baseej had no time for levity. They were pursuing a mission even more important than breaking the Ramazan fast. The youths were soon joined by two older men—burly Ali and grim Muhammad—the hostile komiteh members who had faced Karim at the National Security Council. Armed with 9-mm German automatics, they had finished breaking their fast, and were galvanized—ready and eager to arrest Mansour's American wife. The CIA spy.

The four men moved in. In a gesture of stunning disrespect, Ali grabbed her shoulder and tossed aside her veil. They reacted in shock at the sight of an old woman.

Screwing her eyes shut, Fatima grasped the fabric and re-covered herself quickly. But not before all could see her terror.

Karim was indignant. "What is the meaning of this!"

Ali glared at Karim. "Where is your wife?"

Karim squared his shoulders. "You put your hand on a woman of my household? How dare you insult me this way?"

"Begging your pardon–*Mister* Mansour–but I must repeat: Where is your wife?"

Karim held his ground. "And I repeat. Your behavior is intolerable! However, if you must know, my poor wife is home ill."

Muhammad regarded him through narrowed eyes. "A pity. We should like to express our condolences." As he indicated their minivan, he allowed Karim a glimpse of his weapon. "And you will kindly accompany us–to show us the way."

E would never forget that last look before he left her in the dim passageway. A look of infinite love, infinite commitment. As she had emerged onto the street–now in a black chador–E saw the two baseej following Karim and Fatima. Of course, they didn't notice her–just another shrouded woman. For once, it was a good thing to be invisible in this society. Shuddering, she turned the other direction and hurried inside a tan Toyota, which then sped away. Huddled in its back seat, E prayed to the only God she knew, a generous, compassionate, *loving* God who saw all and understood all.

Rostam, Karim's trusted servant, gripped the wheel. Periodically checking his wristwatch, he tried to make haste across town. But everywhere the streets were thick with crowds and cars, everyone carefree but him. The old man was named after the great Iranian epic hero, a lion of a man, a champion of good. Now he must prove worthy of his namesake, for he was charged with a dangerous task–to save his master's beloved wife. He had doubted the young American in the beginning, but first his wife's heart had softened toward her. And then his own. The world was a tragic place, though, so much could go wrong.

E was heartsick. Wrenched from her husband, alone again. In devising the plan, her anger had met his realism. There would be an escape–but not together. Not two veiled women—but one. Only her. Swaddled in the heavy folds of her chador, her eyes barely visible, she watched the long, tree-lined avenue fall away. As they approached Mehrabad Airport, her earlier confidence was tempered by the knowledge of their razor-thin margin for error. The timing must be perfect—or all would be lost.

Just outside the main entrance, Rostam checked his watch again: Late. He switched off his lights and turned right, squinting at the way ahead. It was very dark, with but few stars. Insh'Allah, they would not be seen. He raced along the empty access road, stopping in the shadows of a small poplar grove at the far reaches of the airport.

Rostam got out and rushed across the dry, hard-packed soil to the wire security fence surrounding the dim airfield. Through the blackness, he saw moving lights: a jet turning from its parking pad onto the taxiway—heading directly toward them.

As he pulled out his wire cutters, E flung open her door. He shook his head. "You must please wait here—inside—in hiding."

E longed to lose herself in action, to escape the fears tormenting her. But she knew Rostam was right. So she huddled in the back seat, watching him slash at the fence with wire cutters—oblivious to everything but the increasingly loud roar of the plane.

The komiteh minivan pulled up outside the gate. Ali brushed his bulk past Karim and with the others at his heels hurried through the courtyard.

"Welcome to my home," Karim said.

Ali was already at the entrance. Sickened that such ill-bred men held such power, Karim watched him remove his shoes, knowing it was merely habit, not courtesy. His spirit was heavy.

"We are most anxious to meet your famous American wife," Muhammad sneered.

Karim followed them inside the Western-style sitting room. He didn't care to invite them into the traditional reception room with its pillows and bolsters, where he knew they would be more at ease. It was an awkward moment as everyone stood there. The two baseej looked at all the furniture—the armchairs and carved tables, the big ebony piano. Their eyes widened, then narrowed at the display of wealth.

Wrapped in her chador, Fatima slipped into a corner ready to be of service. During such dangerous times, not only women needed protection. She began to pray for them all.

Karim continued to stall. "My guests? Will you take tea?"

"Regretfully we must refuse–time is short." Muhammad stared at Karim. "Now where is your wife?"

"She is bedridden."

"Then you will please take us to her."

This was the highest of insults. Male outsiders were never allowed in the women's quarters. "You know that is not permitted. Besides," Karim looked down, "it is her time of the month, and she has asked to see no one."

The men exchanged angry, embarrassed glances. "We would see her now," Ali demanded.

"I will try to persuade her." Karim swallowed his anger and appeared conciliatory. "Please. You must take some tea, and I will bring her to you."

Muhammad regarded Karim evenly. "There is no need to trouble yourself on our account."

"It is not for you, but the honor of my household. Please sit. Fatima will bring tea and I will return with my wife." He nodded to the old woman. Their eyes shared a moment, then he turned away.

As Fatima scuffed off in her house slippers, the men moved to the sitting area, trapped by ingrained patterns of polite behavior. They took their seats, shifting uncomfortably on the hard chairs. Karim left the room under their baleful gaze.

Almost. Rostam dropped the wire cutters and with a grunt, began ripping at the fence. Beyond thought, beyond pain. He may have been old, but he was strong. He struggled with the stubborn metal until the hole was just big enough. Hands bloody, he dashed to the car, grabbed E's wrist and pulled her back with him. They stared at the approaching jet then exchanged frantic looks. Only minutes remained.

Hampered by her chador, E fought her way through the jagged opening, finally making it to the other side. But with her first step she stumbled as something tugged against her. She turned and saw the fabric caught on a razor-like shard of metal. At that moment, she hated the veil with every drop of passion inside her. The more she pulled, the more the fence pulled back. Her mind almost dissolved in panic. *Leave the damn chador behind. Run!* Yet her rational side warned how exposed she'd be–a blond figure in the middle of the runway. *Don't risk it. Don't give up. Keep fighting!* She took a calming breath, then began working her fingers into jagged wire.

Bloody fingers and jagged metal and black polyester-silk.

Rostam knelt on the other side of the fence, struggling with all his might to free his master's wife. This young woman who did not deserve to die in a foreign land. Alone.

She heard the growing roar and glanced over her shoulder. The plane was thundering down the taxiway at its furthest point from the tower—and nearest to her. About one hundred feet. She should be climbing aboard now, instead of trapped at the fence.

Thirty meters. But not getting any closer. Squinting at the figure in black, the pilot began the turn toward the takeoff runway. Captain Hoffer frowned. There was some problem; something was holding her back. If she did not make it, he doubted she'd have another chance. How much more could he stall, though, without causing trouble for him and his crew?

Nearing retirement, Franz Hoffer had been flying in and out of Tehran for many years. He and Karim Mansour were good friends, but it was the offer of additional incentives that cinched the deal. The pilot had big plans for his retirement villa in Marbella. If Lufthansa squawked, this would be his final flight. He'd leave happy, along with his flight crew.

One last tug. And then she was free. Weightless, it seemed, racing from the fence.

Rising to his feet, Rostam watched her disappear into the night. He reached a wounded hand in his pocket and pulled out his old wooden tassbeads. He knew Ramazan was a period for doing virtuous deeds. He had been called. As had his wife. Now, it was in the hands of Allah.

Captain Hoffer saw her dashing for the plane. He looked at flight attendant Jan Linz and nodded. The round-faced young woman hurried from the cockpit.

Air traffic controller Sadegh Bazargan stared through the tower's large window into the still night—made even darker by the thick cloud cover muffling the starlight. A glance at the clock had told him it was past the 12:25 a.m. departure. Pulling at his beard, he spoke to the Lufthansa pilot. "Lufthansa Flight 601—already you have been granted clearance for takeoff. What is reason for delay?"

Hoffer grabbed some air. Copilot Gunther Kohl bit his last nail to the quick. "Tehran—Lufthansa 601 heavy. Red light on rear exit—we're checking. Request two-minute delay."

Karim knew every corner of this house, even in the dark. He made his way along the hall, then downstairs to the basement where he grabbed his French passport. Slipping his feet into an old pair of shoes, he entered the room with the long-forgotten pool. A narrow stairway took him underground to the tunnel that once supplied the household water. The opening was small and he had to crouch to enter. The ceiling that had been tall when he was a child now pressed down upon him. Hunched over, he stumbled through the dank darkness, desperate to get to the other end—the hidden opening in the alley.

The same tree-lined alley where he used to hide and play. So long ago. Karim looked in both directions. No one. He entered the old Paykon and sped off, turning left at the end of the roadway. The street was empty. For the first time, he allowed himself the hope of success. He prayed that Allah the Merciful would grant him the privilege of rejoining his wife and growing old with her.

Clutching her hem, E dashed across the tarmac, fixated on the silver plane. She heard the increasing power of the engines and raced faster. Her breath and the jet roar became one. Then the rear stairs began lowering—a vision that expanded and filled her universe. The veil fell to her shoulders as the wind tossed the hair around her face.

Duty controller Bazargan glanced at the clock, then the radar screen. Fortunately, there were no other aircraft in the system—only this one on the ground. He was alone in the tower, traffic light this Ramazan evening. As he turned his head back toward the window, he blinked, sensing rather than seeing a sudden movement. A flash of gold?

Lifting the binoculars around his neck, he focused and scanned the field... the hangars, the aprons, the parked planes and the Hajj terminal. Other than the flapping windsock, he saw nothing but his suspicions and let the glasses drop.

Frowning, Bazargan twisted the hair of his beard, pondering the situation. The Mehrabad komiteh still watched him due to his past association with the Shah's airport administration. He could not risk an error. He shook his head. It was only an instinct, but Insh'Allah, his instincts had never led him astray. Something was very wrong. He clicked the microphone button. "Lufthansa 601—takeoff clearance now cancelled."

Hoffer saw that E had almost made it, her arms outstretched to catch hold of the stairs. Just seconds away. He spoke into his headset, clicking

his transmit button on and off to simulate bad transmission. "Tehran–
Lufthansa 601. Transmission garbled. Unable to receive you clearly. Please
change frequency. Repeat..."

As E grabbed onto the stairs, she felt them retracting. The plane was
accelerating. *Please, God.* Then her foot found the lower step–and up she
went. Flight attendant Jan Linz reached down, gripped E's arm and yanked
her aboard. The stairs folded shut, sealing the cabin. The jet thundered
down the runway and lifted off.

E clutched her throat, gulping in air. She ripped off her torn chador,
still gasping, then collapsed against the cabin door. As she sank to the
floor, she burst into great sobs of relief and despair.

Oblivious to E's bloodstained hands, Jan hugged the girl and tried to
soothe her, shouting above the roar. "I've heard of those brutal husbands,
dear. But you're safe now. It's all over."

Karim had one thought–to disappear into the vast city, where a guide
awaited him. A guide who knew every mountain pass. Just as he reached
the end of the street, two vehicles whipped around the corner in front
of him, blinding him with their headlights–forcing him to stop. A third
vehicle blocked him from behind.

A disembodied voice came from the first car, a Renault. "Get out.
Your hands up. *Please.*"

Karim recognized that voice. He felt an awful sadness mixed with a
sense of absolute finality. But also, a bitter triumph: The plane would have
left by now. She was free. Calmly, arms raised above his head, he stepped
into the harsh glare. Waiting.

Hassan emerged from the Renault, automatic pistol in hand. The same
Hassan–his own brother-in-law–who had warned him to trust no one. The
two old friends locked eyes, understanding what was to be.

"And what of my sister, your wife?"

"She will mourn you for seven days–until the Shabba Haft rituals. These,
I will naturally permit her. Perhaps even the fortieth-day observances–to
be held in your former home, which as next-of-kin my wife and I will
inherit. A fitting dwelling for the new Deputy Minister of the Interior,
don't you think? And if Nasreen is not properly grateful, I will take a
second wife. Or divorce her."

Karim lowered his arms... staring into his old friend's gun. He stood
still and tall–beyond fear–his heart untouchable. He filled his lungs with

the breath of life, then let it out. Nasreen was beyond his protection now. But Evelyn was safe. His wife.

"*She* will be dealt with later." Then Hassan lifted his weapon and shot the fugitive. "It is the will of God."

The will of God. As Karim fell on the dark street, he raised his eyes to the streetlight and in its glow saw the face of his beloved. She was smiling at him. He cried out for her once, then died.

Chapter 27

Frankfurt, Germany

E dragged herself into the arrival area of the Frankfurt airport. It was shortly after five-thirty in the morning local time. At the sound of her name, she raised her downcast eyes. There, a vision in red, stood Monique.

She embraced E, kissing her on both cheeks. "*Ma chère*, Evelyn. How happy I am to see you."

E pulled back sharply, as if bitten by a snake. The Frenchwoman's stream of brittle chatter barely registered.

"...Lovely as usual. Must be exhausted–"

"How dare you?" E's brain was racing to catch up. This was the friend who had betrayed her so. "What's your angle this time?" She glared as Monique fell silent. "How can you face me?" The horror intensified. "No. How can you face yourself?"

Monique smiled and opened her palms. "I can hardly blame you for these unpleasant feelings. One must be realistic, though. *N'est-ce pas?* Of course I adore Kari. Such a charming man, and so handsome, is he not? But I am sorry to say, he is also a criminal." She took E's arm and began to move her along.

E did not resist, too numb to care.

"Although I am here at his behest, you know. It was Kari who contacted me. He who requested my help. So I have come. To help." She checked her watch. "You are booked on a connecting flight to London leaving in twenty minutes." Then Monique paused, her glib smile fading. "I am loyal to my friends, *ma chère*. This is my small way of making amends."

"A reborn Mother Teresa?" E shook off her arm. "Give me a break."

Monique shrugged. "Of course, you must thank also your friends in Washington, who provided additional assistance–especially to the pilot, I understand." She stared down at her manicured red nails. "Evelyn, I wish to explain. I was given no choice. I too have been under their control." Her pace slowed, her eyes distant. "Many years ago–"

"Spare me–please."

"I will not. Listen first. Then judge me." It was a time Monique would never forget. Her fledging travel agency was dying. She was desperate for backers. Then they came along. The Americans didn't ask anything at the time, and very little over the years, so it was easy to forget their "relationship." When they came calling, though, there was no choice–she was obliged to comply.

E cut her off. "It was a filthy thing to use me like that. It doesn't matter what Karim did. I love him. He is the only one who cares for me, more than himself. He arranged my escape, despite his own jeopardy." Her eyes turned hard. "I've read Dante, Monique. There's a place of honor for you all in the ninth Circle of Hell."

"It is normal you feel this way." Monique resumed her brisk, efficient stride. "But one of 'us' does not deserve your bitterness. Your old friend, Nick Daley."

"Who?"

"*Pardon.* I mean–Nick Ross. Since you left, Nick has remained in contact with me. About you. Always wanting news of you. Always hoping…." She gave E a quick sideways glance. "He is a sincere man, perhaps too honest for his own good. In fact, he almost resigned over you, Evelyn. He said he had promised to leave you alone. His boss, the old *salaud*, told him a pro never promises–unless his fingers are crossed. That's when Nick said thank God he wasn't a pro. That he had finally gotten uncrossed and intended to stay that way." Monique paused again and reached for E's hand. "I do care for you, Evelyn. Despite what you may think. It is all a great pity. But… *c'est la vie.*"

E pushed her aside, not even listening. Yes, she had questions–Nick *Daley?*–but her mind was elsewhere, along with her heart and soul, back in Tehran.

They had reached the Lufthansa boarding area. Monique handed E her ticket and boarding pass. E left without a word, without even a farewell glance.

Lost in melancholy, she was barely aware the plane had taken off. Still staring out the window… at nothing… seeing only condensation, translucent over early morning mist. Some of the anger had dissipated by now. What was left was an awful sadness. And profound loneliness.

Karim. Her husband. She wondered if she would ever see him again—and feared the answer. Her world had closed in on itself, losing its light. Silent as the grave.

The man in the white shirt next to her looked around the plane. Everyone, including the cabin crew, was still buckled up from the takeoff. Quickly, he leaned closer, immobilizing her with his powerful body. His left elbow pressed her shoulder hard against the seat. His left hand covered her mouth.

"Death to the Great Satan! Death to American spies! Long live our great Islamic Republic." His voice rose with passion. "*Allah-u-Akbar.* God is great."

The fierce words poured down on E, smashing their way into her consciousness. She looked at the man, then at the shiny metal above her heart—ready to plunge—then back up into his eyes. She saw only dark hatred—and that darkness became her reality.

Suddenly a tall figure appeared—a sandy-haired man wearing cowboy boots. Nick glanced at E's terrified face, then grabbed her attacker, wrestling him to the aisle floor.

Again, the man shouted, *"Allah-u-Akbar!"*

A shiver of panic ran through the plane. Then screams. The cries quickly subsided as the passengers shrank into petrified silence.

E was staggered. *Nick?* Not again? And why? The grim look he gave her explained nothing. Except that he was here.

The assassin rolled on top of Nick, arm upraised… As the dagger slashed downward, Nick drove a knee into the man's groin. He recoiled and Nick grabbed his wrist, twisting it—forcing the blade up and away.

"*Yes.*" The assassin stared at the blade coming at him. "Kill me! I go straight to Paradise. I am great hero, great martyr! Kill me!"

Nick thrust the dagger deep into the man's throat. He felt the sticky warmth of blood spill over him.

With a blissful smile, the assassin looked at Nick, his gaze losing focus. *"Allah-u-Akbar."*

Nick rolled out from under the dying man as blood continued to spurt over the horrified passengers along the aisle. Over E.

E looked down at the dark stain on her sleeve. The brighter red on her forearm. Her hands, only recently cleansed of Rostam's blood–and her own. *More blood.*

Nick grasped the edge of the seat and pulled himself up to face her. His chest rose and fell. "Good to see you again, E." He said it softly. Then was still.

She stared at him with a fury as violent as that of the assassin. He had saved her, but so what? For what? The fury took hold of her and shook her and her insides were dissolving, but she wouldn't cry. "You bastard. You rotten bastard."

Their eyes locked in silence.

He had no answer–because it was true.

Washingon, D.C.

Nick didn't knock. And he didn't kick down the door. Although he came close. Then he slammed it behind him–hard–disturbing Stiles's concentration.

Jay pushed the chessboard aside. "Ah. I see you saved our girl. To fight another day? I don't remember sending you to Frankfurt for that. Maybe it was mixed in with some other papers I signed regarding her extraction. What the hell. You got the job done and we're one agent the better for it."

"You sonuvabitch. You set her up."

"What makes you think that?"

"She wasn't passing papers. And you know it."

"Well, okay. It wasn't about her, though. But her husband? We couldn't very well have him going around buying chemicals for weapons, could we now? I could care less if they gas Iraq, but I do worry about some fringe group–some terrorist cell–getting their hands on that nasty stuff." Jay sat back in his seat, a smug expression on his face. "So to get to him, I may have had to use her–but that's water under the old bridge. The mullahs did our job for us. I cancelled the search for Karim this morning." He flashed a pleased grin. "And we got her out, didn't we?"

"Thanks to Monique."

"It was my budget."

"You asshole." Nick felt the rage building, but wouldn't let it out–yet. "How'd you do it?"

"Simple. They were watching your girl. I had one of our people bump into her in the bazaar, scattering papers about. She helped him pick them up."

"Yeah. And?"

"He was arrested a few minutes later. They discovered a diagram of one of their air defense sites among the papers. They shot him, trying to escape." Jay shrugged. "But it confirmed she was a spy, and if Karim was playing house with a spy...?"

"Two for one, huh? No wonder we have trouble keeping agents in Iran. You burn them as fast as we recruit them."

"Actually, four. Well, three, so far. The couple that worked for Karim? She helped your girl escape, so they hanged her. That was unfortunate, but her husband is still on the loose. As to the guy in the bazaar, he was low level. The good news, though, we've preserved our primary source."

Nick didn't bother walking around the desk. He reached across and dragged Stiles over it, sending photos, paper and computer monitor tumbling. He also didn't bother with his fists. As soon as Jay's head cleared the front of the desk, Nick brought his knee up into his face—hard. By the time Stiles hit the floor, he was unconscious.

He remained out cold for three minutes. Nick waited. Finally, when he saw Jay's head begin to move back and forth, he walked over and kicked him in the gut. "Did I get your attention yet?" Jay groaned. "You know, Stiles, I feel sorry for you. You don't have the decency to know just how wrong it was. But then, decency has nothing to do with it. Not at the Company."

"Not our mandate," Jay croaked. Down but not out.

Nick wanted to kick him again, but held himself back. "I should have walked away long ago. I thought about it, but I'm glad I didn't. At least in this case, I was there when it *really* mattered."

Jay slowly got to his hands and knees, then rolled into a sitting position. He glared up at Nick. "I don't know whether to simply fire you, or lose you in some Federal prison someplace."

"You can't fire me. I quit. The letter is on your desk." Nick glanced about the disarray. "Or was."

"It's next to my shredder."

"I suppose that depends on how you want to leave your office. On your own two feet, a wheelchair or a body bag." Nick smiled coldly. "No, you won't make good any threats. I know who you are, Stiles. What you are. Beneath all that bravado—and all the other bullshit—you're a coward. That's why you're here and the people getting their hands dirty are out there."

Jay narrowed his eyes. "A born-again moralist? Who you kidding?"

Nick met the man's gaze, then reached down and helped him to his feet. "Yeah. Maybe I am. I've tried to make amends, you know. For all of us. You were pretty cavalier about risking E's life. Then again, the only life you worry about is your own, isn't it?"

"It was for our nation—our security!"

Nick opened the door to leave, but turned to face Stiles one last time. "Isn't it always about national security? What are you going to do, Jay, when your nation runs out of citizens for you to set up to be killed?"

He turned and left. The office. The building. His old life.

Chapter 28

Bali, Indonesia

A few months later

Nick moved to the door of his whitewashed Balinese bungalow, its thatched roof supported by bamboo center posts. From his veranda, he stared for a moment at the gently bobbing sea, thanking God for his second chance. He had lost himself in the deceptions and deceits, the circuitous way they moved about their tracks. Until finally he grew to wonder if even they knew where they were going, or when they intended to get there. He knew they didn't care *how*.

But that was behind him. He had learned much since that life. He had learned to have no regrets. Things happened in their own way. For their own reason.

Nick stepped down onto the warm sand and felt the caress of the breeze on his bare chest, under his knee-length sarong. Then he saw her walking along the shore. Every sight as dazzling as the first. That night at the Indian sculpture exhibit, a young goddess unaware of her power. And today–goddess eternal–a white blossom behind her ear, her fluid hips draped in batik. Her arms full of orchids, she was barefoot and free.

And he intended to keep her that way. Before they dropped out of sight, he'd managed to protect her Swiss assets. It pleased him that she had come out of it fixed financially for the rest of her life. He knew she didn't much care, but it helped his own conscience, which needed all the help it could get. The getaway itself had been no big deal. They'd executed their disappearance via a series of quick, anonymous moves designed to leave no trail.

But the Company had a long arm. And he'd lost his protection on the seventh floor–at least, until someone up there needed him again. For now, though, he was on their shitlist. They wanted him for assault, which resurrected the old "rogue operator" rap. They wanted her, too, for a major debriefing–what his KGB friends used to call "squeezing the sponge." They'd pick her brain till she saw stars. He knew their mindset. They had "a lot invested in her." She was simply an asset, too valuable to waste. Nothing personal, just a matter of "national security."

Well, no. They'd messed with her head too much already. Still, she'd proved she could take it.

Nick smiled. Despite her trauma, E had landed on her feet and reacted with the efficiency of a cat. He'd been impressed by her escape strategy and felt a moment's pride. Her innate quick wit and good instincts had been honed into real skills. The smile faded. But that was all in the past. He only hoped she'd never have to use those skills again.

As she glided along the shoreline, Nick stared in wonder, a barefoot goddess bearing white flowers.

E felt his gaze and knew he was thinking about her. It was a good feeling, but she didn't want to lean on him too much. She knew that would be the easy thing to do. Too easy. What she needed to do, she had to do alone. She needed to get off the roller coaster and stop. Just stop, dig in her toes and breathe. And gradually begin putting the pieces of her life together. Only then might she feel whole again. Centered. Only then might she find her own peace.

She was grateful they had come to this place, this healing place. A generous place that asked only that she take in the beauty, and walk along the sea. Then the foam reached up to kiss her feet, making her feel as ever clean and refreshed. Renewed. She marveled at the simple goodness of her life, each day flowing into the next, a routine that wasn't routine at all.

That's what she liked about living here, the simplicity. She liked the harmony and gentleness of the island. Its serene, smiling people and softly terraced hillsides. The brilliant sunsets reflected in shimmering rice fields. Ducks parading home after a day's grazing. The sweet, deer-faced cows, so sacred and secure. Her own little thatched cottage, surrounded by mango and banana trees. A tiny courtyard with an outdoor shower.

And a kind neighbor, a friend. E looked at Nick as she drew closer, feeling a warmth that came only partly from the sand. He was handsome in a quiet way. A nice man. Good, too. What her Pop would have called decent. She'd always known that. Still knew it, despite learning that Nick Ross was really Nicholas Ross Daley. Just another lie, like the one about him playing shortstop same as brother Bobby. That was in D.C. way-back when, just a little white lie designed to get on her good side. Although that one had really gotten to her–why, she didn't quite understand. She remembered how she'd let him have it. He had looked right at her–his eyes naked–his soul, too. *I wish to God, E, that had been the extent of my lies.* And he meant it, that she knew.

But she was not ready to say goodbye to Karim–her Kari–her husband, with his true and faithful heart. Nick had told her of his lonely fate. The loss still cut like a wound. The emptiness would not recede.

"Fancy meeting you here," Nick said lightly.

E nodded, then included him in a glance that took in the sweep of sky and sea, the bright flowers and cascading greenery. She felt the tender touch of the breeze. "Beats Paris any day. Even Alert." It struck her, then, that of all the men in her life, Nick knew her the best. He knew where Alert was. *He knows who I am.*

At that moment, her past rushed over her like a great wave. This life she had led. It was strange and amazing, an amazing journey. To start from there–and end up here. Or at least, pause. That was it: this place was a deep breath of now.

From afar, the pure, tinkling tones of the *gamelan* wafted through the balmy air, joyous, almost a musical laugh. But her eyes were somber and she didn't smile. Nor did she speak; these days her words were few. E was trying, trying to find acceptance, some kind of meaning. And trying to be fair to Nick. *Nicholas Ross-now-Daley.* A good man who had always been there when she needed him. Even when she didn't know she needed him. Suddenly, a smile broke through.

Like a ray of luminous sun through the clouds.

Nick grinned back. "Maybe you'll drop by my end of the beach more often?" He could feel her pain, the changes she had gone through, was still going through. Maybe even those she hadn't yet faced. He understood her so well. And, he'd waited this long–he would wait as long as it took.

She understood, too, how long he had waited. "Maybe. Don't have too many options."

"A beautiful woman always has options."

"You could tell me a couple."

"Anytime."

"Later." E cocked her head and looked at him—then really looked at him. She had come to trust him again. Maybe that was the basis for everything else. But it was still too soon.

"Anytime, E. Evelyn."

She filled herself with sweet air... then from somewhere heard her Pop's words: *Don't think about where you were—think about where you are.* "I'm heading up to the temple to make an offering. For my past—and future—lives." She handed him a long-stemmed white orchid. "Care to join me?"

"In this life or the next?"

She met his quiet gaze. She knew, and he knew. But only the gods really knew.

Close—but not quite touching—they moved down the beach in silent understanding.

The End

About the Author

Diana Chambers has always been a bookworm. As a child she wandered the musty aisles of libraries, drawn by the promise of discovery, distant lives and distant lands. She has traveled widely, including many far corners of Asia.

An importing business in India led to a Hollywood design career, which led in turn in writing. Research for various projects put her on the road again. She loves spicy food and her bag is always packed.

Her work has been praised for its riveting plots, unusual characters and deep sense of place. A member of Writers Guild of America, Sisters in Crime and Mystery Writers of America, Diana lives in a small Northern California town with her husband, arty daughter and brilliant mutt, the best writing companion ever.

For more on the author, please visit www.dianarchambers.com, www.facebook.com/DianaChambersAuthor and www. twitter.com/DianaRChambers

Read more about Nicholas Ross Daley—and his secret mission in Afghanistan.

STINGER

By Diana R. Chambers

The intrigue begins in Peshawar, Pakistan, a small dusty Silk Road town that has once again become a crossroads of invaders and spies following Russia's 1979 invasion of Afghanistan, just across the Khyber Pass.

When a secret shipment of Stinger missiles goes missing, CIA officer Nick Daley becomes entangled in an unusual triangle with determined San Francisco journalist Robin Reeves and her former Berkeley lover, Jamal, now an elusive Afghan leader with a price on his head.

These characters lead us into a realm of mystery and betrayal, where hidden agendas provide their own kind of veil until the truth is revealed in a shocking climax.

"A superbly crafted and highly recommended political thriller, *Stinger*... is a ripping good novel of page-turning suspense and plot-twisting intrigue."

— James A. Cox, *Midwest Book Review*

"The first book in the Nick Daley series is a captivating and thrilling excursion... When I put (it) down at the end, I had to say 'Wow.' Then I went in search of the next book."

— Randall Masteller, www.spyguysandgals.com

"Forget 'armchair adventure'—this is an edge-of-your-seat action thriller. If it isn't true, it sure as hell could be."

— Charles Benoit, *Relative Danger, You*

www.ingramcontent.com/pod-product-compliance
Lightning Source LLC
Chambersburg PA
CBHW020412180626
46812CB00003B/943